Irish Stories and Plays

PAUL VINCENT CARROLL

Irish Stories and Plays

New York, 1958

THE DEVIN-ADAIR COMPANY, *Publishers*

This volume is dedicated to the
memory of

MARY PEARL

who shared with the author the
joy and the travail of
its making.

Vitam Aeternam dona ei, Domine.

Acknowledgments

The following stories by Paul Vincent Carroll are published here for the first time: "Me Da Went Off the Bottle," "The Stepmother," and "My Learned Friend Hogan." "Home Sweet Home" has appeared in *Esquire Magazine,* and "She Went By Gently" in an anthology, *44 Irish Short Stories,* edited by Devin A. Garrity, and in *Irish Writing.* "Maisie Was a Lady" and "Dark Glory" have appeared in the London periodical *Lilliput* and "The Virgin and The Woman" has been previously published in a London wartime anthology.

Among the plays, "Beauty Is Fled" was issued by Samuel French Ltd., London, and by Julian Messner, Inc., New York, who have kindly allowed us to reprint it here. "The Conspirators" was previously published as "The Coggerers" by Random House, New York. They too have been kind enough to allow us to add it to the present collection. "Interlude" has been issued by Samuel French, Ltd., London. "The Devil Came From Dublin" has not previously appeared in book form, but it has been produced in London and Dublin with considerable success.

Contents

STORIES

Home Sweet Home 3
She Went by Gently 13
Dark Glory 22
Maisie Was a Lady 32
The Stepmother 43
My Learned Friend, Hogan 68
Me Da Went Off the Bottle! 76
The Virgin and the Woman 86

ONE ACT PLAYS

The Conspirators 109
Beauty is Fled 131
Interlude 155

THREE ACT PLAY

The Devil Came from Dublin 179

Stories

Home Sweet Home

Martin sat staring moodily into the fire—a man not in the humor to speak or to be spoken to. Not that he considered himself superior or inferior. He could read but little meaning in such names. It was just that he felt pushed by his nature into a place apart from people who bought and sold and sinned and did penance. And he communed with himself and was fond of it. A thin, gaunt woman moved about and rattled things. He did not like her. Before God he knew it. Before God he knew that if Sarah, that laying-out woman of the dead, came to deck her out for the exit of her crabbed soul he would in his communing dare to be glad. Yet two years ago he said to this woman, "You are young to be a widow and your man is now thirteen years drowned in the channel. What better could you do than make yourself my wife."

Martha had looked at him minutely, at his moody eyes and the stoop of his shoulders, and saw he was a man of the hearth, not a flighty man or one who would roam about in search of sexual illusion. He remembered her sensible eye on him and the woman's intuition in her feeling about him like a discovering finger.

They were married in the small church at the second turn of the road to Avoree. But in scarcely no time he found her out. He had thought her a mannerly woman, one who would respect that in him that was untranslatable. But she wasn't and she didn't. And she talked too much for a woman —in fact even for a man. He considered she should remain deferential to that in him which as a woman she could not understand. But in this matter she had neither manners nor courtesy.

Once or twice when he was foolish enough to give her a deep thought, one that took much drilling and searching for, she guffawed and said, "Ach, behave yourself." He was hurt —so hurt that he vowed in his quiet way never again to cast one of his pearls at the feet of such a heathen.

Of late she fell to arguing a lot, not that he ever verbally countered her. But his silences, his patience, his forbearance, were like oil that lent fluency to her vituperation. Especially was this so on a market day when after selling some fowl and a basket of eggs she returned with flushed cheeks and her mouth loose. On these occasions she ate, talked and scratched her hair concurrently—she gobbled rather than ate—so that the picture of her became to his mind like a burning thing, pressing itself more and more maddeningly on his consciousness.

The fingers of his mind, thwarted yet indefatigable, forever kept picking at the knot that is so easily tied and so seldom unraveled. His preoccupation with that knot gave birth in him to a few original thoughts, inflammable enough to burn the roots of the low village houses if they were known. But he was a man of silence in spite of her ill-timed flippancies, her waving aside of his considered opinions, her joviality that played havoc with his dignity, her imperious way of rasping "Martin," that jolted him into acquiescence when with a quiet snap of his fingers it should be vice versa.

It was a disturbing state of affairs to Martin that he could not come home of an evening and improve his spouse's undisciplined mind. For instance now, Martin was aware that the wind had a taste. He once mentioned such a fact to her and the uncouth creature spluttered into her cup of tea. He saw her in that moment as a reproach to the age that produced her. Yet it was true about the wind. And what was more it tasted differently in different places. He never yet tasted it on Murdock's Hill above the town but a riot of wild heather surged about his perception. In the valley below Ardmahone it had a tang in it, salt, a touch of tar, a bit of hempen rope, a coating of seaweed. And not two miles away you couldn't mistake the peppery sprinkling of lime through it as it flung itself onto the crags of Nitsley. On the road beyond Cabintown could any man in his senses deny the privet scent and the blue musk aroma? But what was the use? That his wife considered profundities such as these fit material for undisguised levity was a barbarous state of affairs. Of course the wind was only one of many things. But what was the use?

This brings us to the point that in the face of such discordance Martin could no longer believe before God that his union with this woman was a union at all.

If there was any logic in life—and there was bound to be after thousands of years of its development by man—no good could come from a continuance of such a union. He had read in papers where men and women had had their unions nullified by the sin of adultery. But to Martin adultery was a mere venial transgression in comparison with the enormity that made his home a study in contradiction. A wiser age would relegate adultery to the place now occupied by drunkenness and ha'penny nap, and bring forth into the new light, the enormities now classed with the trivialities of everyday life.

On account of his belief in this prophecy Martin decided that as neither before God nor man was he conscientiously compelled to continue such a coupling—he would no longer call it a union—he would put on his cap and walk out of the home he had raised and leave it to perish as a thing of evil.

What preparations he made towards this end were few. A folding ruler, his jackknife, a turn screw, a handful of nails that jingled in his trouser pockets and his cap. The cap was important, as when donned it was really the symbol of parting. In fact Martin gave it a grave deference, even as it hung a thwarted thing on the exact and particular nail hammered by his wife into the fourth board in the wall nearest the door. She even occasionally made fun of it, in fact on one occasion she put it on her own head backwards and leered at him in anything but a mannerly way. Of course, she could never see the significance of his cap as the rightful crown of her spouse and that as such it was important. There was not what one would call a sense of symbolism in her at all. As Martin said, it was all a question of "feel," of inward perception. She was gross, and as such, God help her. *He* couldn't.

On the third day of March, with the ushering in on the heavenly floor of the new moon, Martin's smoldering resolve suddenly burst alight. In an instant born of fire he realized that he had sufficiently added and subtracted, had weighed long enough on a balance. The instant was timed providentially insofar as its birth coincided with his wife's absence at the market in the town, and as the instant in question hurled its fiery radiance upon him he resolutely put on his cap ere it died. No part of him betrayed him except perhaps his eyes. They were ablaze. But he drew heavy

6

lids over them, secreting them. At the low door the wind
met him with sudden encouragement. Instantly he tasted it
and translated the taste. In the glory of it he realized his
parting was devoid of pity for the woman he once fondled
as if she were a holy thing. It was regrettable but it was
true.

"They're harvesting hay," he told himself, "in the fifty-
eight acre field on Lord Orr's estate, forty miles away."

He resolved to strike off in that direction. The way lay
over the river at the bottom of Terry O'Kane's barley field
and thence cut a winding path through Tippen's wood and
over the left shoulder of Slieve Ruadh to the level vale that
was now invisible to him. With the help of God he would
see it at the dip of the next sun. The closing in of the night
upon it would be a matter of great visual feasting. He hoped
he would confront the sight alone; most people though
trained in the Mass to give a bowed deference to the mysti-
cal, were incongruously unmannerly in the presence of such
a natural sacrament. In that lay the secret of many failures,
the ruin of many temples.

On the green bank of the river he came upon a man idly
stretched out, his hand cupped behind his neck and his
eyes searching the waters from under the rim of a very
battered hat. Martin recognized him at once as the "Thread
Man." That was what people called him over the ground of
four counties because he offered for sale a stock of rough
linen thread and great-eyed needles at the cottage doors.

Martin sat down beside him and awaited the return of
Terry Kane's boat now approaching from the opposite bank.

The Thread Man plucked a blade of grass, stuck it in
his mouth and eyed Martin. What conclusion he came to he
reserved for digesting with the wisp of grass.

"Are you for crossin'?" he asked as effortlessly as he
could.

Martin nodded his assent.

7

"Is it for the town of Kildare you are bound?"

"For anywhere at all," returned Martin.

The tramp eyed him again.

"It's a wonder to me," he commented, "a tame little man like yourself would spend a penny ha-penny crossin' the river and you goin' to just anywhere at all. Isn't there a world of places this side o' the water, if that's the way o' it?"

"I'd rather the river behind me," muttered Martin.

"Um," said the Thread Man. "A river behind is a river between, what do you say?"

"Maybe," said Martin.

There was a pause. The Thread Man chewed at a blade slowly.

"Does your woman know you're taking a stroll to—to anywhere at all, and the water behind you?" he said with a hint of insinuation.

Martin stared at him, his eyes on guard.

"My woman?" he repeated. "What woman?"

The tramp leered a little under the stubble on his cheeks.

"The woman of your bed and board," he said.

"How did you know I was married anyhow?" challenged Martin, not a little angry. The tramp's smile was now a something, half pity, half contempt.

"You just—know," he answered. "If a man secures his woman from other men with a ring, a woman secures her man against her sisters by branding him all over."

Martin caught his breath.

"With what?" he questioned angrily.

"What? . . . What a stickler for names you are. How would I know. There's surely ten thousand things in the world without a name at all."

Martin felt himself quivering with rage before the insinuations of the other.

8

"I—I don't like you," he said at length between his teeth.

"That's too bad," answered the Thread Man, seizing a new blade of grass.

"You're just trying to be smart," pursued Martin. "What evidence have you at all I'm a married man?"

"If it was a crime," said the Thread Man, "I have more evidence that would hang you on a forty-foot gallows."

"Out with it," cried Martin, now thoroughly roused, "prove it."

"Prove it, is it?" said the tramp, one eye closed, and the other running Martin over like an electric torch. "Look, to begin with, the droop of your shoulders where you've given up resistin' her. You're hers. And that habit you have of squinting all in a minute to the side, the way you be watchin' her. And the way your ears are cocked out the way a bit with you always expectin' the rasp of her voice at you. And the wee black mark there in the neck of your shirt, the exact shape of your chin, when you'd be broodin' at the fire, thinkin' to find a way where there's no way. And the cowed look in your eyes, with just the one spark in them that goes as quick as it comes. Ten times there since you sat down, you flipped a fallen bit of a leaf off your trousers and twice you rubbed the green glaze of the grass off your sleeve. And look at the inside of the turn-ups in your trousers—not as much as a burnt match in them nor a speck of sand nor nothin'. Sure you're an open book to me. And me not sayin' a word about your hand-knitted socks nor the wee patch in your shirt that was done with a number ten needle that only a woman's finger can manage."

Martin lay crushed. It had gone far past the moment for anger. He was speechless, impotent.

"God's truth," he said grudgingly at length. "I'd never have thought it. You're a noticin' man, I'll say that for you."

9

"I'm not more noticin' than the next one," commented the tramp. "If between this and—and anywhere at all, there's one woman among all the women we meet that doesn't notice what I notice, you can hit me a flyin' kick in the stomach."

But Martin had no desire to risk his chance of such a reward.

"It's no use so. I must stay where I am," he said slowly, rising and shaking the damp of the grass from him. The tramp too lurched to his feet.

"That's a truth," said the tramp, "that you got brave and cheap. Did you ever see them brandin' sheep?"

"Often," said Martin.

"They're not in it with men," commented the tramp. "The next time the preacher in the chapel talks about the mark you get in the soul at your christenin' that can never be rubbed off, think the same thing of the brandin's your woman has put all over you. For it is gospel too."

"You seem to be a knowledgeable man at any rate," said Martin half admiringly.

"I gained it dear and I'm passin' it on cheap," responded the Thread Man. "Five years ago when I murdered my first wife—"

Martin felt suddenly weak at the knees and stifled a cry.

"Aye," continued the tramp calmly. "She was a damn nuisance; I had a little farm then. I bought a vicious baste of a mare and sent my woman out to the stable to get a tin-can I left lyin' nicely at the mare's tail. The baste got her with the right hind leg . . ."

"Ugh," said Martin sickeningly.

"No need for that," said the Thread Man. "She felt nothin'. All over in a tick. I thought I was free then, but in nine months another one seven times worse was hoppin' cups and things off me head."

"Did you—kill her too?" Martin managed to slowly gasp.

"I tried to," answered the tramp decisively, "but the very divil himself was guardin' her. She wouldn't go near the stable, she wouldn't look down the well, she wouldn't help me to fix the patch on the roof. A wise one I'm tellin' you. I'm goin' home to her now in the town of Kildare, and there's a grand battle before me. When you came along, I was workin' out a plan of defense. I was feelin' that if I captured the kitchen and forced her back into the room I would be in command of most of the artillery—"

At this point a hail from the water's edge interrupted him and Terry Kane beckoned to them with an oar. The sight of the boat sickened Martin so that instinctively he turned his back to it.

"I think I'll just go—go home," he said, strangely hoarse.

"I'm for the same place," said the tramp, "so I can't complain either. But do you know what I am goin' to tell you, as a branded fellow creature: There's a wise age ahead of us will do away with the cruelest of all things on earth, the thing called home. I wish the high God had seen fit to hold back my birth a bit longer."

In a daze, Martin retraced his steps to his home. As he entered his house an involuntary shivering took possession of him so that his legs wavered and his fingers blundered impotently with his cap. His wife, vigorously alert and loquacious after a day of mighty talk at the market diagnosed him with one penetrating glance.

"I'm going to be sick," said Martin uneasily.

She jerked up his chin with a sweep of her arm.

"Show me the color of your tongue," she rapped out, and when Martin listlessly presented her with that ornament she greeted it with an ominous snort. In a few minutes she had divested him of coat and shirt, had forced him

11

down on the threadbare couch and he felt her strong oily fingers massaging his chest and back. They seared his skin like a fury.

"God help you, you poor idiot," she kept muttering between vigorous strokes; "you'd be a tramp on the road only I'm lookin' after you, and as thievin' and godless a wretch as the Thread Man himself."

With that, she dragged his trousers off with what was the very negation of mock modesty and trundled him into bed. As he lay deciding how many grains of truth were in his wife's assertion, she appeared from the fireplace with a tumbler of salts and a bowl of hot, buttery gruel.

"N-n-no," he protested feebly. "I'm better," and instantly he dived completely under the bedclothes.

A huge hand dived after him and reappeared with his chin in vice-like fingers. She tilted up his head with a mighty forearm.

She Went by
Gently

It was close on three when
the knock came in the night. She was out of bed on the instant in her old flannelette nightgown, with her silver-grey
hair tossed down her back. The night-light was flickering
quietly as, in the shadows by the elm tree outside, she discerned Manahan's unshaven face under the battered hat.

"The pains is bad on the girl," came his voice. "I think
maybe it's surely her time."

"Go before me fast and have plenty of hot water," she
answered. "I'll be at your heels with Frank."

She heard his foot in the night hurrying off as she drew
on her heavy dress over the nightgown. Himself stirred and
put his beard irascibly outside the blankets.

"You'll go none," he snapped. "A slut like that, that gets
her child outside of priest and law. Four miles uphill on a
mountain road and the mists swarmin'."

"I'll go," she said quietly, and crossing, she ruffled

Frank's unruly hair on the little camp bed. "Be risin', Frank, and let you carry the lantern for me to Manahan's."

"If there was just a drop o' tay before we'd start, ma," he protested sleepily.

"There's no time, son."

"A grand pass we've come to, in this country," grumbled himself. "Encouragin' the huzzies and the sluts to be shameless. I'd let her suffer. A good bellyful o' sufferin' would keep her from doin' it again."

He moved coughingly into the deep warm hollow she had vacated in the bed. The strictures of his uncharitable piety followed her into the silver and ebony of the mountainy night. She went gently . . . her feet almost noiseless. There was an inward grace in her that spilt out and over her physical lineaments, lending them a strange litheness and beauty of movement. Frank was a little ahead of her, swinging the storm lantern. He was munching a currant scone plastered with butter. His sturdy little legs took the steep sharp-pebbled incline with careless grace. Now and again, he mannishly kicked a stone from his path and whistled in the dark.

"Careful now, Frank, in case you'd slip over the bank in the dark," she admonished.

"Och, ma," he protested, "the way you talk! You'd think I wasn't grew up. It makes little of a fella."

She smiled and watched him lovingly in the silver dark. He was her youngest. The others had all followed the swallows into the mighty world. Martin was in America, Annie in England, Matthew in Glasgow, Paddy in the Navy, Mary Kate a nursemaid in Canada, Michael was at rest somewhere in Italy. His C.O. had said in a letter that he had died well. If that meant that he had had the priest in his last hours, then God be praised, for he was her wayward one. She preferred him dying full of grace to dying full of glory. . . . But Frank was still with her. He had her eyes and gentleness and the winning tilt of the head. It would be good to have him to close her weary eyes at the end of all . . .

They had now crossed the cockeyed little bridge over a dashing tawny stream and the mountains came near her and about her like mighty elephants gathered in a mystic circle for some high purpose. Everywhere in the vast silvery empire of the dark there was the deep silence of the eternal, except for the rebellious chattering of the mountain streams racing with madcap abandon to the lough below. They were the *enfants terribles* of the mighty house, keeping it awake and uneasy. Now and again a cottage lifted a sleepy eye out of its feathery thatch, smiled at her knowingly and slumbered again. All of them knew her . . . knew of her heroism, her quiet skilled hands, her chiding, coaxing voice in the moments of peril. . . . In each of them she had been the leading actress in the great primitive drama of birth.

The climb was now gruelling and Frank took her arm pantingly. The lantern threw its yellow ray merrily ahead. All would be well.

She ruffled his hair playfully, and smiled secretively under the black mask of the night.

At a mischievous bend on the mountain path, the Manahan cottage suddenly jumped out of the mist like a sheep dog and welcomed them with a blaze of wild, flowering creepers. Inside, the middle-aged labourer was bending over a dark deep chimney nook. A turf fire burned underneath on the floor. From a sooty hook far up, a rude chain hung down and supported a large pot of boiling water. She nodded approvingly and donning her overalls moved away in the direction of the highly-pitched cries from an inner room.

"If there's anythin' else I can do . . ." he called, half-shyly, after her.

"Keep a saucepan of gruel thin and hot," she answered. "And put the bottle of olive oil on the hob in case we'd need it. Play about, Frank, and behave yourself till I call you."

She went smilingly to the bed and looked down at the flushed tearful face, the big bloodshot eyes and the glossy tossed hair of the girl. No more than eighteen, she thought, but a well-developed little lass with a full luscious mouth and firm shapely breasts. Jim Cleary who skipped to England in time had had a conquest worth his while. . . . The little rebel, caught in the ruthless trap of Nature, grabbed her hands beseechingly, held on to them hysterically and yelled.

"Oh, Maura, ma'am, please, please, please . . ." she sobbed.

Maura chaffed her hands, soothed her gently, clacked her tongue admonishingly and pretended to be very disappointed at her behaviour.

"Now, now, now, Sadie," she reproved her. "A fine soldier *you* are! When I was here at *your* comin', your mother, God rest her, bit her lip hard and said no word at all. Come on now, and be your mother's daughter."

"Ah, sure how could I be like me poor dead mother, and me like this, and all agin me?" sobbed Sadie.

"Am *I* agin ye, child?" soothed Maura, "and I after walkin' four miles of darkness to be with you!"

The tears came now but silently, as Maura's skilful hands warmed to her work . . .

Frank remained in the kitchen at a loss until suddenly the door opened and a large nanny goat sailed in with perfect equanimity and balefully contemplated this stranger on home ground. Frank looked askance at her full-length beard and her formidable pair of horns, but this was of small consequence to the goat which advanced on Frank and in the wink of an eye had whipped his handkerchief out

of his top pocket and stuffed it in her mouth. Frank's protest brought an assurance from Manahan who was stooped
over the fire bringing the gruel to the boil.

"She'll not touch you," he said without turning his head.

"But she has me handkerchief," protested Frank.

"Ah, sure isn't she only playing with you!" returned
Manahan heedlessly.

But by this time the goat had consumed the handkerchief with terrific relish, and was about to make a direct
attack on the sleeve of his jersey. Frank dashed for the door
with the goat after him. In the little yard he dived behind
the water barrel that caught the rain-water from the roof.
The goat snuffed past him in the darkness, and Frank
hastily retraced his steps to the kitchen and barred the door.

He was just in time to see his mother put a generous
spoonful of butter into a bowl of thin steaming gruel.

"Go in and feed this to your daughter, and coax her to
take it," she directed Manahan. "She's quiet and aisy now
and all will be well." He obeyed her shyly and without a
word.

"You must be a big grown-up fella tonight and help
your ma, Frank," she said.

"Anythin' you say, ma," he answered. "What is it?"

The baby had come forth without a cry. It was limp
and devoid of any sign of life. She carried it quickly but
calmly to the open peat fire, as close to the grimy chain as
the heat would allow. It was naked and upside down. Frank,
under her calm directions, held it firmly by its miniature
ankles.

"Be a good son now and don't let it fall," she warned
him, and plastering her own hands with the warm olive
oil, she started to work methodically on the tiny body. Up,
down and across the little chest, lungs and buttocks went
the skilful fingers rhythmically until the newborn skin glis-
tened like a silver-wrought piece of gossamer. The long

minutes went by heavily. The oil lamp flickered and went out, leaving the dancing rays and shadows of the fire to light this crude drama with its eternal theme. Five minutes, seven, ten . . . without fruit or the promise of fruit. . . . But the moving fingers went on with rhythmic ruthlessness, searching for the spark that must surely be hidden there in a fold of the descending darkness. Frank's face was flushed, his eyes gathered up with the pain of exertion, his breath coming in spasms. On his mother's forehead beads of sweat gathered, rivuletted down the grey gentle face and flowed on to the newborn body to be ruthlessly merged in the hot oily waves of her massaging.

Then suddenly, as the tension had reached almost to the unbearable, a thin, highly-pitched cry came from the tiny spume-filled lips. She seized the baby, pushed Frank from her, turned it upright, grabbed a chipped, handleless cup of cold water and even as the fluttering life hesitated on the miniature features for one solitary second to receive its divine passport and the symbol of its eternal heritage, she poured a little of the water on the tiny skull and said, "I baptise you, in the Name of the Father and of the Son and of the Holy Ghost."

She wrapped the little corpse in the remnant of a torn sheet, without tear or trace of any sentiment, placed it in a drawer she took from the crazy wardrobe, and having made the Sign of the Cross over it gave it no further attention.

When she saw that the bowl was almost empty of gruel, she chased Manahan out with a gesture and settled the little mother comfortably. She was adjusting her wet, tearstained hair over her pillow when suddenly she felt Sadie's arms tightly about her neck. Her big eyes were quiet now and the pain and the travail were gone, but the tears came rushing from them again as Maura kissed and soothed her.

"I wish I had me mother," she sobbed. "Maura, ma'am, I'm goin' to be a good girl from now on."

"You have never been a bad one, darlin'," coaxed Maura, tucking the faded bedclothes into her back. "A wee bit foolish maybe, but the world and the years will learn ye. Sleep now and I'll see you tonight."

She re-donned her old black cloak in the kitchen.

"I'll tell Maloney to bring you up a white box," she said to Manahan. "It will save you the journey down."

On the mountain path she went noiselessly, with Frank a little ahead, carrying the extinguished lantern. The dawn greeted her from the heights with far-flung banners of amber and amethyst. The heights themselves ceased from their eternal brooding for a brief moment of time and gave her a series of benign obeisances. The racing rivulets tossed her name from one to the other on the Lord's commendation. The sun himself, new-risen and generous, sent a very special ray of light that caught up her tossed hair and rolled it in priceless silver.

"Why do men lie prone in their beds," she murmured, "and the great glory of God washin' the hills with holy fire?"

Shamus Dunne was taking in his two nanny goats for the milking as she passed his cottage.

"The blessin' o' God light on ye, woman," he said, touching his wind-swept hat.

"And on yourself too, Shamus," she answered. "How is the little fella now?"

"Ah, sure isn't he over a stone weight already. Ah, woman-oh, wasn't it the near thing that night? Ah, sure only for yourself, wasn't me whole world lost?"

"Arrah, men always think the worst at such times," she answered smilingly. "Sure, there was never any great fear of the worst that night! Herself, within, is much too good a soldier for that!"

Frank had now discovered a salmon tin and was kicking it vigorously before him. She took out her rosary at the bend where the path dips perilously between two ageless boulders, and as she trudged along, she began counting the beads effortlessly. There on the heights at dawn, caught between the gold and the deepening blue of day, she might have been a pilgrim out of a Europe that has long since vanished, or maybe a Ruth garnering the lost and discredited straws of the age-old Christian thought.

Frank had now lobbed his salmon tin on the lofty fork of a tree, and when she caught up with him, he took her arm undemonstratively. Himself would be up now, she thought, with his braces hanging, and maybe a hole in his sock that she had overlooked. He wouldn't be able to find the soap and the towel even if they were both staring at him, and of course if he blew the fire, even with a thousand breaths, it would never light for him. . . . But no matter now. Thanks be to God, there was an egg left in the cracked bowl that would do his breakfast. If the little white pullet in the barn laid in the old butter box, Frank would have one, too, with the help o' God. . . . When the cock himself laid an egg, Glory be, *she'd* get one all to herself!

They crossed the rickety bridge, as the dawn was losing its virgin colour. Frank saw a squirrel and rushed ahead of her. She paused for a moment and contemplated the restless waters. They looked to her like a rich tawny wine poured out of some capacious barrel by some high ruthless hand who had suddenly discovered the futility of all riches. A May blossom rushed under the incongruous arch and emerged to get caught between a moss-covered stone and a jagged piece of rock. There was a turmoil and pain for a moment, and then it freed itself and rushed on. She wondered if it was the little soul she had lately saved, rushing on in a virgin panic to the eternal waters. . . . Maybe it was. . . . Maybe she was just an imaginative old fool. . . . Ah, sure what harm anyway to be guessing at infinite mysteries, and she so small on a mountain road?

Himself met her in the stone-floored kitchen. Indeed,

yes, he was trailing his braces, and the sulky fire was just giving a last gasp before expiring.

"I suppose you saved the slut's bastard," he commented acidly.

She bent on her knees to blow the fire aflame again.

"I saved him," she answered, and a flame leaped suddenly upwards and made a sweet and unforgettable picture of her face.

Dark Glory

I MET him where the road bends towards Rioch and Rossnacree. He wasn't there one moment, but the next he was. He may have come out of the line of old salleys or indeed maybe from the boreen on the left where the thatched cottage lay hidden in mist and foliage. But anyway, there he was. Complete, I'm telling you, in the garb of a jockey, but tattered and with the mud of nine counties on it. The squat riding breeches, the short severely-shaped jacket over the worn blouse, even the peaked skull cap. In his right hand a frayed whip and under his left arm the worn saddle and rusted stirrups.

The air had the sensuous Irish warmth in it, and I wiped my brow fretfully. He watched me with the full perkiness of a robin.

"Man, it's a dry day," I said.

"There's a cure for that in the clump of salleys not fifty paces on," he returned. "Danny always keeps a wel-

come sup of ten-year-old for them that's civilised enough to
relish the difference between a pure potstill malt and that
Scotch grain with the whiffs of smoke out of it."

"You'll need to guide me," I invited.

"I will and welcome," he slapped back at me.

He was right about Danny whom we found behind a
formidable barrier of barrels of double X, and we laid into
the goblets of Irish malt in spite of the early hour.

"You'll be across in Mappin's Hotel," mused the jockey.

"I am."

"With them film people from London, I suppose?"

"That's right."

"I hear the Director fella is lookin' for a few jockeys to
ride the Ennis races of 1888 all over again on the race course
of Mullingar, God help us."

"That's true enough."

"Boys-o-boys, it's a great and terrible wonder the mira-
cles them fellas can perform with a camera and a case o'
brandy. You're maybe the Director yourself?"

"I am not. I'm one of the writers."

"Ah. . . . And are ye a good writer or a bad one?"

"I think myself, I'm quite a good one."

"Ah . . . that's not the best o' news surely, because
they be sayin' in the snugs that the good writers never have
a penny and the bad ones can't count theirs."

"Never mind. I have enough anyway to do further
justice to Danny's special."

"If you have, well sure, thanks be to God. You're a
dacent man anyway. You have a native tongue in your
head, too."

"I was brought up in Dublin."

"Dublin. . . . Aye, aye. . . . The Phoenix Park . . .
Baldoyle . . . Fairyhouse . . . Punchestown. . . ."

He lifted the worn saddle to his cheek and cuddled it
as a mother would with her infant. The wrinkled eyes saw

me no more. I watched them covertly as they grew to terrifying life and, in the mirror of reverie, become powerful and eloquent and purposeful. Vividly reflected in them, I saw the tensely-poised, ecstatic crowds, the white far-flung railings, the riot of gay colour, the sudden electric ascent of the starting gate, the flash of a dozen stream-lined bodies illustrating the royal poetry of motion. . . . The full minutes passed.

He lifted his glass reverently and drained it in salute. Shamefacedly he restored the worn saddle to the security of his tattered oxter. I signed to Danny to fill the glasses.

"I'm maybe forgettin' me manners," he said with genuine Irish courtesy.

"Were they . . . great days?" I ventured.

"Ah, coloured days they were. . . . It's a strange thing that colours die slowest of all in a man's memory. I remember now, as I do me prayers, the white star on Silver Witch's forehead. The day I had to give her a touch of the whip to win the last lap at Punchestown, I kissed the star that day meanin' I was sorry. Ah, sure we knew every move of each other . . . we two. It was only that once I laid the whip on her. . . . And I'll surely carry to the grave me memory of Roisin Dhu's dyin' head on me lap the day she broke her leg at the Regulation jump at Baldoyle. . . . The gun-shot and the tears and the men's eyes avoidin' each other. . . . But for the life of me now I can't remember what me mother's face was like. Although, mind you, I pray for her soul passin' the chapels on the road. But it's a strange thing. . . ."

"We'll drink," I said, "to the colours that don't die."

The toast pleased him, and I could see that I had won his regard.

"Did you never marry?" I asked, as I again gave Danny the high sign.

"Ah, indeed I didn't," he answered. "It's a strange thing . . . marriage, a very strange thing. But I hitched up with a girl once . . . a fiery little filly that got wrinkles abusin' me for me high spirits and me low manners. Women always like a mannerly man, with a train time-table in one pocket and the Ten Commandments in the other."

"What happened to her . . . the girl, I mean?"

"Ah, sure I can't remember. She either died or got married. If I was never to drink that ball o' malt before me there, I couldn't tell ye. Begod, she . . . she maybe went to America. That's just what she did surely. She went to America. Sure in them days they all went to America."

As we were about to leave, Danny handed the jockey a small parcel.

"Put them sandwiches in your pocket, Martyn," he said. "They'll keep the malt out of your head if the sun fiercens."

"Can I pay for those?" I interposed.

"You can not," retorted Danny, a trifle severely, I thought. "Martyn Cliffe owns a slate or maybe two on my oul' roof, don't you, Martyn?"

"Them was the days, Danny," said Martyn, pocketing the sandwiches.

The Irish rain was falling in a fine silvery spray as we hit the winding roadway.

"If you like, Martyn," I said, "I'll ask the Director if he'd engage you for this race we're going to shoot. The money's good."

"You have the good nature of the race in ye," he answered. "The last coin I earned was a year ago when I broke in a chestnut colt for the American gobdaw that bought Clontibbert Castle and planked two concrete round towers on the roof to make it look Celtic. I didn't like him . . . he once got up on the wrong side of a fine bay he had, and anyway, he mixed ginger-pop with his malt. But it was a fine colt. . . . Tell me now. Who has the Director fella engaged for the race?"

"So far, three locals," I answered. "Joe Crimpsy, Tim Boland and the Cock McGee."

"They're not jockeys," rapped Martyn.

"Well, they said they were."

"Tcha! Isn't that like the English! They'd believe anythin'. Three point-to-point amateurs with jelly knees and duck backsides! Is the day to dawn when the thirst for a jingle in me pocket on the long roads would tempt me to ride in the company of cripples? Tell me that!"

"But, look, Martyn," I coaxed. "I'll try to get you the winning horse."

"Well, there's maybe consolation there. . . . You're a dacent fella, mind ye, and none better. But of course, the oul' blood's in ye."

"Of course, you must understand that when you come near the camera, the star actor will take your place on the horse and flash past the post."

"Flash, did you say? An-an-an-an-actor! Flash!" Martyn stood outraged on the roadway. "Do you mean he'll be dressed as a jockey . . . pretendin' like?"

"But of course, Martyn, that's the story, you see?"

"And how the hell could your actor-fella *flash* past the post if he can't ride, will you tell me?"

"The Director, Martyn, can manoeuvre the camera in such a way that the horse on the screen looks as if he's going like sheet lightning."

Martyn spat on the ground.

"Yous all ought to be shot," he ejaculated. "Nothin' is safe from yous, or sacred to yous. Everything yous use, yous make a fake of it. If yous'd leave racin' alone, I could give yous the pardon I'd give to a fool, but look at yous! To every dacent person breathin' Irish air, a race horse is somethin' not to be belittled before either man or the Man above. Has a fine woman more grace than it or a fightin' warrior more strength than it? And has it less beauty, will you tell me, than all them great figures that do be standin' in the sun of foreign cities? And has it, or has it not, the grand blue blood in its veins that we all had ourselves before we doped our wine and watered our whiskey? No man will answer me that! I'm not goin' to your hotel. I'm on me way, and sweet bad luck to yous all."

With that, Martyn strode off into the rainy mist in a great fury of snorts. Heavy with his drunken castigation, I lit a cigarette and dawdled pensively after him. There was no hurry. The Irish rain meant four things on any location . . . inactivity, bad-temper, poker and piling expenses. At the bend of the road to Mullagh, I came upon him under the drenched lilac blossoms. His temper had passed, and he was gentle and wistful.

"I didn't mean *you* at all now," he apologised. "And anyway, I was maybe forgettin' me manners."

I swept aside his apologies and took him laughingly by the arm. But he wouldn't come to the hotel. Where the roads divide he took my hand in deep affection.

"Where do you live?" I asked him.

"Nowhere at all," he said simply. "Every time I get a little place of my own, I fidget and fidget for the road. And every time I'm on the road I fidget and fidget for a little place of my own. Sure it's just the way some of us is built. And didn't the Man above make us all, anyway. I'm headin' now for Ballinasloe where the horse fair is tomorrow, and after that I'll make west for Galway. Please God, I'll be in time for the races."

We shook hands again.

"You've been a dacent fella to me," he said. "Tell me now, have you a pound on ye?"

The malt and the Irish rain were playing havoc with my

prudence. I whipped out a greenback. He seemed surprised when I held it out to him.

"Put it in your pocket," he said, "and let ye not misconstrue me meanin'. Tell me now, have you a fiver?"

"I have."

"A tenner, maybe?"

"I could manage it."

"Is there twenty pounds between you and the Poor House door?"

"There might be."

"Good for you. Now, listen. I'm goin' to repay your kindness. Put it on Dark Glory in the three o'clock race at the Phoenix Park tomorrow. Not the pound, mark you, or the fiver, nor the tenner, for begod, I'll not have Dark Glory belittled before me. The darlingest little filly that the Man above ever lent lightnin' to. The twinty pounds or nothin'! Promise me!"

"Is she as sure a cert as that?" I ventured.

"Sure? Dark Glory, is it, sure? Is the lightnin' sure when it strikes? Is the hawk sure when he stoops? Are the angels sure when they open up the dawn on the roads? Listen!"

He cocked up his ears in a listening attitude and his eyes saw a host of vivid things that were hidden from me.

"Listen! Listen! There they are now," he cried. "They're shoutin' themselves mad! There's a flash of shadow and gold at the white rails. . . . Dark Glory! Dark Glory! Dark Glory! . . ."

The tears were coming from his eyes and mingling with the rain-drops on his cheeks, as he gripped my arm.

"Don't make little of Dark Glory," he said brokenly. "Only one man ever done that, and the spit from a dacent man's mouth is his portion this day. . . . Tomorrow at three, remember. The twinty pounds or nothin'. And tell nobody. It's for you alone for bein' dacent and gentlemanly. There's the oul' glory of the race in ye!"

The next moment he was gone, and the gentle mist had claimed him . . . his saddle under his arm, and his whip smacking the leg of his breeches.

In the hotel lounge, I found everyone from the Director to the clapper-boy grimly playing poker, and for the thousandth time I thanked the God who didn't give me a poker face. I waited until the tension broke, and old Shamus came dodderingly from the bar with a fresh round of drinks.

Withholding such a terrific piece of inside information from the boys would be unforgivable, I thought. They were a lovable gang and made grand company. When Shamus had shuffled off, I burst out with the whole story. The effect was chaotic. Chairs were pushed back, resolutions made to take the cars to Dublin tomorrow for the races at the Phoenix Park, daily papers with racing cards were whipped out of pockets or retrieved from the waste baskets.

"What course did you say, the Phoenix Park? And what race? The three o'clock? Dark who? Who's riding her? What's her weight for the mile and a half? What's she standing at?"

The horrible moment came when I became conscious of a dozen pairs of sarcastic eyes leering at me. I felt myself blushing like a schoolgirl, as the papers whizzed past me on their way to the waste baskets again. I feverishly searched the list of runners again, but there was no Dark Glory amongst them. It was Frank, the Director, who laughed first. And oh, Gosh, what a laugh! And it was followed in rapid succession by the Camera man's horse-like whinny, the Art Director's volcanic rumble and the Associate Producer's inhuman cock-a-doodle-do. Then the sarcasm followed.

"How many doubles did you stand him, old boy?"

"There's one born every minute."

"Irishman falls for the blarney. What chance has a mere Englishman? Answer in five seconds."

I crawled away to the other end of the bar where, in a secluded seat, I could mentally kick and miscall myself to my heart's content. Yet I hated to think that Martyn was just a common bum, with a repertoire of highly-coloured tricks that ensured him a daily skinful of malt. Yet facts were facts, even if my self-esteem erected rows of very silly excuses. Yet those tears in his eyes as he stood hearkening to the vociferous acclaim of the crowds in his vision as Dark Glory flashed by, were they all just part of the impertinent play-acting?

Old Shamus brought me the brandy silently.

"Have you ever heard, Shamus, of a horse called Dark Glory?" I asked him.

"Ah, indeed, I have, sir," he said tiredly, and the wrinkles on his old face creased into a smile. "You've met Martyn Cliffe then, sir?"

"Yes, I have. How did you know?"

"Ah, sure poor Martyn and Dark Glory are always in the one breath in these parts, sir."

"But Shamus, if Dark Glory is not running tomorrow at the Phoenix Park, where *is* she running?"

Shamus almost dropped the symphon of soda.

"I beg your pardon, sir!"

"Am I to take it, Shamus, that Martyn's mad?"

"Ah, indeed, he is, sir."

"Then there's no such horse as Dark Glory?"

"There was, sir. But that's goin' back . . . och, more than fifteen years now, sir."

"Shamus!"

"Indeed yes, sir. You see, sir, Martyn loved horses more

than he loved anybody or anythin'. But he wronged one of them. Ah, sure he was the pride of Ireland then."

"He wronged Dark Glory?"

"Ah, indeed he did, sir. He fell for a heavy bribe, and he pulled her in the three o'clock in the Phoenix Park more than fifteen years ago. Ah, sure she was the grandest little bit of dark lightnin', sir. I lost a pound on her meself that day."

"He made her lose the race?"

"Indeed, he did, sir. The Stewards found him guilty and he was warned off the turf for good, sir. He loved that horse and hated money and gain from that day on. The heavy drinkin' followed, sir, and the poor head went wrong. . . ."

"But Shamus, he told me to back her in the three o'clock tomorrow!"

"And why wouldn't he, sir? Sure he's still ridin' her. Indeed, sir, he'll ride her again and again until the day he dies. . . . A little soda in the brandy, sir? Thank you, sir."

Maisie Was a Lady

Wʜᴇɴ Maisie said "Yes," Jem, the silly ass, danced with ecstasy. But, then, Jem was always regarded as not just "all there" in Kilmistogue. Young, lean, awkward, mentally immature and aloof, his predominant passion was Maisie, that sexy soufflé of concentrated femininity, with the tight-cut skirt, the perfectly carved legs and the tossed hair of a sorceress.

Up to this, Maisie had whizzed dagger after dagger into poor Jem's craven heart without one iota of mercy, and joked about him to her more elderly male friends, whom, for some high reason, she always preferred, especially if they were comfortably-off traders in the straggling little town. I'm afraid her morals were none too good, or at least so it was reported by the vast majority of dames on whom Nature had played the dirty in the matter of legs and curves. But there is no doubt she had been maid successively to Crone the draper, Joe Mooney that kept the cycle shop and Andy Marron the lame tailor . . . all elderly men with watchful wives who, in the fulness of time, heaved Maisie on to the sidewalk.

She was now with Phil Murtagh, the grocer who also employed Jem as a counter-hand. Whenever she came downstairs from the living quarters to order groceries for the domestic board, she cocked her retroussé nose in the air and imitated the Duchess of La Rochette in the "Smart Girl's Journal." Always as she retreated with her groceries up the steep stairway, Jem used to watch the rhythmic movement of her perfect calves and imagine himself rescuing her from the blazing remnants of a ten-storey building with Kilmistogue looking on. He envied the pot-bellied Murtagh who used occasionally, after a few double Irish, to cup her pert chin in his podgy hand and give her virtuous advice as father to daughter. As these occasions became more frequent, Mrs. Murtagh watched her chance, and one day when she found a safety-pin open in her crying baby's napkin, she was delighted. She fired Maisie on the spot, and Murtagh himself knew from her eye that silence was ever golden.

Round the corner, Adolphus Menzies, the burly dentist, was advertising for a smart receptionist, and when Maisie presented herself in a short well-cut navy skirt and a blouse that was generous to a fault, she was engaged on the spot.

Jem, who was continually mentally rescuing her from every danger, from earthquakes to White Slavers, shamelessly pilfered from his employer chocolates, cigarettes, kirby grips, shampoos and soap flakes, and laid them at her dainty feet without hope or expectation of thanks or reward. Then one day as he slipped her a tube of beauty cream out of a job-lot that Murtagh had picked up on the quays of Dublin, she favoured him with a miraculous smile and invited him upstairs to her little attic. Jem trembled with ecstasy. It was incredible, but dammit, it was true! On the way up, as the stair was steep and the view heavenly, Jem threw his moral resistance over the crazy banisters. She seduced him in five minutes, although poor Jem thought it was he that was to blame, but that is neither here nor there. He went home engaged to her. He was a new man. He stepped on the pavement with mature deliberation. He swept his hat off perfectly to Mrs. Walls who kept the Post Office. He patted Joe Slaven's bull-dog and called him "oul' boy." His mother had tea and a pancake for him. He told her meditatively and with becoming dignity that he was shortly going to marry Maisie. His mother, who knew every game in the eternal jockeyings of her sex, whipped off her red slipper and beat the hell out of him. He went to bed black and blue but impervious to pain. His manhood was intact, and indisputably he was on the up-and-up.

A week or so later, Maisie burst into tears in Jem's manly arms and told him her awful secret. Jem soothed her chivalrously, kissed her hair and assured her that even though cash was short and altars high, all would be well.

He confided in his mother, who again gave him the slipper with might and main. His mother's vituperation and the sheer ferocity of her blows gave birth in Jem to a terrible, an incredible, an appalling suspicion. Weary of her tongue and smarting from her violence, he swept into the street. He was a man. He must do the things a man would do. He must, in short, get drunk.

In Paddy Murnaghan's bar, he was received with an ovation by the cream of the locals, and their applause increased as he tossed back ball after ball of Irish malt.

"Begod, Jem, I never knew it was in ye!"

"I always say ye can't keep a good man down!"

"What are ye goin' to call it, Jem?"

"Faith, aren't you an example, Jem, to them in this place that's twice your age and not a rockin' cradle nor even a sixpenny napkin to the credit of their manhood!"

The iron was now deep in Jem's soul.

"Yous can laugh," he cried, "but I'm not as big an ejot as yous take me for. I'm not marryin' Maisie, and when she takes me to the Court, me mother will have her grand-uncle, Michael Joe Doran, the solicitor in Dublin to defend me. And believe me, when Michael Joe with his lashin' tongue and his spakes out of the lawbooks, gets Maisie in the box, he'll not be long gettin' out of her the names of some of the fine gentry in this place."

The speech was so electrifying that Andy Marron, the lame tailor, dropped his crutch, Joe Mooney spluttered into his pint, Crone the draper knocked over his whiskey, and old Murtagh bit the end off his pipe.

Some days later, Jem, who by this time had told Maisie where exactly she got off and why, was sitting alone in his mother's cottage when suddenly a paper wrapped round a small stone came through the open window and landed on the table beside him. Recovering from his fright, Jem un-wrapped the paper to find a message for him in sprawling block letters.

"Come down, Jem, to Phil Murtagh's old barge at the landing place on the canal tonight at nine, and you'll maybe hear something that's good for you."

At nine o'clock he was in the shadow of the black hulk of Murtagh's barge. In the dim light he discerned a beckon-ing finger, and he followed it on board and down the steep dilapidated stair to the small cabin beneath that was lit by an overhanging paraffin lamp. Five men were seated round the heavy table playing cards, and drinking tumblers of whiskey. Jem recognised them as Murtagh the grocer, Crone the draper, Mooney the cycle dealer, Andy Marron with his crutch and the burly Adolphus Menzies, the dentist. They gave Jem a riotous welcome.

"We always had a great wish for you, Jem, and for your father before you, before he fell off the railway bridge," announced Crone. "Hadn't we, pals?"

"We had, we had!" chorused the pals.

"And we're all for peace, progress, sobriety for others, the oul' sportin' instincts and the good o' the family. Aren't we, men?"

"We are, faith, we are!" chimed the men.

"Peace with the wife. Peace with the priest. All for one and one for all, and keep it a *man's* country. Look now at the state of England and America with unmannerly wives hoppin' things off the heads of their dacent men before God! Am I right now, pals, or am I wrong? Let yous tell me!"

"You're right! You're right!" roared the pals.

"Then we'll drink to them sentiments, pals, with a small thimbleful of Irish dew."

They filled the tumblers and clinking them thunderously against Jem's mug, drank copiously. Then they coughed, blew their noses and eyed Jem out of limpid, benevolent eyes.

"We'll now come to the matter o' Maisie," announced Crone.

"Yous will not!" growled Jem.

Crone looked at him out of large soulful eyes with a pained expression on his face.

"We can surely, Jem, discuss a proposition in a . . . a Christian spirit," complained Crone coaxingly. "Now, Maisie is a nice girl. A bit high-spirited, I'll grant yous in all fairness. But did any of yous ever yet see the spirited little filly that hadn't a grand streak o'fire in her teeth and in her tail? Now, I'm askin' yous! Man to man."

"It's true, it's true," chorused the company.

"There's not one of us here but would drag her to the highest altar in the country, toot-sweet, if only polygamie and the new dacencies of the twentieth century could be got out of the way in a lawful and Christian manner. But unfortunately that's not to be thought of."

"It is not, faith," affirmed the chorus.

"Jem, there, is the only man here in an enviable position . . . sound in wind, limb and energy and blessed with free will and the full pleasure of a rovin' eye."

"So that's what yous are up to," shouted Jem.

"Sure you don't understand us at all," complained Crone. "If it was an oul' spud like your dad, God rest him, it would be different. Sure, man, Jem, there's money in it. We're generous friends and neighbours, all of us."

"Money?" queried Jem. "How much money?"

"There's twenty pounds apiece from us, man. Sure I'm tryin' to explain and you that headstrong and fiery."

"Twenty apiece, is there?" countered Jem. "And I'm to stick Maisie for the rest o' me natural! Yous are grand fellas surely. Good night to yous."

"Thirty, then, Jem. Sure we'd not make little of your father's son. Sure now, don't be makin' us bargain like packmen sellin' oul' rags."

"Sixty apiece, or nothin'!" roared Jem.

"Sixty!" The company rose to their feet and wiped their brows. "Do you want our poor wives and kids to go straight to the Poor House?"

"To hell with yous!" roared Jem again, and dashed for the staircase which he pretended to find too steep for rapid ascent. They were around him in a moment, cajoling, beseeching and complaining. Jem sat on the lowest rung and played delightfully with them. They mopped their brows, whispered hoarsely to one another and drank more whiskey. Jem watched them impassively but his mind was working fast. Five times sixty pounds, he was thinking, would make him comfortably off. And Maisie was a good looking little stepper in spite of the trouble she was in. A fellow couldn't have everythin' in this world . . .

They gave in wretchedly. On Jem's rigid instructions each wrote, signed and handed to Jem a personal I.O.U.

pledging himself to pay Jem sixty pounds as a wedding present on the morning he married Maisie. Jem had them on
toast, and he was determined to keep them there. He threw
back another mug of malt, lighted a cigar, pocketed the five
I.O.U.'s, grinned at them provocatively, waved them an ex-
travagant good night, and went off chuckling. At the Post
Office corner, he met Maisie looking worried and distraught.
Her impertinent eyes flashed daggers of fire at him and she
was about to miscall his seven generations in the public
hearing, when Jem precipitously gathered her in his arms,
called her his adorable little pet, smothered her with kisses,
and told her he had been troubled with his conscience, and
was about to do the right thing by her before all men.
Maisie, in a transport of delight, hugged him hysterically
and, taking him to her attic, thanked him as only a woman
in trouble can. Before he left her, the date of their marriage
was fixed.

The local priest, a charming little man who read Bernard Shaw all day, and had a powerful passion for race-
meetings, told Jem, when he called at the presbytery, that
he took a very poor view of promiscuity in any shape or
form in his parish, but nevertheless commended him for his
exemplary adherence to the moral code and fixed his marriage for two weeks ahead.

The following day, Jem took the now radiant Maisie
to Crone's drapery shop where she ordered her new going-
away suit with all the hauteur of a young duchess.

"Is your mother paying for this suit?" asked Crone
cautiously.

"She is not," said Jem.

"It'll be cash in advance," warned Crone.

Jem surreptitiously showed him his own I.O.U., and
whispered hoarsely in his ear.

"Take it out of your I.O.U. on me weddin' morn."

Jem departed with Maisie for the shop of Andy Marron, the lame tailor. As they entered, Andy hobbled towards them on his crutch.

"I want to be measured for me weddin' suit," announced Jem. "And I'll also be wanting two shirts and pyjamas and a couple of yon red ties with the Round Towers on the front of them."

Andy put the tapes on Jem.

"Is your mother paying for all this?" he asked.

"She is not," said Jem.

"It'll be cash in advance. Times is bad," announced Andy and suddenly found himself staring at his own I.O.U. concealed in Jem's palm.

"Take it out o' that, on me weddin' morn," said Jem.

Emerging into the street, he put a loving arm around Maisie, and led her into Joe Mooney's cycle shop where in high glee they selected two highly decorative cycles with racing handles.

"We'll have a cycling honeymoon," said Jem suddenly.

"Darlin'," said Maisie, "the wonderful brainwaves you have. But dearest lovingest, I do hope the cycling won't do baby any harm."

Before Jem could be husbandly-wise on this particular subject, Joe Mooney nudged him on the arm.

"Cash down on the spot," warned Joe, and found himself staring at the secretly-exhibited I.O.U., like a rabbit staring at a stoat.

"Stop it out of that on me weddin' morn," whispered Jem with a grin, as he followed Maisie into the street where they mounted their brand-new bicycles, took hands ecstatically and swept rhythmically out of sight.

Jem never heard of the Song of Songs, but all through the next week his heart kept singing it gloriously. On the evening before his wedding day, he dressed in his new suit and shirt and went off whistling to meet Maisie by appointment under the salley trees by the canal. She wasn't there, but ah! She was worth waiting on. He lit a cigarette and visualised her tossed wilful hair, her limpid eyes, her sweet impertinent mouth, her shapely legs and ankles. The three hundred pounds that were as good as in his pocket were, to be sure, a secondary consideration, but nevertheless they added to the grand harmony in Jem's heart.

He awoke from his reverie to behold Maisie approaching in her new bridal-blue, going-away suit. But what was the matter with his eyes? She was on the arm of the burly Adolphus Menzies, the dentist! Jem steadied himself against the trunk of a tree. As they passed him, chattering and laughing together, Maisie did not give him even a passing glance. His eyes goggled, his hair became full of electrical disturbances. He raised his voice in a hoarse, dry croak. She swung round tempestuously. Adolphus went discreetly on out of earshot.

"Well, well," said Maisie with perfect equanimity, "if it isn't Jem Doran. Well? What do you want? You're always annoying people!"

"Ah . . . Um . . . Aye . . ." said Jem vaguely.

"I'll have none of your Ums and Ayes," said Maisie peremptorily. "What do you want?"

"We . . . we . . . we're gettin' married in the mornin', Maisie darlin'," gasped Jem.

Maisie threw back her maddeningly impertinent head and laughed heartily.

"Marry *you*, Jem Doran, is it?" she taunted. "Not if you were the last pair of trousers in secula seculorum after an earthquake, you daft, silly, skinny, wet, desiccated piece of mush brought in by the bloody cat. Go on, go home to your ma. I saw the doctor yesterday for a check-up before the honeymoon, and he laughed at me fears and said there was nothin' wrong with me health at all, if you know what I mean, and that all I needed was a good iron tonic to fortify me agin the villainies and calumnies aimed at me respectable name in this town. I'm marryin' Adolphus next week."

"You're what?" roared Jem. "You're not marryin' him in *that* suit!" Jem seized a generous fistful of her skirt and held on to it like a leech. Maisie snarled, bit, scratched and cried out to Adolphus.

Adolphus retraced his steps, socked Jem on the jaw with a terrific left, and put him peacefully asleep under the salley tree.

Twenty minutes later, the slow pattering of the rain awakened Jem. He sat up and stared around him with one eye . . . the other one was lost in swollen blue folds of flesh. He pulled out his five I.O.U.s and regarded them woefully. His voice broke, his active eye dropped scalding tears on their grandiose flourishes.

"Begod, I'm ruined, that's what I am!" he cried, "ruined and murthered . . . ruined and murthered . . . Three hundred darlin' pounds down the drain without even one binge out of them! I'm goin' mad, that's what I am . . ."

At the cottage, he found his mother out, and he was glad, for now they spoke little and seldom, on account of Maisie. He sat morosely down and put a piece of raw steak to his eye. He was thus engaged when the door was suddenly burst open and Crone, Mooney and the limping Marron rushed in upon him, tossed him on the floor, denuded him of everything but his cotton underpants and went their way, followed by Mooney with the bicycle he had captured from the side of the kitchen dresser.

Outside at the corner, they took the five I.O.U.s from a pocket of Jem's new suit, tore them up and scattered them to the winds.

Just then a cheery hello greeted them from the distance, and looking up they saw, perched gracefully on a new bicycle, a sweet, svelte figure in bridal blue riding by with pleated folds sweeping back in the wind displaying a pair of perfect silken legs.

"Hello, boys," Maisie called out. "How's the huntin'?"

They stared after her wordlessly.

The Stepmother

THEY called him Timmy the Shanks, obviously because he had sparrow ankles and thin lanky legs. But it was his face that captured you, with those woeful blue eyes, half mischievous, half fearful of the queer untranslatable world of the Dublin quays on which he lived, with his widower father, who kept a ramshackle tobacco and sweet shop in one of the murky, sun-starved streets. He remembered, a year before, sheep-faced men in dark clothes bearing his mother's body away in an ugly-shaped box that had been sprinkled with holy water by a whitehaired priest who clapped him on the shoulder and said, "Sure isn't me pal, Timmy, twelve years now, and nearly a man, thanks be to God." He didn't understand it at all, and he cried a little in his small room, for she had blue forgiving eyes and a way of disarming his childish fears. Besides, she hadn't finished the story she was telling him night by night about the lovely Niamh who took Ossian away on the white steed to a

land where there was no death and no one ever grew old.
. . . Without her he went timidly on, translating the dark
shapes of the night into monsters of evil, a prey to the
vivid imagination she had so tenderly bequeathed him.

His chief pal at the Christian Brothers' School was Buster. His father, a kindly, stolid, unimaginative shopkeeper,
didn't much approve of Buster, for he was a few years older
than Timmy and besides Buster's father was in and out of
jail through a weakness of his for relieving people of their
superfluous possessions. But Timmy couldn't help liking Buster, and the friendship persisted.

The crisis in Timmy's life came when one day, returning from school, Buster showed him, outside the doors of
the grimy Births, Deaths and Marriages Registry, a notice
framed in glass informing all and sundry that his father,
Jeremiah Clooney intended to wed a woman called Lena
Lanningan, described as a spinster.

"Haw, haw, haw!" laughed the tougher Buster, "you're
goin' to have a stepmother, Timmy, oul' scout, and you
know what that means!" Timmy looked fearfully at Buster
as he grinned fiendishly and slapped his cheeks mockingly.

"Me dad wouldn't do that, Buster," said Timmy. "Me
mother's only a year dead."

Buster laughed sarcastically.

"Gar! He's been courting her for months in MacLark-
ey's Cafe at night when you're in bed."

"What's she like, Buster?"

"Terrible! Face like a hatchet! Eyes like gimlets! Ha,
Lena Lannigan! She's the dame will lannigan *you!*"

Timmy went home full of dark forebodings. His father
was weighing sweets in the shop and he didn't dare question him. He went upstairs to the ramshackle little flat
above where Mrs. Galgoogley, the plump widow who cleaned

up for them daily, was laying the tea table. She had reasonable expectations that Jeremiah would eventually marry her for Timmy's sake, and as a consequence she was fulsome in her endearments to the little chap, and occasionally tried, much to Timmy's alarm, to smother him between the mounds of her ample bosom.

"Timmy boy," she greeted him amorously, "I have a cake for your tea with strawberry angels and fairies on the top of it."

"Please, Mrs. Galgoogley," said Timmy, "I'll wait for me dad coming up. I have a sore head with the sun."

Timmy ran into his tiny bedroom and shut the door against the menacing world. He got out his mother's book and went into bed. It opened at the bright picture of Niamh on her white steed rushing on over clouds and windgusts to the Isle of Youth. He remembered one night objecting that a horse couldn't *fly*. Her white arm was around him clothed in the white lawn sleeve of her nightgown that had funny little lace ruffles and ribbons. "Well, Timmy Clooney," she had said, "I like *that!* Let me just tell you, me bucko, that my grandfather had a dog that could smoke a pipe, and my own mother had a mirror that could tell her everything that I was doing behind her back! And as for the ass that talked back to Balaam. . . ." He fell into a fitful sleep with the tearstained picture pressed to his face.

Meanwhile, Jeremiah had come up from the shop and was morosely nibbling at his evening meal. Mrs. Galgoogley had advised him to let Timmy sleep it out, in case of a touch of sunstroke.

"I think he's missing his mother around," she said meaningly. "You might be the better of gettin', by the grace of God, a good sensible new mother to take care of him."

"I was just thinkin' that way, Mrs. Galgoogley," answered Jermiah. "The boy needs a mother."

"Well, Jeremiah," she suggested jocosely, "when you're

eye starts rovin', let you give meself what the Yanks call the once-over! I have a nice little sum tucked away and I'm a widow now five years."

Jeremiah paused with the cup halfway to his mouth. He coughed and blew his nose with embarrassment.

"Indeed, no man could get a better woman than yourself, Mrs. Galgoogley," he said lamely, "but sure I didn't know you were that way inclined, if you know what I mean. So when Lena Lannigan that's from me own town in Limerick agreed to take the plunge with me. . . ."

Mrs. Galgoogley's mouth narrowed, and her eyes glinted.

"Do you mean that thing with the black mop of hair that I thought was your daughter by an earlier marriage?"

"Sure I thought you knew," apologised Jeremiah, "and aren't the banns up at the Registry Office?"

"You thought I knew, did you? Jeremiah Clooney," she replied witheringly, "and I slaving here at two bob an hour with—what I might rightfully call justifiable expectations!"

With that Mrs. Galgoogley lifted her shopping bag and with a snort that shuddered the rosebuds on the wallpaper swept through the doorway. Jeremiah mopped his brow, grinned sheepishly and poured out a fresh cup of tea.

The next day, Mrs. Galgoogley got her revenge and she savoured every second of it. Timmy had just come in and was toying with a slice of toast, when she touched on the question of his father's new marriage.

"So it's true then," said Timmy sadly. "I saw their names on the notice boards."

"Aw, God help ye, you poor motherless waif," ejaculated Mrs. Galgoogley darkly. "Lena Lannigan of all people! A gadabout that came to Dublin from her own place with swarms of stories round her name—chucked out of her own town, I daresay, for villainies that I daren't mention to an innocent."

46

"Is a stepmother bad, Mrs. Galgoogley?" asked Timmy fearfully.

"Did you ever find one that was good?" she retorted with a snort. "Whisht, child, in case I'd be uncharitably provoked into tellin' you what they really do, in secret of course—like tyin' you to the bedpost all night, or even makin' you eat caterpillars and worms in your lettuce. That poor little chap that died in hospital last week full of cuts and bruises . . . but I'll say no more. . . ."

That night at supper, Jeremiah discussed his coming marriage with a hail-fellow jocoseness that rang far from true. Timmy's reactions were deplorable even when Jeremiah slapped him hilariously on the back and promised him his new mother would have a wonderful electric train for him as a present.

"But, dad," suggested Timmy innocently, "if we could just make it an aunt or—or something instead of a mother. . . ."

"But good gracious, man, you have only your Aunt Dolly in Limerick and I wouldn't have that sourpuss here for a fortune. She's been on the hunt for a man since I was the size of a drumstick."

"But if Mrs. Galgoogley could come oftener . . ." persisted Timmy.

"Don't mention that battleaxe to me again," ejaculated Jeremiah. "Never passes through the shop but she swipes a quarter of tea or a Swiss rolly-polly! No, no, Timmy, boy, your new mother's a smashing girl that you'll love, and you're to meet her tomorrow at the top of the stairs in a new suit with a powerful bunch of lilies-of-the-valley. And I'll expect you, Timmy, to be a little gentleman and give her a good hug and kiss."

Timmy stared at his father as if hypnotised, his face a pathetic study in apprehension. That night in his dreams he met the dog that smoked the pipe for his mother's grand-

father, and the dog took the pipe out of his mouth with his
left front paw, glared at Timmy and laughed sarcastically
at him. He awoke in a sweat. The house was deadly silent,
and the old clock in the sitting room wheezed protestingly
as it gave to the world the dark hour when churchyards
yawn. He looked about him fearfully, but everywhere there
loomed the crushing dark that had swallowed up the flitting
reassuring figure of his mother. He closed his eyes sorrowfully. Someone had let him down badly. . . . He didn't
know who . . . but it wasn't fair. . . .

The dawn ushered in a woeful morn, the morn on
which Timmy was to meet his future stepmother. To his
horror he saw that a mysterious hand in the night had
laid his gaudy new suit across his bed-chair. He touched it
with trembling fingers. From the unswept street below he
could hear the fishmongers calling their catches and the
raucous voice of a newsboy shouting the main heading of
the morning paper. Then suddenly he became aware of
shrill whistling under his window. He opened up and looked
down. It was Buster. There he was with his sinister grin
and his wide protruding lugs.

"Ho, Timmy the Shanks, I've been whistling my head
off for you," he complained. "I thought you was dead—murdered, if you get what I mean." He winked horribly and
Timmy felt the butterflies in his tummy. The newsboy passed
calling forcefully. "Do you hear what that chizzler is calling?"

"I can't make him out," said Timmy.

" 'Schoolboy's body found in cellar. Stepmother accused,' " announced Buster with a knowing shake of the
head. "I suppose you'll believe me *now*."

"But it can't be, Buster!" cried Timmy. "She daren't!"

"Do you want me to sock the chizzler on the chin and
call the Dublin Daily Chronicle a liar?" rapped Buster. "Do
you happen to have a cellar in there?"

"My dad has one under the shop," said Timmy.

"Makes it dead easy for her," announced Buster with a shrug. "Poor oul' Timmy, you're as good as a goner already!"

"But the police, Buster . . ." squeaked Timmy, now thoroughly aroused.

"The police can't do a thing until after—your body is discovered," said Buster with great calmness. "I know all about the law from my Pop—he's in and out of the clink like a pendulum. Hello! There's the bell. I'll be late. So long, Timmy. At least we'll have a day off for your funeral."

Buster with a broad grin slouched off leaving Timmy frightened and distracted at the window. He shivered as he surveyed the tiny room and the closed door. There was only one thing for it now. His Auntie Dolly in Limerick. After all she was his mother's only sister and if she was quarter as good as his mother, she'd understand. He dressed feverishly in his familiar togs and tossed the new suit under his bed. Surreptitiously he made his way down the stairs and was in the act of racing for the street when his father who was carrying cartons of cigarettes from the cellar called him peremptorily. Timmy noted that the cellar trapdoor was yawningly open and below it looked sinister and dark where foul deeds could be done in secret and never discovered. One look at it decided him. He dashed for the doorway, and in a moment was scampering down the street, falling over beer cases, jumping across orange boxes and dodging fruit lorries. Emerging into the broad O'Connell Street of Dublin he landed with a lithe spring on the platform of a bus. Timmy meekly held out the bright sixpence he had earned the previous day for delivering papers.

"All the way, to Dublin Airport, son?" queried the conductor.

"Oh, I'd love that," said Timmy naïvely.

49

The passengers, noting his blue eyes and his pleased innocence, were interested and amused.

"Does your mummy know you're goin' to the Airport alone, sonny?" asked a motherly woman with a shopping bag.

"Sure me mother's dead," said Timmy artlessly. "Me dad's to get me a new mother soon."

That was the beginning of it! Eyes got suspiciously wet. A woman muttered something about the villainies of men, and had a dozen nods from her neighbours. A scarecrow of a man with a battered hat and a neck like a strangled chicken coughed asthmatically and said: "Sure let it not be said of us that we let the motherless orphan leave us without a wee jingle for his pocket!" And in a moment he was going round with the dilapidated hat into which pennies and small silver poured with crazy Irish abandon.

Half an hour later Timmy was nonchalantly seated on a couch in the huge waiting room of Dublin Airport, musingly filling each pocket in turn with the proceeds of his *tour de force* on the bus. Outside, great planes swept down from the sky and as he watched them with large innocent eyes his boyish heart danced and was glad. Life for the moment was good. And sure maybe something would happen —it always did, he ruminated, in his mother's stories.

And something *did* happen. From the loud-speakers came the dramatic call:

"Passengers for Flight 452 for Limerick Airport will now embark."

Timmy listened with a lump in his throat. He thought of Limerick and his Auntie Dolly, and all the rich people who would travel through the air on Flight 452. As he heaved a heavy sigh, a stewardess in Aer Lingus uniform entered briskly, reading a passenger sheet in her hand. She had a lovely face and lo! she eyed Timmy with a bewitching smile. Timmy grinned sheepishly back.

"Ah, there you are, my little man," she said briskly. "I have instructions to collect you and set you down at Limerick. This way, now, old chap, and be quick. We have only a minute!"

In a moment she had Timmy by the hand and she was sweeping him as it were through the air. He tried to give voice to his slow wits, but she shook her head peremptorily and rushed him onwards. It reminded him vaguely of the day his mother, with a lovely blue dress and a veil over her eyes, swept him on to the train for Cork and told him he was a pest and gave him a lollipop and a bull's-eye and a coloured book with a wolf with a poke bonnet in bed on the cover of it. . . . But that was long ago . . . so long that it was just like a story that wasn't true. . . . He came to his senses when he found himself seated in a deep chair with a belt round him that imprisoned him. He saw the top of a steeple passing him, and wondered how he got up so high. His wonder increased when the vision in the uniform smiled beautifully again and presented him with a delicious strawberry ice. Then as in a great glass he saw far below the magic that men wrote about—the lakes and the blue mountains and the mad riot of colour that shot through everything and finally the lordly Shannon like a great gleaming ribbon in the hair of a queen. . . . He felt drowsy and slept, till a gentle hand on his cheek awoke him. It was so cool and sweet. For a moment he thought it was his mother's hand and that the picture engraved on his heart of the sheepfaced men bearing away the ugly-shaped box was a horrible dream. But the lovely lady in the uniform was nice all the same and she spoke to him gently.

"We're just coming in to land, Jim, old chap," she said. "I'll bet you'll be glad to meet your mother."

"But sure me mother's dead, Miss," explained Timmy lamely, "and I'd hate to meet me stepmother. And if you please, Miss, as I was trying to tell you, you have me name wrong. Sure it's not Jim, but Tim I am all the time."

The stewardess eyed him problematically, and consulted her sheet.

"Wait a minute now, sonny," she coaxed. "Isn't your name Jim Connors?"

"Indeed, Miss, and it's not, and it never was. Sure I was always Tim Clooney. Sure me pals all call me Timmy the Shanks."

Timmy regarded her out of wondering eyes. The stewardess stared at him nonplussed, got promptly captured by his comical face and broke into peals of silvery laughter. She touched him maternally on the chin.

"Timmy, old boy, trouble's my twin brother," she sighed. "And I'm certainly up to the eyes in it this time. But no matter. We'll have you sent back to Dublin on the next plane."

When they landed she hurried him from the plane and placed him firmly in a deep chair in the waiting room of Limerick Airport, complete with one enormous sandwich and a glass of milk.

"Don't move out of there, Timmy," she announced, waggling her lovely finger at him, "till I come back for you."

Timmy nodded meekly as she ruffled his hair. But Dublin meant his gimlet-eyed stepmother and the thought of her brought back the butterflies to his tummy. He gulped down the milk, stuffed the sandwich in his pocket, and with a countenance as innocent as a cherub's, swept through the folding doors and disappeared.

After wandering for an hour on the open road, Timmy finally came to a little cottage, on the rustic seat of which a little old woman was sitting busily knitting. She looked up at him and smiled with strange sad eyes.

"Well, little man . . ." she said.

"If you please, ma'am," said Timmy, "could you ever tell me where the town of Limerick is?"

She laughed tiredly and pointed to the spires in the near distance.

"Sure there it is yonder, sonny," she answered. "Sure if it was any nearer it would fall on you! And what might you be wantin' in the town of Limerick?"

"I'm lookin' for me Auntie Dolly," said Timmy simply. "It's maybe that you know her."

"Ah, sure there's dozens of Dollies in the town of Limerick. What is she like?"

"Me father says she's mad lookin' for a man," supplemented Timmy. The old lady laughed wheezily.

"Sure aren't they all, son," she said. "And wouldn't it be the poor world if they weren't. What does she do for a livin'?"

"She makes hats in a wee shop beside the Shannon Bridge."

"Ah, sure if she does, you can't miss her. Did you come the wide road from the Airport?"

"I did, ma'am," answered Timmy.

"Did you happen to see my son, Oweneen, on the road? A tall chap with a fine chest and a great shock of hair on his brow."

"I did not, ma'am," said Timmy. "Small men only I saw and them stooped at their work."

"They're not makin' them like Oweneen any more," observed the old lady wistfully. "He went away, and he told me to knit a pullover for him. He said he'd be back by the time I was finished it."

"And have you finished it, ma'am?" queried Timmy.

The old lady laughed indulgently as she regarded him.

"You're such an innocent little codger. . . . Sure how could I finish it and make a liar of Oweneen?"

Timmy regarded her quizzically.

"But if you come to the end and if he's not here . . ." he began, and the old lady smiled again.

"I always rip out the second-last row and do it again," she explained. "There's no one will say my Oweneen is a liar."

"But when did he go, ma'am?" inquired Timmy.

"He went yesterday, son," answered the old lady.

"But sure if he went only yesterday, ma'am . . . and you knitted all that since yesterday. . . ."

She laughed again indulgently.

"What a little codger you are!" she exclaimed. "Sure it wasn't *yesterday's* yesterday that Oweneen went. It was the yesterday of the years. . . . But sure you'll not know until the years learn you. . . . Are you springing a surprise on your Auntie Dolly?"

"I am, ma'am," said Timmy doubtfully. "And it's that that's worryin' me. Do you think she'll be glad to see me?"

She smiled at him with deep yearning.

"'Tis maybe she will, by the grace of God. . . . If she isn't glad, let you trot back to me and I'll give you a bite and a sup, and if Oweneen isn't back, I'll maybe give you his pullover."

Timmy thanked her with innocent grace and trotted on to the town of Limerick where he inquired his way to the Shannon Bridge. There sure enough he saw a small milliner's shop with the name DOLLY DONEGAN over the door.

"Sure that's me mother's name," enthused Timmy, and made for the door. On the shop wall were scrawled in chalk in drunken letters the words: "Dolly Donegan loves Grundy the Grocer." Timmy was digesting this tremendous allegation with a sheepish grin when the door suddenly opened and he was enveloped in a tornado of flying arms, legs, skirts and a perilously dancing bosom. He felt himself getting well and truly spanked on the bottom. The tornado was his angry auntie, Dolly Donegan, who was having a troublesome time with the local schoolchildren. Unfortunately for Timmy, she mistook him for the ringleader, and hysterically presenting him with a wet rag ordered him to rub out the offending libel instantly. In a daze, Timmy complied, and was then bundled into the shop and thrown across a couch. He was next aware that his furious auntie was bearing down on him with a cane and a series of deplorably fluent ejaculations. His slow wits finally coined a single word:

"Auntie! . . ."

"What!" ejaculated Dolly, rolling up her sleeves.

"If you please, ma'am, if you'd give me a wee minute . . ." began Timmy, but she raged at him afresh.

"Don't you dare call me 'Ma'am.' I'm a Miss. Never had anything to do with any horrible man!"

"But if you please, Miss, I'm your nephew Timmy from Dublin and you're my Auntie Dolly," blurted Timmy.

Dolly stared at him with goggling eyes.

"Are you me poor darlin' sacrificed sister, Philomena's only child?" she gasped.

"That's me, Ma'am—I mean Miss," stuttered Timmy. "I ran away to see you because me dad is marryin' a new woman."

"What!" bellowed Dolly. "The scoundrel! the villain unhung! the reptile! I always suspected that fellow wasn't a spit in the eye off bein' a Mormon! I advised poor foolish Philomena to give him the back of her hand. I have no hesitation in sayin' he poisoned your poor mother with an overdose of "Heavenly Slumber" sleeping tablets!"

"Please, Auntie, it was all arranged that I was to be buried in the cellar," sobbed Timmy. "Me pal Buster swore it to me and crossed his heart."

With a wild movement born of maternal hunger, Dolly seized Timmy in her arms and imprisoned his head between two highly-generous breasts.

"Me poor darlin', lost, emaciated and destroyed innocent," she sobbed. Timmy grinned sheepishly on his heaving pillow and was glad.

The days that followed were red letter ones for Timmy. She dressed him in a new suit, filled his pockets with jubejubes and bull's-eyes, made fairy tea-cakes for him in the oven, bought "The Adventures of Battling Brooster" for him, chased him all round the flat in his pyjamas before he went to bed, and swore that she'd get her pal, the Chief of Police in Limerick, to have his father transported to Devil's Island for breaking his mother's darlin' heart. And all went merry until Grundy the Grocer called to deliver Dolly's usual order of groceries. He eyed Timmy with a watery eye, and wasn't impressed. He knew Dolly had a comfortable nestegg salted away in the savings bank, and he had made up his mind to make a good sensible marriage deal with her. Timmy was a complication he hadn't foreseen. He loathed children anyway—they were troublesome especially if involved in a marriage proposal. His mean liverish mind started working on how best to eliminate Timmy. Timmy's reaction to Grundy was equally unfavourable. His child's mind rightly interpreted the mean sallow face, the drooping moustache, the lanky wet hair, the soiled grocer's coat. . . . He hoped Auntie Dolly wasn't in love with him.

But Timmy's hopes were vain. That night, excited by the superhuman exploits of Battling Brooster he couldn't sleep, and he became aware that Dolly was in jocular conversation with someone in the little sittingroom. He recognized the fruity lisp of the elderly grocer. Their voices came to him only too clearly.

". . . and to tell you the truth, Dolly, I dawdled round to you because I couldn't sleep," he heard Grundy saying.

"And what kept you off your sleep, Jem Grundy," asked his aunt tartly, "except of course your bad conscience?"

"Ah, sure God help me, Dolly, I'm mad in the head

about you," said Grundy mournfully. "I was wonderin' in me poor mind if you'd marry me."

"I'm a good girl, Jem Grundy," he heard Dolly saying, "and no good girl is easily taken."

"Stop your tantrums now, Dolly," came the funereal voice of Grundy. "I'm in a terrible masterful mood the night and I'm not to be denied."

Then he heard Dolly sigh a long meaningful sigh.

"Ah, sure, what's the use of me fightin' you, Jem, if you're in the masterful mood," she said shakingly. "Kiss me this minute, and destroy what little is left of me resistance."

To the sound of smothered sighs and laughter, Timmy fell into a fitful sleep. The rainbow world of his Auntie Dolly was falling darkly apart.

The next day he noticed that his auntie's eye had a new gleam. Her step had a new litheness and she unmelodiously hummed "Drink To Me Only With Thine Eyes." Suddenly while she was trimming a hat she turned to him and gripped him by the elbows.

"Timmy," she announced, "I'm goin' to marry Grundy the Grocer, God help him, and you and I are goin' to live at his grand place over his fine shop."

"He won't want me," said Timmy. "He'll want to send me back to me dad and me new mother."

"Over my dead body," rapped Dolly.

But Timmy was right, for a few nights later he was an innocent eavesdropper of a heartbreaking conversation. He lay back with large hurt eyes on the cosy pillow and listened to the conversation that filtered through to him. Grundy's voice was stern and he could hear him disgustingly sucking his wet lips.

"Timmy's photo is in the Dublin papers, Dolly," Timmy heard him saying. "It's breakin' the law hidin' him here. I'd smack his spoiled backside and pack him back to his da."

"Try it, Jem Grundy," invited Dolly with trouble in

her voice. "Put a finger on him and Dolly Donegan will be up for the murder of the meanest oul' arse-and-pockets in Limerick town!"

Timmy grinned sheepishly. If only . . . ah, but sure didn't God make women to want men in the strange union that he didn't understand. The next sentence from Grundy petrified him.

"What might you be goin' to do with him when we get married?"

"Take him to live with me of course," answered Dolly. "I'm not likely to get any children of me own from a wizened dried-up oul' scarecrow the like of yourself!"

"Me foot's down," announced Grundy with funereal emphasis. "I'm goin' to see that that chizzler is sent home and no nonsense."

That was enough for Timmy. In a jiffy he was out of bed and feverishly donning his clothes. When he opened the window Limerick town was immersed in shadow and mystery. A vision of his stepmother with gimlet eye and hatchet face gave him the courage he needed. He climbed agilely through the window, balanced himself, hit the street rhythmically and was off like a hare on his travels again.

Instinct rather than discretion led him to the railway station where he found himself casting a pair of innocent and inquiring blue eyes on Joe Rafferty, a veteran engine-driver who was busy oiling his engine preparatory to a non-stop trip to the ancient town of Tipperary. Joe had just had a couple of pints against the rigours of the journey, and he was still licking the stray blobs of Guinness from his enormous moustache, when he became conscious of the winning blue eyes.

"And how do you like me oul' girl, Matilda Jane, sonny boy?" he asked wheezily as he landed a tobacco spit on the gleaming piston rods.

"She's terrific," enthused Timmy.

"Twenty-five years together now, me and her," ruminated Joe, "but she's soon for the scrap heap, and a lousy new Diesel is to take her place. That's the way of the world, son. Dead and forgotten and get on with somethin' new."

"That's how it is with me dad. He's forgotten me dead mother and he has a new woman."

"The villain!" roared Joe, tugging his moustache violently. "What is she like?"

"I didn't wait to see, sir," supplied Timmy, "but me pal, Buster, says she's a horror."

"I can well believe it," vociferated Joe. "The same stepmothers are the curse of the country. So you ran, did you?"

"I did so," said Timmy. "I wanted to get to me Uncle Tom in Tipperary. He's an engine-driver too."

"Tom what's-his-name?" queried Joe, sailing a stream of tobacco juice across the funnel.

"Tom Donegan, sir. Sure he's me dead mother's brother."

Joe dropped the huge oilcan and grabbed Timmy by the hand.

"Put it there, mate," he ejaculated. "Sure Tom Donegan and meself have done the main lines for more years than I remember. Get in there beside me, pal, till I land you plop on Tom's doorstep."

As Timmy ecstatically mounted the tender and found himself confronted with a gleaming line of brass levers, he knew that never in his coming life, long or short, could this mighty moment be superseded. His wildest dream had come true, and when Joe made him draw down a lever that released a whole tornado of sound and steam he was in the seventh heaven. As they moved out of the station on the magic wings of adventure, Timmy found himself believing in everything, even in his mother's grandfather's talking dog with the pipe in his left paw.

"Hold tight, son, on the bends," roared Joe at him

above the whistling wind, "for it's a mighty tricky way to oul' Tipperary."

But fear was a stranger to Timmy, as they swept through the countryside and whizzed through tiny country stations. Timmy danced and waved to passersby and dreamed of his showing Buster how to work the levers. On the plain of the Golden Vale, Joe handed him over the controls, and with gnarled, oilstained hands gently over the tiny ones of Timmy, they raced between the ancient ruins and rolled through the coloured countryside. Then as they hit the shoulder of the mountains, Joe took over, and Timmy held fast to the iron girding. But at the sharp and treacherous bend to the left for Arrandell and Urney, tragedy waited. The engine lurched violently and Timmy, caught off his guard in the ecstasies of his experience, was suddenly heaved over the edge of the tender. He hit the grass verge with a force that made his body rebound and go rolling down the embankment where the rows of cruel ageless stones awaited him. They seemed to rush at him like angry bloodhounds and beat him about the body and face. But a kindly dark robe came over him protectingly and he felt himself falling pleasantly downwards to the gnarled roots of an old oak tree, and there at the foot of it, with a pipe in his mouth was his mother's grandfather's dog. Timmy got to his feet apologetically and grinned sheepishly.

"Gosh, what a man!" commented the dog sagely, taking the pipe philosophically in his left paw and sitting back with a grunt on his back legs. "Why, you're worse than a March hare!"

The conversation with the dog was long and whimsical, and during its course, a whitehaired country doctor leaned over a prostrate little body and said, "The spine is affected. This is a job for the Mater Misericordia Hospital in Dublin, and he'll have to be moved very carefully." Timmy was arguing with the dog about March hares and

talking cockatoos while two powerful headlamps lit the
Irish countryside and a white ambulance sped past to
the prayers of rural strangers who blessed themselves at the
sight of it and murmured, "May God give him back his
health and if He can't may He give him a merciful hour."

Timmy was listening to a learned dissertation from
the talking dog on the absurd pretensions of woman-spoilt
budgierigars and certain spurious breeds of tomcats who
pretended to tell the future by tapping with their left paws
at the full moon, as white-masked doctors and nurses were
fighting grimly with a certain big black hound that they
called Death in the operating theatre of the biggest hospital
in Ireland. And it was hours later when Timmy awoke and
found himself looking inquiringly into a very sweet face
that had the queerest little frilly cap perched perilously on
the curls of her shapely head.

"Don't move, Timmy, boy," she said gently.

"She's terrible like what me mother was," thought
Timmy, and with a sigh he went back to the talking dog
who by now was striking a match on his backside and re-
lighting his pipe with the air of a philosopher who has
long ago learned to tolerate the idiocies of the adult world.

"As I was saying . . ." resumed the talking dog, but
Timmy's mind was coming and going unaccountably and
the dog was getting impatient with his inattention when
he awoke again to find the vision with the frilly cap perched
on her curls putting a small spoon in his mouth that tasted
of the honey his mother used to give him long, long ago
before he knew that death and ugly-shaped boxes existed.
Timmy tried to speak to her.

"Just call me Sister, Timmy," she said gently. "And
your poor father's been here for hours and hours. Don't
you want to say hello to him?"

Timmy gripped the neat wrist with the starched cuff
enfolding it.

"Is me stepmother with him?" he queried breathlessly.

"She is not," said the Sister. "We don't allow stepmothers in."

Timmy remembered just seeing his father bending over him, and his drowsy face getting wet with tears. Then he went back to the talking dog who by now was dispassionately dissecting the claims of Pegasus, the famous Classical Flying Horse, and the Irish White Steed, both of whom he alleged existed only in the magnificent and pardonable imagination of rural folks who had never been contaminated by the idiocies of what learned bags-of-wind called Education. Timmy was just beginning to tell him that his mother was a firm believer in the White Steed and that if he had the nerve to take it on himself to call his dead mother a liar, or worse still, a romancer, then it was time for a proper showdown, when the Sister tapped him with a spoon on the jaw, and he found himself eyeing her with naive innocence and eating what he took to be corn flakes.

"Joe's been in and out like a pendulum," whispered the Sister. "When are you going to let on you know him?"

"Joe?" inquired Timmy vaguely.

"The engine driver," said the Sister. "He calls you his footplate pal, Timmy."

"Let Joe in, Sister," pleaded Timmy, grasping her white cuff, "but please don't let me stepmother near me."

"Catch me!" said the Sister gently. "I always throw stepmothers off the roof."

And with this assurance, Timmy with a sleepy grin was away back to his pal, the talking dog who by this time had his tail in his mouth and was playing on it a hilarious rendering of "Here's a Health to You, Father O'Flynn."

"That was a favourite of your mother's grandfather," said the dog wiping his tail carefully and putting it back between his legs. "The oul' devil—he drank both meself and himself out of house and home. I even had to go out and scrounge bones off the neighbours. That was how I got killed."

"Killed?" echoed Timmy incredulously.

The dog laughed indulgently.

"What an innocent you are," he ejaculated. "Did you not know I was dead?"

"I did not," said Timmy, wide-eyed with wonder.

"Ah, indeed I am," said the dog ruminatingly. "Going on twenty years now."

"And am I dead too?" asked Timmy fearfully.

"Well, you're not two licks of a marrow bone off it," said the dog. "But I don't like the way you keep running away. . . . It's maybe that surgeon that's patching up your spine will bring you back to the fooleries of the daily round up yonder."

"Do—do—do you ever see me mother?" asked Timmy breathlessly.

The talking dog took a flea out of his left ear and stamped on it.

"She's not around this part," he said hesitantly.

"What does that mean?" asked Timmy.

"Well, you see," answered the dog, peering into the bowl of his blackened pipe with a quizzical eye, "the oul' Colonel and meself were two pretty hard cases and . . . if you know what I mean. . . . But I did see her once in the distance when she was paying a visit with a lot of others to see what ill-spent lives lead to, and she pretended not to know me, but I put me tail in me mouth and I gave her a few bars of "Rafferty's Racin' Mare." *That* I might tell you put the cat among the pigeons. She lifted her gorgeous veil and grinned at me. After that there was seven thunderclaps and lightnin' flashes that burned the moustache off me. That night the sermon was on *me!*"

Timmy was just beginning to ply the talking dog with further questions when he opened his eyes and found himself gazing into the furrowed weather-beaten face of Joe, the engine-driver.

"Me oul' pal," Joe was repeating, and it was awful to see him trying not to cry like a baby. Timmy saw his own small wasted hand lying in the gnarled paw that often drove Matilda Jane from Limerick town through Ballyeffelstown, Cornapuffle, Slieveangrien, Ballymac, Lissnacree and Urney straight into old Tipperary.

"What are you cryin' for?" asked Timmy simply.

Joe wiped his face with an oil-soaked handkerchief.

"It's Matilda Jane," said Joe, his voice breaking embarrassingly. "I saw them takin' the funnel off her this mornin' and unscrewin' her wheels. And you should hear the jokes they were makin' about her! The same men, Timmy boy, would laugh at their own mothers' funerals. Forgive me for blubberin', Timmy, but they say there's a boy in every man that never grows up. I saw Matilda Jane long, long ago, in shining brass and copper, and the Mayor of Limerick called her 'The Pride of Ireland.' "

Timmy rubbed his great fist soothingly.

"The new Diesel engine will be like a stepwife to you, Joe—just like me with me new stepmother," said Timmy sadly.

Joe clenched an enormous fist.

"I'll never acknowledge one of them," he ejaculated. "I'd rather be dead."

"Neither will I," said Timmy thinking of his stepmother. "I'd rather be with the talkin' dog."

But in the days that followed, Timmy paid fewer and fewer visits to the strange dog with the clay pipe and the burned moustache, and paid more and more attention to the sweet-faced Sister with the cool hands on his brow and the funny little frills on her cap. She had given him her solemn promise that his stepmother would never get near his bed and she had even promised that she would take him to a little place at the coast where they could hire a boat and go fishing for sharks and whales and elephants. Timmy knew of course that this was just silly, but coming to him in the gentle voice of the Sister he couldn't for the life of him reject it and he sank down into sleep with a queer little smile.

But as he slept, a grave conference was held over his bed. On one side was the gentle-faced Sister with her fingers in Timmy's curls, and on the other a stout little man in a white coat who had a severe Imperial beard and a pair of stern owlish eyes that wouldn't know a tear if they saw one.

". . . and I have gone as far as I dare," the Surgeon announced dispassionately. "The injury to the spine may or may not be permanent—it is a matter for the patient himself. If he has the positive will to walk, he will walk, but if he hasn't, then—I'm afraid he will never walk again. . . ."

The Surgeon regarded the Sister with keen emotionless eyes. She nodded gently, and as he adjusted his glasses, he noted that a tear fell from her and tarnished the impeccable whiteness of her collar.

"Very unprofessional, Sister," he remarked brusquely, and in a second he was gone.

It may have been days or even weeks afterwards— my memory is hazy now—but Timmy woke one fine morning to find his pal, Joe, and the Sister whom he now adored, manipulating an electric train that careered round a circular line that was laid out on the polished floor. Timmy gave such a gasp of delight that the two sprang up with broad smiles.

"Me pal, Timmy," ejaculated the engine-driver. "See what I've brought you."

Timmy's eyes goggled, and something vivid and electric passed through his queer little being.

"Me mother promised me one like that when I reached her shoulder . . ." said Timmy shakingly. "But I hadn't enough time to grow before they. . . . Could I have the engine on the bed, Joe?"

Joe looked forlornly at the Sister who watched Timmy with gentle but firm eyes. She spoke slowly and with an effort.

"You—must—come—for—it . . . Timmy. . . ."

"But if you please, Sister, sure me legs won't walk," said Timmy with a little sob in his voice.

"They'll walk if you say they will, Timmy," replied the Sister firmly. Timmy looked at her beseechingly but beyond a suspicious little quiver of her lips she remained adamant. Joe came with rough tenderness to the bedside.

"Get your teeth into it, sonny, and don't let it get you down," urged Joe, clenching his great fists. "You're goin' to be a man some day."

"I'm waiting for you, Timmy," said the Sister calmly, and she rebelliously wiped away a furtive tear.

"Are you goin' to cry, Sister?" asked Timmy innocently.

"Only if you let me down," she said almost in a whisper.

Timmy, with a queer little smile at her, turned down the bed clothes and bit by bit edged his body to the side of the bed. A minute of torture followed. Then slowly he worked his way to the floor so that he stood supported by the bed. His hands quivered as he gripped the iron rail.

"Me oul pal! . . ." sobbed the engine driver involuntarily, and Timmy smiled ruefully at him.

With heart-moving gradualness he moved step by step to the bottom of the bed, clinging fearfully to the rail. Then turning with great effort he looked forlornly across the—to him—vast floor space that separated him from the

Sister. Their eyes met for a long moment, and Timmy shuddered all over his puny body.

"Courage, pal," breathed Joe, and then he turned his rugged face away. There are some things a man cannot bear . . . things they leave to the bravery of their women. . . . The Sister's face was an eloquent study in hidden suffering. Her voice was low but gently imperative.

"I have said you must come to me, Timmy, and you must come," she said in a strange hushed voice. "I am waiting for you, son."

Timmy looked longingly at her. What miles separated them in his frightened imagination. But suddenly she smiled at him and with a mighty effort of the will he took one brave step into the unknown . . . then another faltering step . . . and yet another . . . A frightened little cry escaped him as he realised he was utterly alone on the polished floor. He was about to collapse when she held out her arms to him and called his name softly. With a wild sob of endeavour he walked stumblingly to her and in a moment he was wrapped sobbing in her arms.

"I done it," sobbed Timmy. "I done it for *you*. . . ."

"For *me*, Timmy," she said softly. "You're my son now, aren't you?"

"If you want me to be," said Timmy appealingly.

"I want you to be, very much, Timmy," she whispered, "because you see, I'm your stepmother."

My Learned Friend, Hogan

Dᴜʀɪɴɢ those years, I had been a Sergeant in Middlestone, and it was only natural that, when last week I got leave after we had convicted Staines of poisoning his wife, I should go back to the picturesque little town that was crazily perched on a lofty cliff that overlooked the Straits, and relax in the sea air and sunshine.

I ran into Hogan in the bar of the Pipe and Horn, and that evening over a Scotch salmon mayonnaise and a bottle of hock, we found ourselves discussing the death of Halliday twelve years before.

I liked Hogan. He was an extraordinarily shrewd type, but winning in manner and personality, and was now a very successful chartered accountant. But in my time there, he had been a junior in the firm of Halliday, Leach and Hogan, which dissolved after the tragic death of Halliday.

"I could never finally believe it was an accident," Hogan said to me as he drank a glass of hock.

"There was never any evidence to the contrary," I answered.

And indeed that was true. During the enquiry into the tragedy, it was elicited that Halliday and Leach were taking one of their occasional walks along the crazy path that wound like a ribbon round the summit of the cliff. It was a very windy day, as I remember, and that fact stood strongly in favour of Leach—that and the fact that Halliday was still weak from a recent bout of influenza.

Leach swore that a sudden vicious gust swept Halliday from his side over the edge. He tried to grab him but it was too late, and to his horror he saw his partner's body rebound off a jutting-out elbow of the cliff and go somersaulting into the angry waters which swept it out of sight in a moment.

Leach rushed down the cliff in a very distraught condition and immediately reported the tragedy to me at the local barracks. I alerted every town and village on the coast, but Halliday's body was never found and we concluded it had been swept out to sea.

I subjected Leach at the time to the most gruelling cross-examination, allowing him no rest, in the hope that he would weaken and give me an opening. But it was all to no purpose. Mind, I admit that Leach was an introvert, difficult, sulky, taciturn and by no means given to loquacity, but he was perfectly frank with me when the question of his business and social relationships with Halliday came up. It was young Hogan—now twelve years older and toying with his hock—who had secretly prompted me at that time to bring up the question of Vera Manners.

I had known Mrs. Manners quite well—a most charming and good-looking widow in the early thirties. Her late husband had owned extensive property in the picturesque neighbourhood and left her very well-off. The firm of Halliday, Leach and Hogan had looked after her affairs. I remembered that there had been quite a buzz of local excitement when she and Halliday had announced their engagement.

But to return to Leach, my incisive questioning concerning Vera Manners was met with a frankness and honesty that amounted almost to naïveté. He quite admitted being in love with her, and in fact a bit jealous of his rival whose smiling charm and personality won the prize against Leach's taciturnity.

"After all," Leach had burst out to me, "everyone was in love with Mrs. Manners—even that young upstart, Hogan."

I knew there was truth in that assertion for I had seen the tell-tale admiration in Hogan's shining eyes. To be absolutely frank, I had been a bit gone on her myself!

At the end of the enquiry, we concluded that Leach was either a totally and entirely innocent man wrongly suspected of a dastardly deed, or the most cold-blooded cutthroat in England. I had personally concluded he was the former. But Hogan had always remained suspicious, and I had naturally put it down to jealousy.

Hogan looked up at me from his strawberries and cream.

"You may have closed the case, Inspector," he said smilingly, "but it was never closed for *me*."

"Sour grapes," I teased, "because you couldn't win Vera Manners."

Hogan pushed away his plate and laughed heartily.

"Shall I tell you the rest of the story?" he queried.

"I didn't know there was anything to tell," I replied, for in truth I had forgotten all about the rural tragedy in the deep vicissitudes of metropolitan crime.

"You didn't know then that Leach married Vera?"

"I did not," I answered sitting up attentively.

"Well, he did, and in fact in a mere six months after Halliday's murder."

"You mean of course his death," I said sympathetically, for I realised that Hogan, for all his charm, still nursed his jealousy.

"Just as you like, Inspector," he replied. "But let me go on. I stayed on with Leach for a spell after his marriage. But Vera became quite a frequent visitor to the office and I fell more and more in love with her."

"Did she know?"

"Doesn't every woman know?"

"Did you declare your love for her, or—do the decent thing?"

He laughed heartily again at my shaft.

"Not in words. But I fetched and carried for her, brought her cups of tea, stamped her letters for her, found her gloves for her when she mislaid them—"

"I know. Go on. Did Leach notice?"

"Of course he did. He became more and more jealous of me, found fault with my auditing, accused me of incompetence, and finally dissolved the shaky partnership between us. After that I set up on my own in opposition to him. I grew to hate the very sight of him. I could see him passing my windows daily—lean, crabbed, surly, wrapped up in his thoughts, and occasionally she was with him, a lovely creature with the limpid eyes of a gazelle and the poise of a duchess."

Hogan's eyes were now flashing with hauteur and hatred. I watched him fascinated, and sipped the brandy the waiter had brought me.

"I was now fully convinced—call it unreasoning jealousy if you wish—that Halliday's death had been no accident. Then one day something happened that spurred me to action. I had a caller. It was Vera. The sight of her set my blood on fire. She looked ravishing in a taffeta dress with a blue fox cape round her shoulders. Her lovely eyes looked tenderly at me from under a seductive veil. She wanted to ask my advice in strict confidence. She could trust me. She had grave differences with her husband on this matter. Would I advise her to sign over a considerable sum in stocks to her husband as security for the purchase of this very hotel that was then for sale."

Hogan's eyes were now tender and indeed almost child-like in their soft memories. I was excited.

"This *is* exciting," I ejaculated. "Go on!"

"I advised her against signing over anything beyond small domestic commitments, but suggested she should buy the little hotel in her own name and with her own securities, if she thought fit."

"Why did you make such a suggestion?" I asked rather sharply, and he again grinned in that subtle way of his.

"Perhaps I had my reasons," he answered. "She tapped my arm gratefully with her beautiful gloved hand. Yes, she would take my advice—and indeed she *did*."

"She what?"

"She now owns this hotel."

I drew a deep breath.

"You scoundrel, Hogan!" I ejaculated, and once again he laughed heartily and signed to the waiter to bring more brandy.

"I was now so deeply in love," he continued, "that I employed all my ingenuity to think up some subterfuge that would unmask Leach."

"And this subterfuge?"

"After weary nights of nervous exhaustion, I found the one that I felt would work, and I decided to embark on what I called 'Operation Leach' without further delay. Next evening as the wintry dark was thickening, and the rain drizzling on the rooftops, I called on Leach just as he was closing. I knew I would find him alone at that hour. I was a bit of an actor in my younger days and it was easy for me to put on the act I staged. As Leach opened the door to me, I staggered past him and collapsed into the old green hide armchair beside his desk. My hair was unkempt, my face pale, my tie loose and irregular. He stared at me in utter disgust.

" 'For God's sake, Leach, pour me out a brandy—quick,' I gasped.

"Leach poured me out a miserly measure and I gulped it down, and laid down the glass with a shaking hand.

" 'And now perhaps, Hogan, you'll explain the meaning of this disgusting exhibition,' he rapped at me.

"I looked at him and feigned suppressed excitement.

" 'I was in Templestone this afternoon on business and I—I saw Halliday,' I ejaculated.

"As I watched him covertly, he stiffened with a jerk. That gave me heart and assurance. I was going in for the kill.

" 'You've been drinking, Hogan,' he growled with rising anger.

" 'No, Leach. On my honour. Just a lager for lunch—no more,' I assured him.

" 'Stupid fool!' he raged. 'It couldn't be Halliday. His body was swept out to sea.'

" 'But it was,' I countered. 'I tell you, Leach, I *spoke* to him.'

" 'You *what?*' he roared, and his eyes bulged.

" 'He pretended not to know me first, but when I insisted he drew me into a shadowy doorway,' I continued grimly, as the drama mounted. 'He looked ill and dishevelled and he bore an ugly gash on his left temple. He gripped me fiercely by the lapels and made me swear never to mention I saw him to anyone—*you* least of all.'

"Leach staggered backwards, and pouring out a stiff brandy, drank it with one gulp.

" 'Why *me* least of all?' he croaked, now deadly pale.

" 'He said he had a rendezvous with you, Leach, in secret,' I explained with emphasis. 'He told me that the fast tide had carried him down the coast. A lifeboat man rescued him and looked after him in his cottage by the shore.'

"Leach suddenly gripped me fiercely by the arms and raged at me.

"'You never liked me, Hogan,' he bellowed. 'Tell me the truth or I'll strangle you.'

"A tussle followed, but being more lithe and agile than he, I succeeded in breaking free from him. At the door where I was comparatively safe from a sudden maniacal attack, I looked at him contemptuously.

"'I'm damn sorry now, that I said anything to you,' I barked.

"His hands were still clawing the air, his mouth gaping, his eyes bloodshot.

"'You hate me,' he raved. 'Why then did you come and warn me?'

"'Because you are in great danger,' I answered. 'I certainly don't dislike you *that* much.'

"'Why am I in danger? I admit nothing. Nothing—do you hear?' he yelled.

"I decided now to throw my last ball.

"'Halliday said he was officially dead,' I answered. 'And that he wanted to remain dead, so that the police wouldn't start looking for him after he had murdered *you*.'

"'*Murdered* me!' he groaned.

"'That's what he said, word for word. I don't know why, but I've warned you. It's your affair, Leach. Good night.'

"As he slumped into the armchair I had vacated, I made a dramatic exit. I went home and waited."

As he stopped speaking, his grin appeared and he gently warmed the brandy with the fingers that encircled his glass. I watched him closely. There was not a trace of nervousness in his poise—in fact his grin was maddeningly evident. I marvelled at his self-assurance, his complete con-

trol of his emotions. I found myself thinking that Hogan
had in him all the potentialities of a highly-dangerous criminal. But I naturally kept my own counsel.

"You waited, you say," I remarked at length. "For
what?"

"What do you think, Inspector?" he answered with a
deepening grin. "I had only to wait about an hour. The
news came through around nine o'clock. Leach had shot
himself dead through the temple. Considering everything,
Vera took it calmly. After the cremation, I advised her to
take a holiday with some friends in Paris, and as usual she
gratefully took my advice. I saw her off on the Golden Ar-
row at Victoria. She looked lovelier than ever in black. . . ."

As I watched him fascinated by his nonchalance, the
waiter presented me with the bill, but Hogan flipped it
from me, signed it with a careless flourish and waved the
waiter away.

"So your hunch was right, Hogan?" I remarked.

"My hunch was right, Inspector, and the case is now
closed," he answered serenely. "Come through with me and
I'll stand you a nightcap."

He escorted me to a beautifully furnished suite. As he
poured the drinks, a striking woman came through from the
bedroom clothed in a delightful dress of white organdie.
She looked at Hogan with adoring eyes and he took her
hand affectionately. I recognised her almost at once as
Vera Manners.

"You've met my wife before, of course, haven't you,
Inspector?" said Hogan, and that devilish grin spread all
over his face.

Me Da Went Off the Bottle!

It all began on the day me da took the pledge. I was just a nipper at the time, chasing A, B and C down the algebraic labyrinths, and calculating how long it took to fill a cistern by the senseless method of leaving an ingoing and an outgoing tap open simultaneously. My elder brother, Paddy, did all the milking and manuring and general slave work of the farm for little or no wages according to the mood of me da. My goodlooking sister, Kay, was mooneyed about Jerry Doyle who was just back from Dublin with a veterinary diploma. My father, Peter, in his sober senses was a martinet, strict to the point of tyranny and given to nagging and girning if everything wasn't just plumb right. But when he was reasonably lit up with a few balls of Jamieson's Three Star, he was as decent and generous a spud as you could get, and it was a delight to hear him singing "Lord Clare's Dragoons," even if he was wholly incapable of singing in time or in tune. On such happy occasions, the family rejoiced and was glad.

I was always the first, little ferret that I was, to announce the glad tidings that me da was on the bottle. "Me da's after comin' out of Mike Regan's pub and he's singin'," I would exclaim hilariously and chuck my Algebra and Professor Meiklejohn's Latin roots into the clothes basket.

"He has a drop in him, praises to God," my harassed mother would say, and put on a kettle of water in readiness for the punch. And mind you, she liked her ball o' malt as well as any woman, only when me da went on the wagon she, poor thing, had to follow suit.

But as ill-luck would have it, a young pioneering priest with a pale tubercular face and the eyes of a zealot came to the parish to assist the old Canon who was a charming old chap who read Bernard Shaw and tolerated everything with the single exception of sexual promiscuity. It was the only sin in the calendar he outlawed, and as he was touching seventy he could never understand what mossy banks and dew-wet meadows were made for. This young priest's father had been a publican, and although the profits from good porter and bad whiskey had paid for his long training in Maynooth Seminary, he had for the drink a hatred that seemed to consume his unhealthy being.

In his all-embracing campaign against it, he selected twelve elderly men, good men and true, to be the spearhead of his open war on Bacchus, and believe it or not he christened them his twelve apostles. They were intended to be a living and eloquent example to the young men of the parish. The old Canon suffered this pioneering activity with a patient shrug and merely removed his bottle of Jamieson from the communal cupboard to a small wall cabinet in his bedroom.

You can imagine our consternation when on one dreary Sunday morning me da put on his swallow-tail suit, with his black Parnell tie and his half-gallon hat and gravely announced to the assembled family that he was St. Peter.

From that moment on, our lives jointly and severally became a living hell. The good old glass of hot malt that submerged the prim Christian in me da and made him charitable and kindly was gone forever, and on his ponderous watch-chain he wore a total abstinence medal the size of a five shilling piece. He became the most cantankerous little spitfire imaginable, totting up poor mother's account books, grudgingly giving poor Paddy a miserable half-crown on Saturday nights, instead of the habitual ten shilling note and a bottle of Guinness, and warning Kay that if she as much as looked the same side of the road as young Doyle was on, he'd hang her off one of the bacon hooks in the kitchen ceiling as a deterrent to fleshly and unmaidenly thoughts and desires. As for me, if he caught me knocking jam jars off the pier of the gate with my catapult instead of finding the cubical content of a pyramid standing on its end, he promised me four of the best on the bottom and a double ration of the same at bedtime.

Of course we all went to mother with our woes and worries.

"Mother, what sort of a man is that you married at all, at all? Were you out of your senses or what? If we slipped out to the dance tonight, mother, could you possibly square it with your conscience to swear that we were over at the Church instead?"

And she, poor thing, would soothe us and beg us to have patience.

But me da's zeal got worse instead of better as the days lengthened into weeks, and the drier his stomach got for want of a rozener the sourer he got in the tongue. But each of the Apostles watched their colleagues with the eye of a hawk and me poor da daren't give in. Mother, cute old thing that she was, used to put a bottle of stout here and there about the house where his roving eye would catch it, but he invariably hopped it venomously off the pier of the gate outside much to mother's chagrin. So logical and sensibly moral was my mother that she even went the length of saying a secret Novena that me da would go back on the bottle; but her prayers weren't heard.

Then one evening, to our horror, he marched us all to church—mother in her sable bonnet, Paddy in his shiny bowler, Kay in her little blue cape and I in one of those infernal skull-caps that were a target for the unprintable eloquence of the less respectable boyos of the parish. And there in the presence of this ecstatic and tubercular-ridden cleric, with me da as St. Peter pompously erect, we raised our lighted candles and renounced forever the works and pomps of the fiend that Satan posted in every beer bottle.

The first casualty under this iron regime was Kay. It came from a kiss stolen by Jerry Doyle behind a cowshed door while Kay was milking our black cow, Roisin Dubh. I was keeping watch for them in fair return for a bar of chocolate, two bulls-eyes, a bar of a sticky sweet called "Peggy's Leg," and a mug of warm milk straight from the generous udder of the said Roisin Dubh. But St. Peter must have been peering through a chink in the dilapidated woodwork of the shed, for he was upon us like a lightning flash.

Kay was seventeen, but seventeen or not, in the presence of us all with her gym skirt drawn up she got six whizzers of an ashplant across her pink bloomers. I remember that evening creeping up to her bedroom with a chunk of bread and cheese and how, shaking with sobs, she put her head into me for sympathy, her big luminous eyes swimming with tears and the long sheeny mane of her hair round her white shoulders. How I hated religion and temperance and all the things that hadn't a little human weakness in them to make them pliable and lovable. I swore to Kay that, if she'd stop sobbing, I'd carry notes between her and Jerry and do it for nothing, and I'd bear twelve of the best from him before I'd give them away.

"And anyway," I added with a wave, "won't you and Jerry be married when they're all in hell!"

This made Kay suddenly laugh and the laughing became so contagious that we had to bury our heads under the bedclothes in case such an incongruous noise should be heard in the sober house of me da.

But it was the quiet sombre Paddy, the inscrutable man of the fields who rebelled. It happened one day when we were all expecting me da home from the fair whither he had gone to sell a fine milking cow and a few yearlings. We were as usual all round mother begging her to ask him to make this concession or that, but of course she could only give us sympathy without promises. It was then that Paddy lifted me da's framed photograph from the mantlepiece— the one he got taken as St. Peter, with the temperance badge prominently displayed on his watch-chain—and in a moment of terrific tension smashed it into smithereens on the floor and then venomously danced on it.

It was a moment I have never forgotten, with poor Kay in the shakers with fear, me mother grovelling on the floor stupidly trying to reassemble the broken fragments and I hopping around like a wasp in a jam jar. To me it was the unfurling of the rebel flag. I looked up at the fine defiant face of my brother. He was Robert Emmet, Wolfe Tone and Parnell all rolled into one. I wanted madly to be ordered to charge!

"Bravo, Paddy!" I burst out involuntarily, and immediately stopped a corrective left swing from mother that left me sitting half-dazed among the milk churns with about as much fight in me as a doctored tom-cat.

"I'll say I knocked it off the shelf myself when I was cleaning," said my mother.

"Lies!" yelled Paddy.

"And how else can we live but by lies?" cried mother, "and the sour puss on your da for want of a drop."

Then Paddy petrified us in earnest. He lifted the heavy poker purposefully and brandished it.

"There will be no lies told tonight," announced Paddy with strange quiet. "I smashed his damned photo and I trampled on it. That's what he'll be told!"

Kay burst into tears.

"Take that poker from Paddy, mother," she cried, "and hide it."

"If you'd touch your da with that, you'd wither," cried mother. "Even Hell wouldn't have you!"

"One solitary word out of him," said Paddy tensely, "and I'll split him open!"

In the petrified silence that followed, Paddy deliberately went to me da's special armchair—dare any one sit in it but him!—and drawing it roughly in front of the fire, seated himself in it complete with the poker, and began to whistle.

By this time mother and Kay were so nerve-ridden that they both had to run to the old toilet in the garden. I went cautiously to Paddy, eager to get rid of this new and dreadful menace. I clapped him approvingly on the shoulder as man to man. "No one thinks more of you than meself, Paddy," says I, "but as man to man and for the sake of the women. . . ."

It was like as if a wind suddenly caught me up in an idle frolic. I landed head first in a large barrel of flour and emerged from it gasping for breath and wildly trying to sweep the flour out of my eyes, ears and mouth. Paddy's maniacal he-haw-haws made me even worse, and the return of Kay and me mother didn't improve the situation. You could have cut the tension with a butter knife, and it became evident to all of us that serious and indeed even tragic happenings were not only possible but probable. Whatever the blazes got hold of Paddy, he seemed determined to pile on the agony, for when poor Kay meekly handed him half-a-crown she had saved up to buy a blue ribbon to freshen up her washed-out blouse, he sent it whizzing viciously through the window. Then with a deliberate and ominous calmness he went to the vegetable barrel, selected a large turnip and cermoniously placed it before him on the top of the oven. With evident relish, he wielded the heavy poker and cleft it in halves.

"What on earth are you at, Paddy?" cried my mother.

"That was just me da's head, Mother," he answered emotionlessly. "It'll be just like that."

I had had enough. I could feel the blood in me congealing horribly. I ran from the house. But I was no sooner outside than I heard in the lane a step there was no mistaking. I dashed back into the house, deftly seized the poker, and flung it through the window.

"Me da's comin'," I cried. "He's in the lane."

Determined to please me da and to be on the right side in the imminent fury, I seized my Algebra study-book and began hysterically ejaculating about two crazy trains, A and B, departing at amazing speeds from two stations, X and Y, on the stroke of midnight. At what exact second would they meet? And how far from station X? . . . Ah, sure, what the hell did it matter where they met and when! Wouldn't they be better to collide decently and be done with it, for wasn't Paddy goin' to kill me da anyway?

Me mother craved and Kay sobbed and entreated but it was of no avail. Paddy sat on in me da's chair, swinging his lanky legs and whistling furiously. Then as the calm of impending tragedy descended on us like a funeral shroud, we heard the familiar step, then another and another till our hearts thumped like hammers. The knob turned awkwardly, there was a little stagger, a slight snort of glee and a sudden miraculous burst of highly-unmelodious song:

*"For never when our swords were set,
   And never when the sabres met,
Could we the Saxon soldiers get
   To stand the shock of Clare's Dragoons. . . ."*

I leaped from my seat at the table and threw the alge-braic book of tortures into the flour barrel.

"Me da's on the bottle," I roared.

Me mother raised her eyes meekly to heaven and crossed her hands.

"Praises be to the high God for His mercies," she whispered devoutly.

The next minute me da was amongst us, clapping us all on the shoulders and greeting us like loved ones back from the strangers.

"Yerra, sit down, da, you'll be dead beat," said Paddy, jumping up from the forbidden chair. But me da gave him a friendly push and landed him back into it.

"Sit where you are, Paddy, boy," he exclaimed. "And there's a fiver for you."

"It's too much altogether, da. I won't take it," protested Paddy.

"There's more where it came from," answered me da, planking a bottle of stout in Paddy's lap. "What did I get, Paddy, for the red cow with the white star?"

"You got seventy pounds for her," said Paddy, with one eye closed.

"Guineas," said me da triumphantly.

"Begosh, da, you were always a powerful man at a fair!" ejaculated Paddy.

"Praises be to God," interposed me mother, who praised God for a most incongruous variety of things.

Then with a twinkle in his eye he looked at Kay who blushed furiously and didn't know whether she was going to be kissed or caned. But in a second he had an arm about her and the big tears were coming unbidden. Then opening a parcel he handed her a lovely summer dress with an alluring green sash on it.

"Mother," said me da, "put this dress on Kay tomorrow because that pup, Jerry Doyle, is comin' here to ask for her. I'm afraid you're goin' to lose your daughter."

And with that Kay ran embarrassed to mother and buried her face in her breast.

"And pup's the word, mind you," continued me da, "comin' up to me at the fair, with a stiff jaw. 'You're not good enough for her,' says I. But he took the wind out of me sails right away. 'Indeed, I'm not *half* good enough for her,' he answered looking me straight in the eye. Now, what can you do with a cute pup like that?"

It was at this precise moment that his roving eye lit on *me* as I stood, robinishly, with my ear cocked for every word. Then suddenly he rapped out at me:

"What's the factors of X cubed minus Y cubed?"

"X minus Y into X squared plus XY plus Y squared," I rapped back at him.

"Good man," he exclaimed, throwing at me a poke of black balls that I caught neatly on the wing. "You'll be a scholar yet. I'll either make a priest or a stockbroker out of you accordin' as God directs me."

He then handed mother a bottle of Irish, winked knowingly at her and went singing into the little parlour.

"Hot water and cut a lemon and hurry," ordered me mother breathlessly. And we all busied ourselves around her in an atmosphere of happiness and relief. It was at this moment that Mrs. Mullen, our nearest neighbour, came in surreptitiously and caught my mother excitedly by the arm.

"I have a terrible bit o' news for you, Mrs. Grady," she moaned. "St. Bartholemew is after landin' in to me, and he's as full as a piper."

84

"Bless your innocence," ejaculated me mother. "Go and have a peep at St. Peter singin' Clare's Dragoons in the parlour. And she poured out two stiff drams which they took with delicious relish.

It was the beginning of normal humanity again. The land became sweeter from the human foibles of the people who toiled it, and the harvest was golden with rustic feasts and weddings. The delicate little priest whose name I forget, having worn himself out advocating a Puritanism that is foreign to the men of the fields, was quietly transferred to be chaplain to a small Convent, and the old Canon stoically rescued his bottle from his bedroom and having restored it to its rightful cupboard, settled down comfortably in his old armchair to chortle over Shaw's strange "Gospel of the Brothers Barnabas!"

The Virgin and the Woman

Martin used to say in his whimsical way to Mary that it must have been a blunder on the part of the Celestial Foreign Office to have dropped him into a family like the Marrons. Mary was the woman Martin loved. She was also the wife of Martin's brother, Andrew. The explanation they gave each other for their coming together was that they were both human in a tradition of brutality, and that humans will find their way to each other. Martin, with his slim body and sensitive nature, was certainly an incongruity in such a house, for the Marrons, sailormen all, had gone down to the sea for generations, believers in tooth and claw, coarse in body and voice, in mind and soul.

Matthew, the second son, lies at the bottom of the Indian Ocean, together with his ship and a cargo of grain; Owen ran disastrously into one of the terrific squalls that occasionally sweep the English Channel in midwinter; Sydney "had it out" with four mutineers off the Brazilian coast and accounted in person for three of them before dying of wounds as his ship entered Rio; Old John, who had fathered them all, furrowed the seas of the two hemispheres for close on forty years, and lived to hand over his wheel to his eldest, Andrew, who was now lying at Bilbao loading up with iron ore. Some months previously he had by sheer brutal appeal swept the virginal Mary Osborne off her feet, and left her in charge of his father, after three months of uncertain matrimonial weather, for a round voyage that included Shanghai, Beirut, Capetown, Bilbao and Cardiff.

The Marron homestead was a rambling place with rooms smelling strongly of wood-rot and tar, and laden with innumerable models of old ships, and a bewildering collection of odds-and-ends brought home by the brothers from all over the earth. On the walls hung flamboyant prints of storm-tossed ships, and crude sketches of the heads of grisly mariners, but most conspicuous of all—the disconcerting enlarged photographs of the sailormen sons and their father, stolid, stubborn and scowling out resentfully.

Built on the edge of the cliff and about half a mile from the spray-swept town of Orm Point, with its mean streets and its straggling sections of crazy houses huddled round a windy pier, the Marron homestead symbolised the mentality of its owners by its pre-eminence, as it looked frowningly down on the roofs of the humbler dwellings and out over the racing spray of the sea.

No enlarged photograph of Martin hung on the walls in any of the rooms. Neither was there one of the miserable woman who had borne them all, except one hidden deep under a pile of rubbish in a moth-eaten drawer in a back room that looked inland on rolling plains. Here lay a melancholy reproduction of her, on a yellowing surface, half-faded and forlorn.

From the day Martin's boyish fingers smashed one of the many nautical models in the front room, because he "hated and hated them", Old John Marron suspected his wife, and as the boy grew fonder and fonder of reading, and of rambling inland in search of tall, murmuring pines, instead of downward to the beach in search of a legitimate Marron's birthright, the suspicion grew to certainty and his dislike of her to hate.

Before long she broke under the strain of those ruthless eyes with the steel-like lashes above them that were like the teeth of a comb combing her consciousness for what was never there. She lived long enough to be assured that at least she had reproduced her hounded sensitiveness in Martin, and, having prayed that the bud might flower and add itself to the stray wisps of beauty she had discovered in life, passed quietly out.

Martin missed her terribly at first, for there was in him that sprinkling of the feminine that makes a man pliable and adjustable. To Andrew and his father that theory was a damnable heresy. It was an insult to the Marron tradition of blood and brutality. They, therefore, with the frankness of the stupid, denied his legitimacy, and illustrated their contempt for him by hurling him out of their way in the house. When his dogged studying eventually earned him an opening on the "Courier", a paper published in the nearby seaport of Orsbycove, their contempt was crowned. A Marron that preferred an office stool to an oilskin! A Marron that was born with a book in his fist instead of a marling spike. Could that be true and Nature remain impeccable? It finally confirmed Old John's belief that his wife had fooled him—once. It seared the thick hide of his pride. Once in a swirl of temper he grabbed Martin by the chest and swung him round in a fury. In such moments Martin tasted fear. And the taste remained with him.

Grasping for some sort of support when the stay of his mother's influence was withdrawn, Martin fell back on Mary

Osborne. Mary, like all virgins, was a romanticist. Her young visualisation of life along the windy coast was like the grey picture that appeared every week in the "Courier", with instructions for the children to colour it. The crayons, used to hide its drabness under the blues and the reds and the yellows, were romanticism. Life needed romanticism, believed Mary, as Martin believed a man needed as much of the woman in him as would make his personality colourful and flexible.

Now, in Martin, Mary discovered a romanticism of a type not easily translatable by her. His young vehemence of word and gesture she could understand, but his gentleness never, and his habitual silences, sitting with her under flowering foliage, puzzled her. Her young spirit, being virginal, understood as yet only the strong positive urge. The subtler urge mystified it. When, therefore, Martin at times broke his silences to tell her that trees were often more sensitive than human beings to pain and loss, and that hills were often holier than the flaunted spires of great towns, she secretly thought him silly. Once she laughed and she saw him smothering the hurt in his eyes. She came covertly to the conclusion that he was effeminate, and when one day he impulsively put his head on her lap as they sat on a cliff, her surmise was confirmed. The pent-up virginity in her could understand his imprisoning of her hands, or his firm fingers forcing her chin upwards till her lips were vulnerable, but his head pressed pityingly against her bosom was to her negative and as yet meaningless. When occasionally he showed her his name in print above a poem or a sketch she was scarcely impressed. Yet when later she saw a snapshot of Andrew in wildly-blown oilskins, holding a ship's wheel in a shower of spray, she was thrilled to the heaving of her breasts.

In Andrew's walk, in his swinging arms, his compelling stride, in the brutality of his chiselled features, in the peremptory vibration of his voice, there was that positive reaching out, that popular romanticism she could easily interpret. From afar he thrilled her, nearer to her she trembled, but the trembling was ecstasy. One day he imprisoned her hands and twisted her arms backwards, so that her young body was impelled towards him. In this there was that glimpse of abandonment she had tasted in a diluted way in the imagination. It thrilled and trembled her young being like a reed shaken in wind. When afterwards he kissed her forcibly till her body panted, she remained against him after he had freed her—helpless and submissive. Martin, seeing all, could say nothing. He let her go.

Soon Martin was to see her coming out of the church on his brother's arm, and the fisherfolk throwing rice and tiny sea-shells. It made him dislike the squinting spire even more than previously, and turned his mind more fully inward to the torment of his being. The wedding night was a torture to him. On his bed he begged God to let him sleep so that he could escape his imagination. When sleep did come, his imagination ravaged it unspeakably. In the morning he found himself covertly watching Mary. But she gave him no sign, not even meeting the quick glance of his eyes.

During the three months that followed, up to the date of Andrew's departure on the circular voyage, Martin—now terribly alone—kept for some masochistic reason a diary of daily events in the Marron household. Only a few quotations need be set down, and parts even of these deleted, in deference to the niceties of contemporary politeness:

> *Feb. 8th.* Found Mary alone and crying. Wouldn't tell me what the matter was. Women sometimes cry like that when they're with child. Please, not that! . . .
>
> *Feb. 11th.* She looks worn. I've got to find out if it's

that. I'll ask her. . . . If it is, I think I'll go away.

Feb. 12. Funked it.

Feb. 14. Ditto . . . Andrew drunk. Sang 'Shipmates o'
Mine.' Tried to lift me by the hair. . . . Terrified.

Feb. 20th. Asked Mary in a round-about way. . . .
Told me not to be silly. Feel like a new man now.
But I keep doubting. Is she lying to me?

For the week following, the diary becomes so pitifully
intimate that it is not quotable. The nearness of Mary to
the boy makes it too terrible a study. But from March 7th
onwards, it is more readable.

Mar. 7th. I love Mary. I adore Mary. I love my brother's wife. God, what have I come to? I should have
cleared out. . . .

Mar. 11th. Tortured. . . . Mary, today, looks womanly and sad. . . .

Mar. 24th. The old man flung a plate of soup at me
today. Andrew lay back and howled. Mary rubbed
my neck with carron oil. . . .

Mar. 31st. Told Mary I loved her. She just looked at
me with her grave eyes and went on washing cups.
I kissed the back of her neck. . . .

Apr. 3rd. Kissed Mary again. She kissed me back, but
very lightly. . . . How quiet and lovely she is now
—lovelier than when she was a virgin. . . . Mary
is a steady lamp shining over a tormented sea. . . .

Before Andrew went off, he took Mary roughly by the
arm and kissed her. He made her kiss him back, his eyes
fully upon her the while.

"Are you—expectin' anythin'?" he asked of her at
length.

She shook her head, looking up at him, a little afraid,

but steadily. Old John ready to accompany Andrew, joined them from the front room.

"It's damned funny, I call it. What have you to say about it?"

"What can I say, except that there is nothing?" said Mary, her voice very quiet. The old fellow, who suspected Mary, laughed as he drew down his cap angularly. Andrew regarded him meaningly.

There was a pause.

"It's maybe," said Andrew grimly at length to Mary, "a matter of you winning the first round, eh? But the knock-out is mine. Sleep on that till I get back home."

Abruptly he took up his kit and stalked off, the old man following with a grunt. Their oilskins flapped noisily in the fresh breeze as they took the steep road down to the town. Mary watched them from the window—huge hulks in the shape of humanity—till a twist of the road rubbed them, as it seemed, out of existence, as being superfluities. She turned to Martin with steady eyes. He came across to her as if bidden, and touched her deferentially.

At Orm Point the old man did not accompany his son to Orsbycove, where Andrew's boat lay, as he first intended, but, having bade him an almost wordless and yet wholly eloquent good-bye at the railroad station, turned about to negotiate the stiff climb upwards to his now, to him, desolate home. His feeling for his son was jealously and devouringly emotional, and emphasised by the fact of Andrew's ship having been once his own. He was aggressively convinced that a vital and inspiring part of the mariner remains in the wheel from which a stupid age-limit regulation hounds his physical presence. That Andrew, his eldest son, in fact almost his physical and mental reincarnation, now commanded his vessel, and commanded the wheel in which there remained so much of himself, was a tremendous satisfaction to him. Indeed, the love—or whatever it was—between them was no mere cord tied with the conventional family knot, but sharing, as they did, that circular symbol of nautical achievement, it bound them together closer even than blood and kindred.

Heavy with the thought of Andrew, he silently crossed the threshold of his home, and emerged from the toss and tumult of his preoccupation to find Martin's lips on the lips of Andrew's wife, and his arms about her.

For a moment he paused—his resolve mounting the crazy rungs of his thoughts—his hatred of Martin, his convinced suspicions of his dead wife, his instinctive distrust of Mary, his belief that she had outwitted Andrew's desire for a son—till on the topmost rung it flared into precipitate action.

He had now Martin across a bench, tearing at him as if he would release the disputed blood in him and let it drip back to its mongrel source. But Mary kept frustrating him, her firm hands tearing at his oilskins, her body, panting and cat-like, interposing itself, her voice screaming like a swarm of seagulls in his ears. From the welter of sound and forces Martin escaped like a scared rabbit, flying from the house in which, from his first coherent hour, he had been denied his birthright.

With his friend Harvey, in the town, he made a makeshift home, and in the house perched crazily on the edge of a cliff Mary remained, under the watchdogs of scrutiny in a loathed pair of eyes that sleep seemed but rarely to visit.

The lovers were not irrevocably separated. Old John sometimes had to shuffle into Orsbycove to study the whereabouts of the "Carroway," Andrew's boat. And, occasionally, he drank himself into unconsciousness. At such times they reached out to each other, and now and again Martin's love for her goaded him up the steep road, usually in the wake of his father's stumbling footsteps. In the silence of the kitchen he always took her hands in his own and looked down at her. She was good to look upon, now that she was womanly and grave. She was like a certain tree that he loved in a valley out of sound of the sea—willowy and strong without showing it. It wasn't that she was merely guileless—Martin believed, like his father, that she had deliberately frustrated Andrew's desire for a son—for guilelessness was a negative quality, but her positivism, the alluring steadiness of her gaze, the strength suggested by the poise of her head, all enthralled him. Incidentally, he knew with the lover's instinct that she would give him sons, and the secret thought exalted his stature and ennobled him.

But although she conferred her love on him and gave him her lips to kiss, she had not as yet consented to go to him, and face a world that was ever over-ready with its branding irons. In addition to this deterrent there was the physical menace of Andrew, who on his return would be sure to seek, not out of love but out of pride, unqualified revenge.

"He might never come home," said Martin to her one day.

"Men like him always come home," she said, quietly.

Martin sighed. "I wonder how it will all end, Mary," he asked.

"As it is fated to end," she answered.

Then their eyes met in the circle of their thought, clung and gravened. He crushed her to him suddenly with passion and she felt and shared his need. The shuffle of footsteps on the road made them delve deep into the long grass. A snort as of a mind forever running on indignation, came to them, and then the unmistakable flapping of oilskins. Peering, they saw Martin's father. He was quite drunk, and the tails of his old sou'wester were flapping violently about him like the wings of angry birds. But neither drink nor idiosyncrasy could rob him of that picturesque brutality that appeals to the virgin of either sex.

"The yellow scum!" he snorted to the winds, as he passed.

"I'll get in before him and you can slip up later when he's in bed," said Mary hurriedly, and with a bound was off through the grass. As she left him, Martin noticed that the sea was flinging up jets of dazzling spray, and out of its torment were coming rapiers of wind—the advance guards of an imminent storm. He sought shelter under a rock that frowned down on him with a detachment that was unique.

Mary had time to divest herself of her cloak—and of all else, for that matter, that was caressing to her thought—before the old fellow blundered in upon her, fixing her with the peculiar stare of inebriated eyes. This last was by now not unusual to her, and she had learned to suffer it. Yet to-night, he somehow seemed to her other than human—the embodiment of some hateful force her mind flung away from. The very air seemed to become charged with his presence and to take on splashes of sudden fantastic colouring. The roar of the rising wind added to her unrest. She lit the oil lamp with fingers not quite steady, as if in an effort to bring back the natural atmosphere she could understand.

He sprawled sullenly into a heavy chair by the fireplace, his oilskins weirdly about him like diabolical robes, his cap down over his brow. She decided to take him quietly.

"You're late tonight," she said. "Where on earth have you been?"

"Down, woman, where the sea spits on things. I like the way it can spit."

His tone stung her to defence.

"I suppose that means you'd like to spit on me?"

"If I had the mind to, I would. You're no good. You'll never be the mother of a man."

She cooled suddenly, seeing the uselessness of her anger.

"It's time you were in bed," she said, quietly.

"Bed . . ." He seemed to echo it. "The prison of the troublesome, eh?" He laughed, maddeningly, as if he could read in her that which was hidden. There was a pause, and then he added, proudly, "You must keep out of my way and not disturb me. I want to sit and think about my—son." He said the last word emphatically.

"If you were fair at all," she said, "you would remember that you have more sons than one."

The remark roused him to a fury.

"Is every man born of a man's wife *his* son?" he roared. "Tell me that, woman!"

She countered rapidly. "Is every woman tied to a brute bound to drown her own nature, and send on nothing of it?"

"You haven't answered me, woman," he insisted. "Come on! Can a mongrel be the son of a giant, and truth still be truth?"

Again she realised her helplessness.

"Are you going to bed," she repeated, calmly.

"Go you. It might be—safer." The sudden insinuation disconcerted her.

In the tenseness of the pause that followed she realised that rain was pattering on the roof. As she drew the curtains she glimpsed the gathering clouds and the anger of the sea below. On the way to her, she felt, were conflict and hurricane. She shivered, and again asked him to go to bed. His answer took away her breath.

"No bed tonight. I'm expectin' my—son."

"What? Martin?" she managed to inquire.

His voice came like a sword thrust. "My son, I said. Andrew."

"Are you mad?" she protested. "Didn't the boat leave Bilbao only last night?"

He nodded strangely. "It did. It will be rollin' through

the Bay o' Biscay now. Rollin', woman—plungin', stag-gerin'. . . ."

Fear came to her now in earnest.

"And how," she managed to ask, steadily, "could he be home tonight, stupid?"

His answer was so calm that it frightened her.

"How do I know how, woman? But he'll be home nevertheless."

She tried by protestation to reason away her fear. "You're talking in your sleep, old man."

"I mustn't sleep. If Andrew were to sleep at that wheel now. . . ."

"Well, you're not Andrew. You should be in bed."

"Maybe I am Andrew. Maybe in a way we are one another." His voice lost its harshness, but not its sinister-ness. "Isn't that wheel of Andrew's my wheel?"

"Oh, go to bed," she entreated. "What's in that?"

"In it?" he retorted, resentfully. "There's part of me, woman, in that wheel. As there's part o' the dead in the things they leave."

In an agony of impatience she flung up her hands.

"Oh, why am I arguing here with an old fool that the sleep's drowning?" she cried.

The word shot him directly upright in the chair, his eyes on her startled. "What in Hell word is that, woman?"

"I just said the sleep was drowning you," she answered, a little afraid of his attitude.

He held her for a moment with his eyes in thrall, then as if overpowered by recurring sleepiness, lay back again impotently.

"Sleep and water," she heard him muttering. "The two tyrants. The one like a cursed woman, quiet and murdering —the other like a man, terrible but fair. . . ."

The sleep—or was it sleep?—seemed to fall about him

like a veil that made him meaningless and uncanny to Mary. His eyes, although still lidless, became unseeing. It seemed to her he was sinking down into some horrible shell that hid powers and values not of her knowing. She became conscious of the growth of her uneasiness. Simultaneously with the deepening of the silence inside came the heightening of the wind-fury without, and the one made the other more awful. She felt as if, in a strange way, the blacks of hate and the whites of love were whirling over and over down some hill of conflicts and that at its feet lay racing waters that would resolve all things finally. The swirl of the sea joined now with the gathering furies, and she knew how the trees were leaning over to the stunted walls and sobbing like human things.

As soon as Martin pushed the door inwards, and stood wind-beaten and drenched before her, it all suddenly translated itself to her in one word—conflict. And the conflict was imminent. In what shape it would present itself to her she was vaguely aware, and yet not aware. She was, woman-like, piecing together—Martin, the sleeper in the chair, herself, and—Andrew, the last-named though he was myriads of miles from the lists. And still more strangely, she found her intuition insistent upon the inclusion of the dead Marrons as well. She saw them momentarily as Macbeth saw the forms stretched out and out. . . . They touched her consciousness and were made potent in her mind. The battle, she sensed, would be more than physical, more even than mental—a thing shot through with forces she had hitherto not met or felt. Yet she was calm, and Martin saw how quiet and steady her eyes were.

She took his hand silently in her own, and led him in, so that he could see the fitful slumber of the old man. Martin's face in the yellow lamplight was weak and small—small enough to be insignificant to one less human than Mary.

There were lines upon it that, as a woman, she knew the meaning of. They touched her pity and her protective instinct. She looked at him out of her tranquil eyes, and miraculously she loved him. The thought made her a taut, leashed life-force wrapped incongruously in soft flesh.

"What made you let him sleep there?" Martin asked, in a whisper.

"He wouldn't move for me," she answered. She caught his sleeve secretively, and her voice was tense. "He said Andrew was coming home tonight."

She felt the jerk of his body, and saw his face discolour in the yellow rays, and his gaze turn backwards towards the door. He was suddenly afraid.

"To-night?" he said, his breath hurting him. "But that is impossible."

"I know," Mary answered. "But he kept on saying it as if. . . ."

"As if what?"

"As if he were sure." She looked at him fixedly, as if she wanted with all her heart to impart some of her strength to him. "You must hold on to yourself—hard, Martin. Do you hear?"

"But, Mary, there's no—no danger, is there? How could there be?" His lips were twitching nervously and his face had no colour now. "Do you know, I—I think that cursed row outside is going for my nerves."

"If there is danger," she answered him, steadily, "we can overcome it together."

The head of the sleeper lurched a little as if it were borne on a heaving medium. She drew him silently into the shadow cast by a dresser of insect-eaten wood. A branch of a tree crashed down the wind. They heard it hurtling past the window. It was a symbol of brutality, and as such they recognised it unerringly. Martin gave an involuntary sob.

"That's how they would treat me," he muttered. "That tree was me, and the wind was them."

The old man's breath increased into weird speech. His eyes, still open, saw nothing of them, but only what was flung to him over wild distance by the potency of some perverted affinity. He seemed uncannily inspired.

"Lift her to it, Andrew," came his terrible low crying. "Lift her to it, man! It's comin', son, and you're right in the way of it. . . . Don't do that, man! Leave that to the scum aft. . . . Marron blood, eh? It's hell but keep your eyes forward there, Andrew Marron, as I bred it in you, I, John Marron, senior. . . . Hold her, lift her, lift her to it, man! Lift her, by the red blood in ye, son! . . . Lift! Lift! . . . Phew! . . . A couple of points now. . . . Steady! Good! . . . Drenched, eh? . . . What in hell about it. . . . Hold that wheel o' mine, Andrew, son. . . ."

They listened to him spellbound, as if witnessing the conflict of ship and water. Martin was visibly trembling.

"He's seeing the ship," he managed to whisper. A frenzied patter of rain on the roof whisked the rest of his words away on the tumult. Mary was leaning forward, intently listening. "They were so—close, the two of them," she heard him sob in her ear. "Maybe he can see. . . . There's such things, Mary, isn't there?"

"There's nothing we need fear," she said calmly, taking his hand firmly to her side. Yet, in spite of her calmness, she was alert in every nerve, and her being seemed in torment. With a start he saw that she, too, had come to believe. It was not raving, then, or a drunk man's talk, but inspired reaching-out. She was now straining forward as if in a theatre, caught up in the dramatic movement.

"Hi, there!" came the raucous voice again. "Where's the hang-dogs that were workin' the pumps? Scum! Scum! Hold her up to it, Andrew! . . . Hit that yellow cur one in the spine. . . . That's it! . . . He was no good! Scum!

Muck! . . . They're taking to the boats, the sons of whores!
. . . She's—God! She's—she's goin'. . . . Hold her, for
God's sake! . . . Look it straight in the face! Spit on it, man!
that's it! Bravo! . . . It's blood that tells, Andrew Marron.
The rest of a man is muck! . . ."

So tense and uncanny had the atmosphere become
that Martin would have fallen down in fear but for the wiry,
capable arm of his companion. The swirl of the waters from
without lifted his imagination into frenzy.

"They hate me, they hate me," he sobbed. "That poor
devil got his spine smashed because there was a little of the
woman in him to make him human. That would have been
me, Mary—me, me! Over the side and to hell, with me! Oh,
God! . . ."

He would have cried aloud hysterically but for her
hand on his mouth.

"Hush," she said, tensely. "He said it was—going. I—
must know." She leaned forward. "Look, look! He's gasping
as if he was struggling in icy water."

"Does that mean—" Martin began, but she stopped him.
"Listen."

The raving voice was now strangely pathetic.

"Aye, son, you're nearly home now. Marron blood, eh?
. . . Sailormen all, they went their way. . . . Strange lights,
them, Andrew, eh? . . . And the cap'n's on the pier. Ready,
son, salute! . . . Aye, Cap'n, he was a son o' mine—a Marron, if you understand. . . ."

The voice ceased on the night. The head fell back as if
with finality. A sudden swirl of wind viciously shook the
casements and hurled itself down the steep road to the swirl
of waters. A moment's interlude of silence followed. Mary
seized it.

"He's gone," she told him, the repressed breath almost
stifling her. "I'm a free woman, Martin."

"You—believe it?"

"I do." The quiet in her eyes made her appear more than human. The light in the eerie room began to fade. Martin noticed it with sudden alarm.

"The light!" he said, hysterically. "For God's sake, Mary, see to the lamp. Keep it burning, or I'll go mad."

"I'll get more oil from the scullery," Mary said, quietly, her fingers touching his face and steadying his quivering nerves. It was then she looked towards the chair. What she saw made her go forward quickly—Martin holding to her desperately. She touched the flesh of the upturned face. It was cold and like wax. She pushed Martin back.

"You were right, Martin," she said. "They were one."

"D-dead?" quivered Martin.

She nodded. "Both dead. . . ."

He stood petrified, the fear frozen on his face as if it were the work of a ruthless and embittered artist. The rain pattered deafeningly on the roof. She gathered him to her in the blackening shadows and coaxed the life and blood back to his features.

"Dead . . . dead . . . the five of them," he kept muttering.

"And I'm alive. . . . They hated me. . . . I know they hate me still, wherever they are. . . . If they could come here, they would—would." His voice rose into hysteria in unison with the shrieking of the storm outside. Her voice, coaxing and calming him, was like a white feather floating in a fury of sound.

"You must hold on to yourself firmly," she kept saying. "We have won, we two, and we must not be cheated. Wait now till I get more oil from the scullery, and then you'll feel better."

She settled him solicitously in a chair with his back to the dead man, and then stumbled over and through the slithering shadows into the scullery at the other end of the kitchen. He looked after her—glimpsed her undaunted head, and worshipped her. How brave she was! She was as brave and as steady and as quiet as the light men kept burning above Orm Point. She would be the mother of his sons. . . . He glanced fearfully at the inert figure, as if expecting a thunderous protest. The light grew dimmer and dimmer. A long shadow passed from the dead man to himself, saluted him with mock gravity and scurried into a coil of ropes in a corner. His half-crazed mind followed it, and was winding and winding the coils round the slippery sides of the shadow, when the wind with an unearthly shriek flung wide the heavy door and raced round and round the gloomy entrance as if it were a host of crazy human creatures, babbling, raving, cursing and expectorating.

Martin jumped from the chair and cried. But the cry did not come. He fell to sudden childish whimpering—his eyes staring and blurred by the strain of his fear. Small, darting streaks of light rent the shadowy tumult, and his distracted mind translated them as inexorable fingers beckoning to him.

"No, no, no . . ." he cried, piteously. "I can't, I can't. . . . It's too—terrible . . . awful . . . awful. . . . Oh, Mary, I'm lost! They've come for me—the five of them. . . . I knew it. . . . I knew it. . . ."

But the babbling grew louder, and the fingers still beckoned. Outside the furies raged.

"Mary," he sobbed, but the sob choked the strength of his cry, and what did escape was swept away and tormented. His fear and terror now possessed his whole being. Compelled by the merciless fingers, he moved a step towards the door, two steps, three steps. . . . He would have fallen down into unconsciousness could he have taken his eyes from the curving fingers, but they held his gaze as if in some horrible vice, and the babbling screamed and howled about his ears.

"Have mercy on me, have mercy on me," he kept whimpering, as he was impelled forward. "I'm not like you. . . . I have never been strong. I can't look on terrible things. . . ."

It was then the fingers seemed to touch him, and the babbling assaulted all his senses, like rowdy men met for summary justice. He felt himself being hurried past the crazy door, and out into a black cavern of outraged and ravaged sensitive things. A vicious blast of rain blinded him. Something invisible that whirled and eddied hurled him forward. He saw the beckoning fingers again on the edge of the cliff. . . . Then suddenly he became aware of a new force that panted and was brimful of tenacious energy. It flung itself upon him and bore him down to the ground. He was dimly conscious that it was dragging him over the wet earth, and that it was soft to the touch and yet radiated strength. In his first coherent moment he heard the clang of the heavy door and the clamour of the disappointed babbling against it. He knew then that Mary was with him and that her warm body encircled his own. He could hear the violent pant of her breath, and when he looked up her face was flushed and her eyes victorious.

"Stay in close to me," he heard her say. "Away in there. Don't look out there or anywhere. Look only at me—at my eyes."

He looked, and saw her heavy lashes and underneath quietening pools of light, untormented by shadow or windgust. He thought again of the quiet bright light above Orm Point. A great sob shook him and ran from his body into hers, making her a partaker of his humanity and his ignobility alike.

"Hold me in close to you, Mary," he entreated her, "and never let me go from you."

Sitting on the damp, shadowy floor she drew his weakling head into her breast and suffered it. Once she glanced at the chair by the fireplace. The form on it still lay inert and grey, but to her it had no significance. To her, and such as her, the dead must be always meaningless.

Ultimately, a watery dawn came forth out of the grey waters. She looked down at the sleeping face and whispered some little thing that perhaps has no meaning in the dictionary of words. She lifted her head to the sorrowing daylight. The dawn is a sad woman, and for a moment they regarded each other—two women who must be about their business. She smiled slightly and, as if in answer, a single shaft of sunlight touched her tossed hair and made it beautiful.

One Act Plays

The Conspirators

CHARACTERS

Brigid Anne Galgoogley (an old Charwoman).

Oweneen (her Son, about nineteen).

Eamonn O'Curry (a Librarian).

Statues of John Mitchel, Lord Edward Fitzgerald, Wolfe Tone, Robert Emmet and Charles Stewart Parnell.

The action passes in the entrance hall of a Dublin City Library, during the morning of Easter Monday, 1916.

This Play was first produced at the Abbey Theatre, Dublin, in November, 1934, under the direction of Hugh Hunt, with settings by Tanya Moiseiwitsch. As "The Coggerers," it appeared in book form in 1939 in a collection of Carroll's plays published by Random House.

Note: This play is fully protected in the United States and Canada. Applications to perform it publicly should be addressed to The Richard J. Madden Play Co. Inc., 522 Fifth Ave., New York 18, N. Y.

The Conspirators

SCENE: *The entrance hall of a Dublin City Library in the vicinity of St. Stephen's Green.*

From L. *to* R. *are five pedestals surmounted by busts of* PARNELL, EMMET, TONE, LORD EDWARD FITZGERALD *and* MITCHEL.

To the back, R., *is a low white slab, made as a base for a reclining figure. It is now empty, its figure having been removed for repair. The names of the patriots are conspicuously inscribed on their respective pedestals. The empty slab bears the inscription "*DAN O'CONNELL.*"*

A door back C., *to the library shelves, and a door* R., *leading outside.*

It is early morning on Easter Monday, 1916.

As the CURTAIN *rises, the stage is half-lit and misty. There is deep silence. Then comes a ship's siren call from the Liffey, then the voice of a newsboy in the distance, "*In-depen'ent and Irish Times,*" then the sudden chirruping of birds from St. Stephen's Green. A clock strikes rhythmically somewhere. The door back* C. *opens and*

EAMONN O'CURRY, *a dark, middle-aged man, comes in, hatless and with pen and papers in his hand. He looks round him. He is nervous.*

O'CURRY. Is there anyone there? (*He crosses to the door* R. *and looks out, then returns to the statues.*) If yous only knew! . . .

(*He looks about him again nervously and goes off, back. MRS. GALGOOGLEY, a worn little woman, comes in* R., *with a duster. She wears a shawl. She goes forward and begins dusting* PARNELL's *face.*)

PARNELL (*as she is about to move up* R.C.). Come back here, my good woman, and put my beard straight.

MRS. GALGOOGLEY (*motherly*). Sure, you're that touchy about your beard, Parnell. (*As she rewipes his beard.*) Sure, God help ye, little d'ye know nobody wears them nowadays at all, except an odd mad fellow here and there. Will that do?

PARNELL. Thank you, my good woman, thank you.

(MRS. GALGOOGLEY *moves on to* EMMET, *wipes his face and regards him sadly.*)

MRS. GALGOOGLEY. You're frettin', Robert, aren't ye?

(EMMET *takes no notice. He is sullen and morose.*)

Sure, God help ye, and you only a child, standin' there forever.

(*She passes on to* TONE, *whom she regards severely.* TONE *grins provocatively.*)

Well, Cock o' the mornin'.

TONE. How are ye, Brigid Anne? Bonjour, madame.

MRS. GALGOOGLEY. Well, aren't you the divil, with that grin of yours and that French lingo. Could you not be sayin' an odd word or two to Robert?

TONE. What's the use, Brigid Anne? He goes on regretting he never got living in a free Ireland with old John Philpot's daughter. Vraiment! La mort vient à tout le monde!

MRS. GALGOOGLEY. Sure, God help him, he's like my

Oweneen the way he frets and fidgets. (*She turns away* R. *towards the empty slab, and looks at it.*) Dan himself will be back from the repairin' men next week. Two of his toes, the American tourists stole off him, and his wee finger and all the curls on the one side of his head.

TONE. The new barbarians . . .

MRS. GALGOOGLEY (*turning, and moving* L.). Faith, no man is a barbarian nowadays that has money in his hip pocket—savin' your presence. (*As she reaches* LORD EDWARD FITZGERALD.) Good mornin', Lord Edward.

LORD EDWARD (*as she dusts him*). 'Morning, Mrs. Galgoogley. Careful with the wound in my neck.

MRS. GALGOOGLEY (*dusting carefully*). I will so. Faith, it was the woeful wound too.

(*She moves on to* MITCHEL, *whom she dusts respectfully.*)

MITCHEL. Blessin's on you ma'am. I always did like a little freshen-up in the morning.

MRS. GALGOOGLEY. Thank ye, sir. I heard a man sayin' yisterday in Jer O'Brien's pub that the "Jail Journal" was the odesee of the Irish race, whatever that means. Does that please you?

MITCHEL. Faith, it pleases me well.

MRS. GALGOOGLEY. But the other man he was talkin' to rared up, and says he, "How could a great Irishman fight agin' the slaves in America and still be more than a spit in the mouth?" And there they were into it like two oul' cats, breakin' faces and glasses and ever'thin'.

MITCHEL. Let them fight away, ma'am. 'Tis only when they can talk without angerin' one another that Ireland will be lost.

MRS. GALGOOGLEY (*wandering across*). 'Tis maybe so . . .

(*She goes off* R. *The morning begins to brighten. The statues yawn.*)

TONE (*fidgeting*). Les morts—ce sont de tristes personages! Que leur blême immobilité contraste avec la souple élégance des vivants! (*He bursts into hilarious song.*)

> There's wine from the royal Pope,
> And Spanish ale shall give thee hope,
> Shall give thee heart and life and hope,
>   My Dark Rosaleen.

MITCHEL. Quiet, Tone, for mercy's sake. That puzzling old fool in there will hear you.

LORD EDWARD. Do you, gentlemen, feel anything strange in the air this morning?

PARNELL. In what way strange, my lord?

LORD EDWARD. A sort of restlessness. Everything seems fidgeting.

EMMET (*lifting his head, excitedly*). That's it! I have been trying to analyse it, listening to this fool here raving in French.

TONE. And what's wrong with the French, will you tell me?

EMMET. Are you pretending you don't know they are now fighting with the British?

TONE. If they are, they have degenerated since Napoleon died.

EMMET. Like our own slaves out there.

PARNELL (*soothingly*). Enough! Enough! I pray you.

LORD EDWARD. There *is* something in the air. I *smell* it. (*All the statues start sniffing strongly.*)
Gunpowder!

EMMET. That's it! That's the way my rockets used to smell in Thomas Street.

TONE (*excitedly*). Vive la République!

MITCHEL. Hush, hush! Let us discuss this matter dispassionately. What is your opinion, Parnell?

PARNELL (*sniffing*). Gunpowder my grannie! It's the Liffey.

(*All laugh except* EMMET.)

TONE.   The Liffey we have always with us. . . . Hush!
Here's old Socrates coming. Stupid old classical bookworm!
I hate a man who can neither fight nor sing.

ALL.   Ssh!

(EAMONN O'CURRY *re-enters, back. A heavy overcoat con-
      ceals his person. He is ill at ease, and shows suppressed
      excitement. He looks about him nervously.*)

O'CURRY.   Are you there, Mrs. Galgoogley?

(*There is no answer. He breathes more freely. He takes out
      his watch and consults it. The statues watch him fur-
      tively.*)

(*Excitedly.*) Eight-thirty . . . and the minutes tick on to
the fateful hour. (*Suddenly, flinging open his overcoat and
showing a Volunteer uniform underneath, complete with
bandolier and holsters.*) The hour will be nine, gentlemen!

TONE (*involuntarily*).   Mon Dieu!

(O'CURRY *swings round in a startled manner, closing the
      overcoat.*)

O'CURRY (*fiercely*).   Is there anyone there? . . .
(*Silence.*)

Good God, I thought I heard a voice . . . as if the dead
spoke . . . the dead that died for Ireland. (*To* EMMET,
fiercely.) You poor pale piece of marble, didn't you say that
if the flag flew over Dublin Castle for a week, Ireland would
be saved?

(*The statues do not move.*)

We'll keep it flying, Emmet. We'll stick it to the mast with
our blood.

(*Noises off, of pails falling. He swings round, his hands at
      the holsters.*)

By God, I'll not be taken. I'll fight for it like Lord Edward.
Who's there?

(*The statues look excitedly at each other behind his back,
      and then resume their poise.* MRS. GALGOOGLEY *re-enters*

115

R., *with pails and mops. He is relieved. He breathes freely and speaks.*)

It's only you, Mrs. Galgoogley.

MRS. GALGOOGLEY. Sure, did I frighten you, Mr. O'Curry? Sure, I'm like an oul' scarecrow anyway.

O'CURRY. It's nothing, ma'am—nothing at all. (*A pause.*) The library will be closed all day of course—Easter Monday. I just came in to get a few papers. When you finish, lock up and leave the keys at the gate-house.

MRS. GALGOOGLEY. I will so. And I hope you'll have a nice holiday. To the country you'll be goin', I'll bet, sir, with Mrs. O'Curry and the children. Och, sure, it'll be the life o' the poor craythurs.

O'CURRY. Well, I don't know that I can manage to-day. I have a bit o' work to do. It will have to be some other day.

MRS. GALGOOGLEY. Sure, won't the work be after ye, sir, and it still not done anyway. 'Tis little ye get, liftin' the hand for others. Look now at them poor craythurs there that gave love and life and all, and sure, God help them, standin' there. . . . Who gives them a look or a word?

O'CURRY. The look or the word is a small matter, ma'am. They belong to the soul—to the thing that is eternal.

MRS. GALGOOGLEY. 'Tis maybe so, but they need dustin' every mornin' all the same.

(*She goes to her knees morosely.*)

O'CURRY. How did Dublin look and you comin' along this morning?

MRS. GALGOOGLEY. Look? Sure, jist as it always looks —like a woman paradin' in all her finery, but a dirty house at home. That's Dublin.

O'CURRY. You didn't notice anything unusual?

MRS. GALGOOGLEY. What would there be unusual? The oul' cabbies blowin' their hands on the quays, and the oceans o' bicycles takin' the breath out o' ye, and Guinness's porter barrels floatin' down the Liffey.

(O'Curry *turns and exits in a brown study, up* c.)

(*She looks after him. Then she tests the water with her fingers, finding it not hot enough.*) Och, sure God help him, sure I think 'tis his stomach that bees worryin' him.

(*She takes the pail and goes off* R. *The statues all become alive instantly and look eagerly at each other.*)

EMMET (*tensely*).   Did you hear? I feel the crash coming. It's here! It's upon us!

PARNELL.   This—is madness, gentlemen!

(TONE, EMMET *and* LORD EDWARD *laugh sarcastically.*)

EMMET.   Same old tune, Parnell. Same old platform stuff.

MITCHEL.   Quiet! Quiet! Let us discuss the matter dispassionately. If a people arrive at the decision that their objective cannot be won by pacific methods they are justified in resorting to—ssh!

(MRS. GALGOOGLEY *re-enters with the pail of water, interrupting* MITCHEL. *The statues resume their poise.* MRS. GALGOOGLEY *starts washing the floor.* O'CURRY *re-enters up* C.)

O'CURRY.   Finish up and get home quickly, Mrs. Galgoogley.

MRS. GALGOOGLEY.   Home? How so, sir?

O'CURRY.   It's—it's going to be thunder and lightning.

(*The statues rapidly regard each other and then resume their poise.*)

MRS. GALGOOGLEY.   Eh? God save us, I dread the thunderin'. Will it be yon forked lightnin' with the tail on it?

O'CURRY.   It'll be every sort of lightnin' you ever heard of. Hurry up now.

(*The statues again regard each other and then are still again.*)

MRS. GALGOOGLEY.   I will so. It's God that's angry with the people. And Oweneen'll be under the bed. The same divil would rather face a regiment o' soldiers than look at a flash o' lightnin'.

O'Curry. Is your son not with you this morning?

Mrs. Galgoogley. Sure, I knew the furnace wouldn't be gettin' lit so I let him lie on. He didn't get in last night till early this mornin'.

O'Curry. What was he playin' at, and he just a young fellow yet, keeping such hours?

Mrs. Galgoogley. Sure, it's a new invention he and Jerry Turley is workin' on, in Con Carey's cellar. Sure, it bees all hours when he gets in.

O'Curry. What sort of an invention?

Mrs. Galgoogley. Och, sure, the little he tells me . . . somethin', he says, to make the sparkin' plugs of a motor-car spark better.

O'Curry. I see . . . Did he say if he was goin' out this morning?

Mrs. Galgoogley. He did then. He told me to leave his breakfast in the oven, and I comin' out; that he had to be up at me heels to do a wee bit o' business in the centre o' the town. But, sure, if it's thunderin', divil the stir he'll stir. Och, sure, what's he but a child?

O'Curry. Oweneen is a man, Mrs. Galgoogley, and a man must prove himself.

Mrs. Galgoogley. Well, sure, so long as he doesn't disgrace me, sir . . .

O'Curry. He'll not do that. (*As he crosses* r.) Good-bye, Mrs. Galgoogley.

Mrs. Galgoogley. Good-bye? Sure, you'd think, sir, you were goin' to the ends o' the earth instead of Rathmines.

O'Curry (*turning at the door down* r.). Well . . . so long, then.

Mrs. Galgoogley. Till the mornin', sir. And tell Mrs. O'Curry I be prayin' for her since her operation.

O'Curry. I will, and thank you.

(*He exits* R., *putting on his hat as he goes.*)

EMMET (*quickly to* MRS. GALGOOGLEY).   Go after him, Mrs. Galgoogley, and wave to him.

MRS. GALGOOGLEY.   How so, puttin' bad in me head, Robert Emmet?

EMMET.   Because you'll never see him again.

MRS. GALGOOGLEY (*starting up*).   What are ye sayin' to me?

PARNELL.   Leave her alone, Emmet.

MITCHEL.   Don't distress yourself, good woman.

MRS. GALGOOGLEY.   Yous are conspirin' there between yous, as if somethin' was there and I not to be seein' it. What are yous at?

EMMET.   My words were hasty. Forgive me.

MRS. GALGOOGLEY.   I will then, and sure, it's not the first time. You're like my Oweneen, Robert Emmet—a hasty little spitfire, and yet a child in ways.

TONE.   Och, you'll be crying in a minute, Brigid Anne. Tant pis! On ne vit que pour mourir.

MRS. GALGOOGLEY.   Och, you! You imp! Divil the word I can have with Robert, without you puttin' in your spake.

TONE.   Come on, and give us one of your old come-all-ye's.

MRS. GALGOOGLEY.   I will not so. And I with not a pick in me stomach but a drop o' tay and the outside cut of a loaf.

LORD EDWARD.   But you promised us yesterday morning, Mrs. Galgoogley, and of course as a lady of noble birth, and as a Galgoogley . . .

MRS. GALGOOGLEY.   That's right. A Galgoogley . . . If I made a promise, Lord Edward, I'll keep it.

TONE.   That's the spirit. Wait and I'll give you your doh.

MRS. GALGOOGLEY.   I can get me own doh, thank you, Wolfe Tone, with your outrageous and Godforsaken French manners.

EMMET.   This is unseemly. I dislike it. I protest.

MRS. GALGOOGLEY (*looking at* EMMET).   Och, he frets,
like Oweneen.

MITCHEL.   You are just morbid and dull, Emmet.
There is nothing unseemly in song. We are not a crowd of
dull Teutons. We are a people of song and beauty. We are
the saviours of idealism in the Nordic jungle. Sing away, Mrs.
Galgoogley.

MRS. GALGOOGLEY.   I'll sing if Parnell lets me. I knew
him the best. One day, as a little girl, Parnell, I touched the
tail of your coat in College Green.

PARNELL.   Thank you for that, ma'am. Sing by all
means, and never—never let us become too respectable.

TONE.   Hear, hear! Give us that one of yours about
Dublin.

MRS. GALGOOGLEY (*standing arms akimbo, in loud come-
all-ye tones*).

> Oh, Dublin is a frowsy dame,
> 'Tis her's the brazen Tartar,
> Her petticoats are Saxon lace,
> Her perfume's Guinness's porter.
> To see her kneelin' at the Mass
> You'd swear she was a martyr,
> Till Parnell in O'Connell Street
> Stares cock-eyed down at her garter.

LORD EDWARD.   Excellent!

PARNELL.   Very commendable!

MITCHEL.   First rate!

TONE.   Splendid. I wish I had hands to clap you, Brigid
Anne. Come on, another verse and we'll join in.

MRS. GALGOOGLEY.   Well, aren't yous the divils for
fun! And amn't I the oul' fool!

(*She starts singing again. All join in except* EMMET, *whose
head is drooped very low.*)

She'll sit on Dan O'Connell's steps,
And froth at Anna Liffey,
She'll coort a bit with Dick Muldoon,
And cod little Father Fiffey.
Oh, Jerry Mooney is her boy,
And Father Matt's her other,
And damn the knowing either knows
Such caperin' in a mother.
She'll take a sup with Jer O'Brien,
And say an Av' with Father Fiffey,
Fill up with spleen in College Green,
And empty all into the Liffey.

(*When the singing stops, all the statues, except* EMMET,
laugh happily. MRS. GALGOOGLEY *regards* EMMET *in a
motherly way.*)
You're vexed with me, Robert, and so well ye might be, makin' an oul' fool o' meself and me oul' enough to know better twice over.

TONE.   Och, isn't your heart alive, Brigid Anne. Never mind him.

EMMET.   It's unseemly and undignified in an hour like this.

ALL.   Ssh!

MRS. GALGOOGLEY (*looking around, from one to the other*).   In an hour like what?

MITCHEL.   Nothing, nothing, Mrs. Galgoogley.

PARNELL.   Now, don't distress yourself, good woman.

LORD EDWARD.   Your life and fate should have taught you discretion, Emmet.

EMMET.   I'll say what I'll say, for woe or weal.

MRS. GALGOOGLEY.   Sure, it's just that you're short in the temper, Robert, like Oweneen. Many's the drubbin' Oweneen gives me, and then he washes the cups and things for me to make up to me.

EMMET. There you are, singing and brawling, and where is Oweneen?

MRS. GALGOOGLEY. Sure, where is he but in bed, and the divil wouldn't waken him, he's that tired.

EMMET. His bed is empty.

LORD EDWARD. Emmet!

TONE. That's not fair!

MITCHEL. Now what's the good in alarming the poor creature?

(MRS. GALGOOGLEY *looks at them all uneasily, one after the other. Fear grips her heart.*)

MRS. GALGOOGLEY. Yous are conspirin' there, and yous have somethin' between yous. (*She watches them with fear.*) Yous think me an oul' hag without feelin' because I can sing an oul' song. But would I not tear out me eyes and give them to Oweneen to see with? Would I not give me heart's blood to Oweneen to live with?

(*A pause. The statues all are very quiet. She stares at them in terror.*)

What's wrong with Oweneen? Tell me! Tell me, or be Jaysus I'll tear yous down to pieces and flitter yous and thramp on yous. (*Her hands are over her head hysterically. Sobs break from her. She turns down* R., *with resolve.*) I must go home quick. I must get to Oweneen. 'Tis maybe that a thievin' cut-throat would turn the handle and he'd be murdered and slew in his sleep.

(*Suddenly there comes the rapid clattering of rifle fire in the distance, and the sharp reports of revolver shots.* MRS. GALGOOGLEY *stops dead. Then backs a pace or two.*)

What was that? Mother of Mercy, what was it? (*Swinging round to face* L.) Tell me?

LORD EDWARD. Be a brave woman, Mrs. Galgoogley. Be a Galgoogley.

MRS. GALGOOGLEY (*appealingly, moving to* C.). I'll be only a woman. . . . Tell me, Lord Edward.

LORD EDWARD. It's what was bound to come, ma'am—guns and the tramp of men again.

MRS. GALGOOGLEY. Merciful God! Oweneen will be killed in his bed.

EMMET. Oweneen is not in his bed. Oweneen is a man. (*Rifle and revolver fire.*)

MRS. GALGOOGLEY. Not in his bed? Have pity on me, Robert. Don't be too hard on me. I'm an oul' woman, wore away with the washin' of floors. Tell me where Oweneen is. (*Revolver and rifle fire.*)

EMMET. Courage, woman. Oweneen's behind the barricades in Stephen's Green.

MRS. GALGOOGLEY (*in terror*). The—the barricades? In the Green? . . . (*facing* EMMET) He's not! He's not! . . . You're my enemy, Robert Emmet, my enemy and Oweneen's enemy. Oweneen's not grew up, he's only a child. (*Turning to face* MITCHEL.) Oh, John Mitchel, John Mitchel, you that saw hearts break! (*She goes to him in tears.*) You that saw lives wither away . . .

MITCHEL (*moved*). My poor woman, what can I say to you! God, have I not seen enough of this? Must I go on seeing it till the last day ends?
(*He bows his head.*)
(MRS. GALGOOGLEY *turns* R., *and moves to* C.)

MRS. GALGOOGLEY (*sobbing*). Parnell! I touched your coat in College Green. I was a little girl with my father. He said, "Touch him, Brigid Anne, he is holy."

PARNELL. I have no words. I have cast them all to the winds. . . .
(*Sudden rapid volley of shots.*)
That, that you hear, is the words of the new generation, and I am too old to read them.

MRS. GALGOOGLEY (*wringing her hands*). Yous knew

this was comin' and yous wouldn't tell me! Yous villains and cut-throats and stinkin' conspirators! I that always had the wee word for yous and the wipe of me duster, when the patent-leather people passed yous and the high men with big books. And did I not sing for yous the song of the greedy oul' bitch that yous all died for.

(*A volley of shots.*)

I know what it is that's up with yous! Yous are jealous of Oweneen and the way his strong arms can fling a hundred o' coal on his shoulder—jealous of the pant of his breath, the cry of his blood and the ring of his heart-beats.

(*Shots.*)

Yous conspired together to get him into that corner there (*she points to the vacant corner*), to be one of yourselves, yous wicked, jealous, dead oul' vagabonds! But yous'll not get him. My Oweneen has warm blood that he will give not to yous, nor to that oul' bitch that wanders O'Connell Street,

(*A volley of shots.*)

but to some little soft bit of a girl who will give him back in exchange the livin' life; do yous hear, the livin' life! I'll go out to my Oweneen now, and I will put my woman's body round his, as it was long ago in the beginning. My seven curses on yous and my seven curses on the oul' bitch yous died the death for!

(*A volley. She staggers across the floor towards the door, wrapping her old shawl about her. The statues look at each other. The rifle and revolver fire is repeated.*)

MITCHEL (*murmuring*). Poor woman . . . poor woman . . .

(*As she nears the door, it is flung back and* OWENEEN, *a boy of about nineteen, staggers in, wounded. He is dressed partly in uniform and wears a bandolier. Blood has stained his tunic. His rifle falls from his hands. He is pale and grimy with powder. The statues lean forward and look excitedly.*)

OWENEEN (*staggering*).   Mother! . . .

MRS. GALGOOGLEY (*staring at him*).   Oweneen! Mother
o' God! . . .

(*She runs forward and catches him, preventing him from
falling. She draws him in, to* R.C.)

What foolery is this you're at now? Am I not always . . .
(*She sees the blood on his breast.*) God! Blood! . . . Oweneen's blood . . . Yous have got him, yous villains and
vipers! . . . Me one little bit of riches that I was hidin' from
yous. Yous found him out; yous ferreted him out . . .

OWENEEN (*weakly*).   Listen to me, Mother . . .

MRS. GALGOOGLEY (*sadly*).   Aye then, son. Put your
mouth into me ear and whisper it anont to them.

OWENEEN.   I want to lie down, Mother . . . Put me
on the floor.

(MRS. GALGOOGLEY *gently lowers his body to the floor. She
puts her shawl under his head and kneeling by his side,
leans over him. Rifle and revolver fire.*)

Mother, I—I'm afraid . . .

MRS. GALGOOGLEY.   Of what, son! Sure they'll not find
you here, unless them villains there tell.

OWENEEN.   'Tis not of them I'm afraid, Mother. It's of
the pain in me breast. (*With weak passion.*) I—I don't want
to die . . . I want to live. . . . I—I—I want to be twenty-
one one day and to—to have a party and singin'. . . . (*His
head falls back.*)

MRS. GALGOOGLEY (*almost insanely, as if talking to herself*).   They've kilt him on me, the villains and vipers! Me
one little dropeen o' gold, me one little sprig with the green
leaves on it. (*She is peering closely into his face, the woman
in her fighting for hope.*)

OWENEEN (*painfully*).   It was all cruel and awful . . .
I didn't know anythin' could be so terrible . . .

(*A volley of shots.*)

I wanted to shut me eyes and call on God. . . . Then the

pain came and I could taste the blood in me mouth . . . and I crawled down the lane. . . . I knew you'd be here. . . . Mother, I want to live . . . I want to sit and think all over again about everythin'. . . . Will I be all right, Mother? Tell me! Is it just the cold of the ground that's got into me bones?

(*A volley of shots.*)

MRS. GALGOOGLEY. Just that, son, with God's help. Sure, if there's a God at all . . .

OWENEEN. What has God to do with it, Mother, when the guns start roarin'?

(*Shots.*)

I'm shiverin' and it's gettin' dark. . . . I wish I could have gone on till I stopped growin'. . . . I'm an inch and a half short of what me da was, and you said I'd be taller nor he was. . . . Twinty-one, we said, didn't we?

(*He turns his head gently and dies.* MRS. GALGOOGLEY *looks down at him tearfully, but calmly. She crosses herself slowly. A moment passes. Shots. She lifts her head fatalistically and looks round at the statues.*)

MRS. GALGOOGLEY (*slowly*). Yous villians and vagabones, yous have taken him from me, with your plottin' and conspirin'.

MITCHEL. You poor lonely creature, my heart bleeds for you.

MRS. GALGOOGLEY. There's no blood in your heart, John Mitchel, to bleed for anyone, so let ye hould your whisht. The oul' whore ye died for drank it all.

(*Volley of shots.*)

EMMET. Slut! I'm ashamed of you! What kind of talk is that for the mother of a hero? You should lift up your heart and be proud.

MRS. GALGOOGLEY. Did Sara Curran lift up her heart and be proud, Robert Emmet, when the dogs licked your blood in Green Street?

EMMET (*tensely*). She did! She did!

MRS. GALGOOGLEY. So *you* think. But she only cried herself sick because her lover was dead.

EMMET. That's a wicked calumny. You ought to be ashamed of yourself. Slut and harridan!

LORD EDWARD. That'll do, Emmet! Can't you see she's distraught?

PARNELL. The poor woman is right. This dying with honour with a bullet in your guts is a relic of savagery. It's time it was buried at the crossroads of the nations.

LORD EDWARD
EMMET } (*together*). Bah!
TONE

(PARNELL *lapses into silence. A silence follows.* MRS. GAL-GOOGLEY *regards them all sadly and then looks down at* OWENEEN.)

MRS. GALGOOGLEY (*resigned*). Ah, sure, God help yous all standin' there forever and ever and no man at all takin' the least notice of yous, and God help me too standin' here with my little dead maneen.

(*Rapid rifle fire.*)

TONE. Sure, if you could only see it, Brigid Anne, your maneen was more than ten Samsons that stayed at home.

LORD EDWARD. We're all proud of him, Mrs. Galgoo-gley. Aren't you, Emmet?

EMMET. I take off my hat in spirit to the men who die for Ireland.

MRS. GALGOOGLEY (*softly*). Do you mean to Owe-neen, Robert?

EMMET. I do. The people will remember him. Put him up here among us. This is his place.

MRS. GALGOOGLEY (*with pathetic eagerness*). Do yous want him? Honest now, and do yous? Sure, he hasn't a clean shirt or nothin' on him?

ALL. Put him amongst us. He is ours now. We claim him.

MRS. GALGOOGLEY. Aye then . . . he's yours. . . . I'll put him there in the vacant place where Dan O'Connell was before the Americans took lumps off him with their penknives.

(*She draws* OWENEEN's *body tenderly towards the low marble slab, and places it upon it. The statues look round at the body as she steps back from him, to* C.)

PARNELL (*gravely*). Gentlemen, we have added to our company an illustrious patriot. I call upon Mr. Emmet to say a few fitting words to mark this occasion.

EMMET (*oratorically*). Gentlemen, no tears for the dead who die for Ireland. Let us rejoice that blood is still rebellious in Irish veins and that the end was not with you or me or any of us—that the end will not be until all our manacles are riven. In spirit I salute this, my brother, who is come to his rightful home.

TONE (*softly*). Le roi est mort. Vive le roi . . .
(*Volley of shots.*)

ALL. Amen. We salute our brother.

MRS. GALGOOGLEY (*softly weeping*). There now, yous wanted him, and yous have him now. Sure, who am I to be grumblin', and I wore with the washin' of floors. Sure, 'tis maybe that I'll be cryin' needlessly on the Liffey quays where the men do be talkin' and spittin', or on O'Connell Bridge with the world and his wife passin'; and forgettin', when I'll be havin' a sup in Jer O'Brien's, that God and the dead know best. Let yous be good now to Oweneen, and I away, and let yous not have him frettin' after me.

(*She looks down at him and smiles, then turns slowly and goes out meanderingly.*)

PARNELL. There is Life going out there—poor, ragged, thwarted, buffeted, beaten and yet living, and with hope in the heart.

EMMET.   And there is the music of Liberty! Listen!
(*From without come the rapid reports of rifles and revolvers and the spitting of Thompson guns.*)
The symphony of Freedom, gentlemen! What notes on a thundering scale! What grand crescendos! And what immortal musicians!

The CURTAIN *falls slowly.*

Beauty Is Fled

CHARACTERS

HANS ERICCSON (an old Toymaker).

DAME ERICCSON (his Wife).

HERR HACHENBLOCH (a Landlord).

EDWIN (a Wanderer).

TAVINTOSK (an Officer of the King).

TWO GUARDS.

EIGHT LIFE-SIZE DOLLS, Children of About Eight Years.

A RED-HAIRED WOMAN.

SILENT PEOPLE.

The action passes in the ancient workshop of Hans Ericcson, in a lonely valley in Europe.

NOTE: This play is fully protected in the United States and Canada. Applications for licences to perform it publicly should be addressed to the Richard J. Madden Play Co. Inc., 522 Fifth Avenue, New York 18, N. Y.

"Beauty Is Fled" appeared in book form in a collection of children's plays published by Julian Messner in 1938.

Beauty Is Fled

SCENE: *An ancient workshop of a toymaker in a secluded valley in Europe.*

Round the floor are rough heavy benches littered with tools, knives, and parts of the limbs of dolls. Small dolls and soldiers are hung on the walls, for sale. An old worn horsehair couch, R.C., *and a rough heavy chair near the bench to the left.*

L., *a doorway of old horseshoe pattern with a surround of rough stone.* R., *a small, diamond-paned window, without curtains. Some sacks of sawdust, etc., about the floor.*

Along the back wall, on the top of three steps, are placed eight cardboard boxes,* tied round the middle with a ribbon. Each is about three feet high and eighteen inches wide. They contain eight life-size DOLLS.

* Producers should note that the boxes have no backs or bottoms, so that the tiny players need not stand inside them except at the moments when the play demands it. The boxes can be entered unobserved from the back, if a curtain surround is used.

The DOLLS, *played by children of about seven or eight years, are dressed in simple satin gowns from throat to toes, with a coloured girdle round the waist and a large bow of the same material in the hair.*

The toymaker, HANS ERICCSON, *a middle-aged man with a beard and very bright eyes, is seated on the couch, dispirited and downhearted. He is sadly contemplating the large* DOLLS' *boxes. He wears old wide corduroy trousers, a coloured shirt, and an old print apron. His hair is tossed and white.*

A moment passes. DAME ERICCSON, *his wife, enters,* L., *briskly. She is dressed in the style of the German country Gretchen, and is vigorous, talkative, and full of self-pity. She regards* HANS *impatiently. He raises his head slowly.*

HANS (*irritably*).   Well, wife. What is it now?

DAME (*at* L.C.).   Has anyone been?

HANS.   No one that would buy.

DAME.   Same old story with *you* always. You'd make one believe all the buyers in the world were dead. (*Moving down* L. *to the bench.*) You'll have to be stirring yourself.

HANS.   If I cut strips off the sky and pulled down the stars to make dolls of them, do you think it would make any difference?

DAME (*fingering toys on the bench, contemptuously*). Not while you go on making baby dolls that nobody wants (*to below the chair* L.). Its toys that move and squeak and run round the table that children want now—and guns and the things of war. (*She moves up* C. *and surveys the eight dolls' boxes.*)

HANS.   I know. I have seen. . . . The times that's in it have taken away the beauty of children. We must all answer for it.

DAME (*vigorously, turning on* HANS).   We must answer first to the landlord. And this very day too. You must just start and make these newfangled things that run round and round firing things like guns.

HANS. I'll not so. There is little enough beauty left in the world for me to make it less.

DAME (*decisively*). Well, there's no dinner.

HANS (*slowly*). Well, if there's none—there's none.

DAME. But—we'll starve.

HANS. We'll not be the first, nor the last.

DAME. But what about *me?*

HANS. You took me for better or for worse.

DAME (*in self-pity*). Oh, wasn't I the fool ever to listen to the tales of you. (*Stamping her foot.*) Listen to *me* now! I could sell those eight big dolls on the steps of St. Peter's church if you'd let me take them into town. 'Tis there the money is! (*She moves down to the chair* L., *and turns.*)

HANS (*quietly*). They will remain. They are worth coming down the valley for. It is in the nature of man to despise what lies to his hand, and to cherish that which he seeks over long roads.

DAME. But, you oul' fool you, who seeks or journeys nowadays?

HANS (*rising*). Only the few, I grant. (*He turns up* c.)

DAME. But we can't live by the few.

HANS (*turning to face her*). There is always a little meal, and a potato from the field.

DAME. And is it to be that—night, noon, and morning —day in, day out?

HANS (*up* c.). You are like the world out there, woman. You have begun to believe that a man lives on what he eats.

DAME (*moving up stage*). Now, I've had enough of that talk. Out of my way. (*She tries to push past him.*) I'm taking those dolls into the town now.

HANS (*barring her path*). Not the eight big ones. I

have given myself too much to them for that. I will sell them only to those who trudge over weary roads for them. Such will love them always.

DAME. The days of trudgin' are over. Out o' me way, you oul' fool!

(*They struggle.*)

HANS. Not on my soul!

(*A long, low sob from the* DOLLS *in the boxes. They cease struggling and look up sharply.*)

DAME (*retreating a pace*). What was that?

HANS. How would *I* know?

DAME (*frightened*). It was like a sob. . . . (*Looking at him.*) I believe you know and you won't tell me! . . . What hidden thing is there in this place that's always frightenin' me?

HANS. There is nothing to know or to hear. I have told you so for years. It's only the wind in the chimney.

DAME (*looking around*). There's a curse on this place —that's what there is. I can feel it. (*She moves down* L.)

HANS. You have neither manners nor sense, woman. (*Moving to below the couch.*) Go away and leave me in peace.

DAME (*turning to him*). I'll sit down and starve to please you, will I?

(*Enter the landlord,* HERR HACHENBLOCH, *up* L. *He is a fat, bearded man, rough and loud-voiced. He carries a large roll of paper and a big notebook.*)

LANDLORD (*up* L.C.). What now! What now!

DAME. Oh, mercy me! The landlord! We're lost to the world now!

LANDLORD (*coming to* C.). Hans Ericcson, it is the eighth hour of the clock according to the agreement whereunder you have subscribed your hand and signature. Have you ten kronen here and now, and in this place, in agreement with the terms herein set out?

HANS. If I had one kronen, I would bless the Lord.

LANDLORD. Then let you look to it!

DAME. Oh, mercy on us, Herr Hachenbloch, and may the sun shine on you and yours always!

LANDLORD. Fiddlesticks, woman! The sun will shine whether or no.

DAME. I will give you a beautiful life-size doll for your little daughter.

LANDLORD. Ppt! A fig for your doll! It's not dolls my daughter wants. It's moving pictures in the parlour, and steel trains that fly round the table, and guns that can fire six glass beads at a time.

HANS (*as if to himself*). Aye . . . 'tis a lost world. . . .

DAME. Could you not give us a day or two more? I'll see my uncle that's married to the woman that owns ten haystacks and a clump of trees on the edge of the wood beyond Titzen.

LANDLORD. Not a minute! Not even a tick of a clock that's ten hours fast! Out you go this very day. There's a man waiting to take this place, that makes cannons with red and gold barrels, and tanks that crawl round a room. There's where the money is nowadays.

DAME (*to* HANS). You could make the like of them if you liked.

HANS. God didn't give me hands for the Devil's work.

LANDLORD. Pah! A man that's wiser than his betters always dies of starvation. And serve him right too. See how wise this will make you. (*He unrolls the sheet in his hand and pins it on the wall, back, to the right of the* DOLLS' *boxes. It is a printed notice. Only the words,* PUBLIC AUCTION, *are visible to the audience.*)

DAME (*excitedly*). What's this you're doin' to us? What is it? (*She moves up* L.C.)

LANDLORD (*returning to* C.). Can't you read, or were you never at school?

DAME (*reading*). "Public Auction" . . . Auction of what?

LANDLORD (*with a wide gesture*). Of all this stock. (HANS *sits slowly on the couch.*)

DAME (*to* HANS). Are *you* listenin' to that?

HANS (*philosophically*). I'm listening.

DAME. You're not doing much.

HANS. There's not much to do.

DAME (*moving down* L.). There's a man for you! (*Turning to the* LANDLORD.) The big dolls too, is it?

LANDLORD. All. To sell without reserve at high noon today, up to the value of ten kronen. These bills are posted all over the town and down the valley.

(*Another long low cry from the eight* DOLLS. *All turn and stare.*)

LANDLORD. What was that?

DAME. It was like a sob. It *was* a sob.

LANDLORD. It was so.

HANS. It was the wind in the crevices of the walls.

LANDLORD. It gave me a start, and I a poor delicate man with a weak heart. (*He turns authoritatively.*) What's here is now under the rule of the law. Let nothing be touched under pains and penalties. Today, at high noon, I will auction, according to, and in the terms of, the Court's decree.

(HERR HACHENBLOCH *gives them a stiff bow, snaps off his big book closed, and goes off up* L., *with fearful steps.*)

DAME. There's for you now! (*She looks at him and wrings her hands.*) Oh, amn't I the poor abandoned woman! (*She weeps, moving up* C., *and turning.*) I'll starve and no one will care. If my mother wasn't dead I'd get her to give you a tongue-thrashing, and if my father wasn't dead I'd get him to wallop you black and blue. (*She moves across*, L., *sobbing.*) Oh, amn't I the poor, poor woman! Amn't I the poor, wronged, innocent creature! (*She goes off, woefully, at* L.)

(HANS, *who has taken no notice of her, nor lifted his head, now rises slowly and sighs. He goes slowly up* C., *turns to the notice and reads.*)

HANS (*slowly*).   To sell at the time, place, and day, hereinunder set forth, the stock, fittings, and tools of the said Hans Ericcson of Marnitzen Valley. . . .

(*A long, low cry from the* DOLLS. *He starts and looks round.*)

HANS.   Tears. . . . Once they sang, but that was long ago . . . when there was magic in the little things. . . . But now all that is gone. We live in a lost world. . . . (*He goes towards the* DOLLS. *He opens the lids, outwards, of a few of the boxes, exposing the standing* DOLLS, *then closes them softly as he speaks.*) My pretty ones. . . . How lovely you are. I have put my best into your making. Sometimes I dream that you live and speak. Maybe you do, if all the old thrilling stories of this place are true. But for that, one must have great faith. One must believe, and this is an age of unbelief. Yet, if the people in my brother's plays can live, *you* can live; and if the beauty in my sister's music can live, *you* can live. (*Pause. He hangs down his head. Then he moves away, down* R.) There is a doubt in my mind. . . . I but dream. . . .

(*Enter* EDWIN, *up* L. *He is a man clothed in a cape and velvet trousers. He is staggering with weariness, and looks unkempt and uncared for. His hair is tossed and there is mud on his clothes and boots.* HANS *turns sharply and comes across to him in wonderment.*)

HANS.   My good friend, what can I do for you?

EDWIN (*wearily*).   Give me sleep.

HANS.   I can give you a bed, but only God can give you sleep.

EDWIN (*staggering*).   Then God is not with me, for sleep has deserted me for many days.

HANS (*supporting him*).   Nay. God is with all of us. What is your name?

EDWIN.   It too has deserted me.

HANS.   My poor friend, you are ill. Have you come far?

EDWIN.   Farther than the valley's mouth, by a long stretch. Beyond that it is dark. . . . I have lost all my memory of things.

HANS.   Have no fear. Quiet and rest will give you sleep and restore to you all that you have lost.

EDWIN.   Aye, but sleep will not come. . . . I count the heavy hours. And oh, those terrible killing bells. . . . (*Indicating the couch*) Can I lay myself there?

HANS.   I am ashamed of it, but it is the best I can offer.

EDWIN.   No man can offer more than his best.

(HANS *assists* EDWIN *to the couch, on which he stretches himself wearily.*)

HANS.   Shall I send word to one of your friends outside the valley?

EDWIN.   I have no friends that I can remember. I am like one lost in a dark mist.

HANS (*as he places the coverlet over* EDWIN).   Then count *me* as a friend.

EDWIN (*wearily*).   Glory to God for that. . . . If I could but sleep now . . . gold for sleep! . . . Gold for sleep! . . .

HANS.   Gold? . . . Nay, my friend. One buys sleep not with gold, but with prayers.

EDWIN.   Then I will pray. . . .

HANS.   Aye, and simply, as children do. And I'll bring you a cup of soup from the stock pot.

(HANS *exits softly* L. EDWIN *turns and tosses wearily muttering to himself.*)

EDWIN (*mutteringly*).   Sleep. . . . God give me sleep. . . . Where am I? What dark cloud is this come upon me? . . . All are gone . . . all . . . all the bright faces, and all the merry music. . . . Is there no one there? . . . Is there no one left to me? . . . Can no one give me a song with sleep in it? . . . Sleep, blessed sleep. . . .

(Very soft music, calling and plaintive, is now heard offstage, after the manner of the following:

Introduction

To be repeated from the double-bar till the dolls have risen.

End of Introduction

As this music gets louder and louder, the eight DOLLS, *life-size, appear on the steps, back, all dressed as indicated at the beginning of the play. Keeping time to the music, they tip-tap across the stage, moving their hands up and down mechanically. When tip-tapping they should not bend their knees. As they come round the couch in a circle, the music stops. They look down at* EDWIN *and at each other in great pity. Then they begin to sing very plaintively.)*

DOLLS.

> Here is a man that has wandered far
> Over the hills of pain and grief,
> Seeking a cure for a sleepless head,
> Seeking a rest from worry and dread;
> Ta, la-la-la; ta, la-la-la;
> Where in the world is his gladness fled?
> Where in the world is so sad a head?
>
> Let him be rocked in a rocky bed,
> Whispering dreams around his head,
> Rocked with a song and the beat of hearts,
> Such is the way that sorrow departs;
> Ta, la-la-la; ta, la-la-la;
> What's to become of so sad a head?
> Look how the joy in his face is dead.
>
> Now are his eyes in the dreaming mood,
> Lidded with lids that droop and hood,
> Over his terror and dread are drawn
> Veils that will lift to show him the dawn.
> Ta, la-la-la; ta, la-la-la.
> Dream of the garlands of song we weave,
> Dream like the birds in their nests at eve.

Song of the Dolls

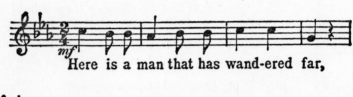

Here is a man that has wand-ered far,

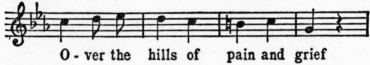

O - ver the hills of pain and grief

Seek-ing a cure for a sleep-less head Seek-ing a

rest from wor-ry and dread Ta la la la

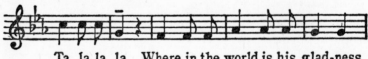

Ta la la la Where in the world is his glad-ness

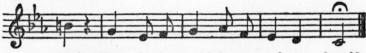

fled? Where in the world is so sad a head?

(*As the song ends, they look down at* EDWIN *again, smile at one another, say "Ssh" in unison. Then the calling intro-*

ductory music begins again, and in the previous manner they tip-tap across the stage, up the steps, and off. The music dies away very softly.

HANS *re-enters,* L., *carrying a cup of soup. He comes to the couch and sees that* EDWIN *is asleep.*)

HANS (*perplexed*). Asleep! . . . What am I to do now, and he starving? If I waken him, he'll die for the want of sleep; and if I let him sleep on, he'll die with the hunger. Now, was a man ever in a worse fix than this? (*He moves down* L., *and scratches his head pensively. A low mischievous laugh from the* DOLLS. *He starts and looks round.*) Did someone laugh? And if there did, what now is there to laugh at in a minute like this?

(*He puts the cup down on the bench.* DAME ERICCSON *enters.*)

Well, wife, what is it now? Am I not perplexed enough?

DAME (*coming to* C.). There's men and women comin' down the road of the black elms to the auction. And right in the middle of them is who d'ye think?

HANS (*irascibly*). If you know, why don't you say?

DAME (*venomously*). That one with the carroty hair that married the man that slaughters the cows in Staroven; and her stepsister that has the dogcart and the licence to sell pots and pans. I'll blacken their eyes like a penn'orth o' tar.

HANS (*moving to below the chair* L.). You'll behave yourself, woman, that's what you'll do. I'll have none of these people saying my wife is an unmannerly woman.

DAME. Ppt! Mannerly wife indeed! I'll be a saint, will I, and thieves and rogues carryin' away my home?

HANS (*indicating* EDWIN). Be quiet, woman, and let the weary sleep.

DAME (*looking at* EDWIN). Is that the man came in? Ppt! I thought you said he was a gentleman.

HANS. And how is he not so?

DAME. A queer sort of gentleman that goes to sleep

145

with his head under his elbow like a baby that was tired cryin'. (*A pause, as she moves above the couch to* R. *of it.*) I wonder if he has anythin' in his pockets that he wouldn't miss.

HANS (*sternly*).   Woman! What—what have you come to?

DAME (*shouting*).   To what *you* have brought me! To the mud that's in a black waterhole at the end of a lane.

HANS.   Enough now! There's always a way out if you'd have faith. But what woman living has that?

DAME.   There's one thing I *have* without any doubt at all—and that's an empty stomach. An empty stomach and a husband all full of himself. I'm a rich woman surely!

HANS (*impatiently*).   Ach, woman, between your tears and your bad manners—

(*Enter* HERR HACHENBLOCH, *the landlord, very aggressively, carrying a sheaf of papers, his large notebook, and an auctioneer's hammer. A number of* MEN *and* WOMEN, *dressed in colourful garments, come in slowly behind him and take up places about the room. They begin inspecting the stock silently. One of the women wears a fiery red wig. She and* DAME ERICCSON *continually exchange aggressive glances.*)

LANDLORD.   Now, now! No hiding of things here, I hope, in a manner contrariwise to the law's decree?

HANS.   We've hid nothing. (*He turns down* L., *to the bench.*)

DAME (*aggressively*).   Do you take us for thieves and rogues? (*She glances deliberately at the woman with the red wig.*)

LANDLORD.   You're worse than thieves and rogues. You're failures. (*Turning vigorously.*) Come in, folks, come in. It's a public auction.

(*The people move and eddy about the room quietly inspecting.* HERR HACHENBLOCH *now stands on the old heavy chair,* L., *and after striking with his hammer on his big ledger, begins to auction. He consults his papers.*)

LANDLORD. To sell here and now without reserve, in the terms hereinunder set forth, the stock and fittings of the said Hans Ericcson under the duress of the Court's decree. (*He catches sight of* EDWIN *asleep on the couch.*) How now? Thunder and lightning! What's this?

HANS (*quietly*). A stranger that was tired.

LANDLORD. Hah! Bad consorting with worse. Birds of a feather. . . . (*The people laugh.*) Why, it's no other than the tramp I turned my dog on, at my door, not two hours ago! By the whiskers of my grandfather, I'll auction *him* too! (*Laughter.*) Ho, there! What am I bid for this ornament on the couch? Come now! What are you waiting for? Don't you know a bargain when you see one? (*Laughter.*) Is there no woman there wants a good upstandin' husband, guaranteed to sleep all the time and give no trouble? (*Further laughter.*)

DAME. Go on, Carrots! There's a chance for you! (*The* RED-HAIRED WOMAN, *at up* C., *shakes her fist at* DAME ERICC-SON. HERR HACHENBLOCH *thinks she's bidding, and bows.*)

LANDLORD. Lady with the aurora borealis hair bids me sixpence! Thank you, lady. (*Laughter.*) Going for sixpence! . . . Any advance on sixpence? . . . Why his hair is worth that alone! . . .

(*Further laughter.* TAVINTOSK, *an Officer, accompanied by two* GUARDS *in uniform, enters suddenly, left.*)

OFFICER (*striding to up* L.C.). Make way! Make way there! (*As they come forward amongst the people.*) Has any of you good people seen the King?

(*All are surprised. They look at each other and murmur in astonishment.*)

LANDLORD (*loudly*). The King?

ALL (*incredulously*). The King?

OFFICER. His Majesty is missing since the third hour of the day beyond yesterday. He has been unwell and has wandered away. We fear he has lost his memory. He has been traced in the direction of this valley.

LANDLORD.   Well, he's not here. This is an auction sale in the terms of the Court's decree as hereinunder set forth. (*Tapping his papers.*) We have a tramp here if he's any good to you. He's going for sixpence. Would you like to bid? He might come in useful as a scarecrow in the royal garden.

(*The people all laugh.* TAVINTOSK *steps down* C., *to inspect* EDWIN, *then exclaims sharply and springs to attention.*)

OFFICER (*astonished*).   It's the—the—the—the King! (*He clicks his heels and salutes the sleeping form.*) Your— Your Majesty!

(*The two* GUARDS, *at the salute, present arms, march one to either side of the head of the couch and stand stiffly on guard. All the people fall back in amazement and stare at the* KING.)

EDWIN (*waking drowsily and rubbing his eyes sleepily*).   Oh, gooseberries and duck eggs! I've had such a wonderful sleep! I feel like a man born all over again. (*He looks about him comically.*) Hello! Where am I? I believe I'm asleep still! Where is my good friend who gave me his couch for a bed?

DAME (*excitedly,* R. *of the couch*).   Sure it's Hans, my husband, King.

HANS (*reprovingly, moving to below the chair*).   Tt! Tt! Will you take care of your manners, wife, before the King! (*Bowing respectfully to* EDWIN.) Your Majesty, your servant!

EDWIN (*sitting up, in surprise*).   Majesty? . . . Good heavens, of course! I'm the King! . . . That's who I am! And I couldn't remember for the life of me, yesterday, who I was. (*He suddenly sees* HERR HACHENBLOCH *on the chair.*) Ha! There is the ruffian that turned me fainting from his door!

OFFICER (*in horror*).   Outrage, Your Majesty!

EDWIN.   Aye, Tavintosk, outrage is the word. Seize him,

Guards! (*The* GUARDS *wheel round and seize the* LANDLORD, *dragging him from the chair to* C.)

DAME (*bursting out*). And he was sellin' you for sixpence, King, to yon red one that buys the pots and pans.

EDWIN. Ha! (*He rises.*) So, you were selling me for sixpence to a redheaded termagant, were you! Blood and thunder! Is your King only worth sixpence?

OFFICER (*horrified*). Outrage ten times ten, Your Majesty!

EDWIN. Never mind, Tavintosk. *He'll* be worth much less than sixpence when I'm finished with him.

LANDLORD (*groaning*). Mercy, Sire, mercy, on a poor delicate man with a weak heart.

EDWIN. I give mercy, fellow, only to the merciful. Away with him, Guards.

(*The* GUARDS *drag him off in a wretched state, up* L.)

DAME. I always knew that fellow was a villain, King!

HANS (*reprovingly*). Quiet, wife, before the King! (*He indicates the people.*) By your leave, Your Majesty, may I send all these people away?

EDWIN. Who are they?

DAME (*again interposing volubly*). A crowd, King, of the biggest rogues and cutthroats God ever put breath in. And if you please, King, that one with the carroty hair—

HANS (*peremptorily*). Woman! (*She stops abruptly at* HAN'S *fierce look.* HANS *bows apologetically to the* KING.) They are the people, King, who always want much for little.

KING. Then I don't know them. Send them away!

DAME (*again forestalling* HANS). Off you go now! Go on now! And yon red one too, and your tails between your legs! Booh-hoo! Booh-hoo! (*She jeers.*)

HANS (*with a hopeless gesture, as the people move slowly across, up* L., *bow to* KING, *and go out.*) Excuse, Your Majesty, this most unmannerly woman of mine.

EDWIN (*smiling*).   Come, come! You're much too strict, Hans, my good friend. Can she make good soup?

HANS (*magnanimously*).   Excellent soup, King, I admit.

EDWIN.   Then I have no hesitation in pronouncing her an excellent woman. Come, Dame Hans, when do we taste your soup?

DAME (*up* C., *enthusiastically*).   Why, in the—the sweep of a lamb's tail, King. (*She crosses to the door,* L., *and turns.*) Do you like it, King, with a wee sniff of pepper, and as much thyme as would—

HANS.   Woman! Your manners!

EDWIN.   I leave it, Dame, to your good self. Far be it from me to seek to dictate to a woman in such an all-important matter. (*He bows to* DAME ERICCSON, *and she gives him an enthusiastic bow in return. Then she glances at* HANS.)

DAME.   Thank you, King. And if you please, King, will you excuse my husband? He doesn't know any better. He never saw much till he married *me*.

(*As* HANS *chokes, she bows again, and with a smile from the* KING, *goes vigorously out.*)

EDWIN (*moving down* R.C.).   And now, Hans, my good friend, while we wait on the good wife's brew, let us have those beautiful maidens in again to sing. (*He sits on the couch.*) Are they your daughters?

HANS (*at* L.C., *astonished*).   Maidens, Your Majesty? Sing? Daughters? I have neither son nor daughter, nothing but a woman that talks as much as ten.

EDWIN.   But this is very mystifying! Who are the beautiful little maids who sang me to sleep?

HANS (*in fear*).   Sang—you—to sleep? . . . (*He looks towards the* DOLLS *in amazement, and back again.*) No, it is impossible. You dreamed it, King. It was Your Majesty's poor sick mind wandering.

EDWIN (*rising to his feet*).   I wonder if it was. . . . I

can't believe it. It was all so real, as I went down, down into sleep. . . . (*He wanders down* R., *pensively.*) I would give much to hear such singing again. (*Turning suddenly on* HANS.) Are you sure you are not hiding anything from me?

HANS (*evasively*). One who has nothing, King, can hide nothing.

EDWIN. Nothing? . . . Pray, make your mind easy on that. I repay good with good. (HANS *bows.*) Make a note, Tavintosk, in your book, that our good friend, Hans, deserves well of us.

OFFICER (*bowing*). Instantly, Sire. I will deliver your command to the Royal Purser. (*He writes pompously in a notebook.* HANS *bows again.*)

EDWIN (*reminiscently*). That singing. . . . That singing. . . . It haunts me.

(HANS *watches the* KING *closely for a while, as he walks discontentedly about.*)

HANS (*at length, cautiously*). There is, of course, the old legend attached to this ancient workshop, Sire, that if you lie on your face and cover your eyes, the dolls will give forth unearthly music, if your soul is worthy to hear it.

EDWIN (*turning sharply*). Ah! . . . And you would hide it from me, Hans?

HANS (*evasively*). It is an old wives' tale, Your Majesty.

EDWIN. I believe you are deceiving me, Hans. You are jealous.

(*A pause. They look at each other.*)
Come! Have you—heard anything?

HANS. Nothing but sighs and sobs, King. It is a sorrowing age.

EDWIN. We two could perhaps strip ourselves of its entanglements and hear. (*He pauses.*) Do they not sing for *you* when you cover your face?

HANS (*sadly*). Only little snatches with the tinkling

of strings. (*Pause.*) I believe it's because of that woman of mine. Her sneering and the bad manners of her, they feel her near and refuse to sing.

EDWIN. Extraordinary! . . . Even if she *can* make excellent soup! . . . But I must hear that song again, if I am to be happy. Go, Tavintosk, and keep Dame Hans in talk. Let her in here and you—die.

OFFICER (*very distressed*). But, Your Majesty, how can I keep her in talk if *she* talks all the time?

EDWIN. Get your words in edgewise, fool.

OFFICER (*bowing, distressed*). This is a most difficult mission, Sire. (*He bursts into tears and sobs.*) I obey, King. I die or succeed for Your Majesty. (*He bows again and exits* L., *weeping.*)

EDWIN (*urgently*). Come, Hans; flat on the couch!

HANS. You on the couch, King. The floor for me. (*As they lie down.*) And put all evil from your heart, King, if kings harbour such.

EDWIN. Kings are but men in the heart, Hans. (*Praying.*) Depart evil and sin and all things not of beauty.

HANS (*praying*). Forgiveness I beg for being hard on my poor, clattering, foolish wife, and for all my many imperfections. Give me a pure heart so that I may hear.

EDWIN. Amen.

HANS. And keep faith, King. Do not look.

EDWIN. A king gives his word.

HANS. And a poor lover of the beautiful gives his. Sssh! Let us be quiet. Let us rest from the fever of the world's mad business.

(*They lie flat on their faces, covering their heads with their arms. Soft music begins as before, getting louder and louder as the eight* DOLLS *emerge, to the time of the music, and circle them. Then moving in circles, they sing plaintively, to the tune of the previous song.*)

DOLLS.

> Where is the wondering world we know?
> Where are the simple things and true?
> Where is the beauty that once we wore?
> Why are the wise ones merry no more?
> Oh, ho-ho-ho; oh, ho-ho-ho;
> Where is the world of the fireside gone?
> Why are the tales in the firelight done?
>
> You that have travelled the weary road,
> Come to the shrine of love's abode,
> Asking a sign that will soothe your pain,
> Seeking the old dreams over again.
> Oh, ho-ho-ho; oh, ho-ho-ho;
> Rest you a little, while rest you may,
> Rest till the dawn lures you far away.

(*As they begin to recede, the soft recalling music recommences, and they tip-tap across, up the steps and off. As the music dies away,* HANS *and* EDWIN *rise slowly to sitting positions and look at each other, their faces diffused with joy. A long pause.*)

EDWIN. Beautiful. . . . I am very, very happy. . . . I am as happy as a child.

HANS (*softly*). I feel as if I had come from a king's feast, and drunk the king's wine. (*Pause. They stand.*) Let no man know of this—our secret, King.

EDWIN (*down* R.C.). No man. (*Turning.*) What does it all mean, Hans?

HANS (L.C., *a little above and* L. *of the* KING). It means, King, that greedy men have swept all beauty out of the world, into little old corners like this, and that the few who still love it, will come after it like pilgrims.

EDWIN. That is the speech of a wise man. Give me your hand.

HANS. If I may, King.

EDWIN. Aye, you may, and freely. (*They clasp hands.*) *You* are a king too, in a beautiful sense. I shall come here often, Hans, and be a better king and a better man for it.

HANS. And I shall be the better for it too, King.
(*They look at each other and smile, softly.*)

EDWIN. I will give you a thousand royal kronen for your dolls, Hans.

HANS (*slowly*). They are not for sale, King.
(*They look at each other again.* EDWIN *smiles.*)

EDWIN. Begone, Satan! Is that what you mean? (*Pause.*) Come! I smell the good wife's soup. (*He crosses* HANS *to the door up* L., *and turns.*) Let us leave beauty to its communing, till the heart of the world opens to it again.

HANS (*looking round softly, as they go off*). Aye then, King. Such a sleep they sleep. . . .
(*They go out. Faint music for a moment on the empty stage.*)

Slow CURTAIN.

Interlude

CHARACTERS

Mr. Farrelly (the local Provision Merchant, Financier and Man
of Property).

Maloney (his Clerk).

Judy Tippin (a middle-aged, demure little Woman).

Tippin (her devil-may-care Second Husband).

The action of the play takes place in a little market town in
Northern Ireland.

Note: This play is fully protected in the United States and Canada. Applications to perform it publicly should be addressed
to The Richard J. Madden Play Co. Inc., 522 Fifth Avenue,
New York 18, N. Y.

Interlude

SCENE: *The business office of* MR. FARRELLY.

TIME: *Early evening in late autumn.*

It is a harsh, solidly furnished room, with a heavy desk and equipment.

There is a door up L., *in the back wall. Another, to a private room, in the* R. *wall. The windows are in the* L. *wall. The desk is* R.C. MR. FARRELLY'S *chair is* R. *of the desk. Another chair at* C., L. *of the desk. A third chair down* L., *below the windows.*

When the CURTAIN *rises* MALONEY, *the clerk, is about to show in* JUDY TIPPIN, *and her second husband,* TIPPIN.

MALONEY (*outside, as he opens the door*). Sure, just sit down, Mrs. Tippin.

(*He enters.*)

In no time at all he'll be in from his tea, and he *might* see you.

(*As* JUDY *and* TIPPIN *enter.*)

Did you say that he *knew* you?

(JUDY *is a quiet, demure little woman.* TIPPIN *is a hulking, lazy, good-natured fellow.*)

JUDY (*moving to the chair* C.). He *used* to know me, but that was when he bought scrap and old clothes.
(TIPPIN *has moved a little down* L.)

MALONEY (*up* L.C., *dubiously*). Aye . . . well . . . I wouldn't like to bet that he'll remember you. Specially when you want your account to stand over.

JUDY (*turning to* MALONEY). Money makes them all like that, Mr. Maloney. Much wantin' more. (*To* TIPPIN.) Stop wanderin' about, Tippin, like a stray ass. And take your hands out of your pockets before Mr. Farrelly comin' in.

MALONEY. And don't smoke in here before him, Mr. Tippin. It makes him mad.

TIPPIN (*meekly*). Is it any harm for me to draw me breath before the *great Mr. Farrelly?*
(*The lights flicker.*)
Hello! What's makin' the lights wink like that?

JUDY. God help us, that's a queer thing . . . the flickerin' of them like yon!

MALONEY. That's three or four times they've done that this evenin'. It's maybe the high wind from the south, or maybe one of the fuse wires that's not all that it might be. Just warm yourselves there at the fire, and when yous hear him comin' up the stairs (*going away*) run across to me in the outer office.
(*He goes out.*)

TIPPIN (*above the chair down* L.). I'll run for no man. I'll walk.

JUDY. You'll *run*, Tippin.

TIPPIN. All right then, Judy. (*Moving up* L.C.) If *you* say it, I'll *run*.

JUDY (*worried*). I wonder, Tippin, if he'll let us off till Christmas with the account. (*She moves below the chair* C.) If God would only put it in his head . . . If he doesn't, there's nothin' . . . nothin' . . .

TIPPIN (*crossing behind her to above the desk*). Well

sure, there couldn't be less so. (*He stands by the chair* R.)
With your worryin' and snufftherin' . . .

JUDY. Y'oul' divil ye, Tippin . . . If the sky fell down,
you'd roll it roun' ye, and fall asleep.

TIPPIN. And you'd tear strips off your petticoat and
start patchin' it up with safety-pins.

JUDY. Wasn't I the fool to have ye! And me brave and
comfortable and me first man dead and all . . .
(TIPPIN *laughs and lights his pipe.*)

TIPPIN (*puffing his pipe*). It must have been the way
I did me hair, Judy.

JUDY (*looking around the room*). It's funny too the
changes that come. . . . The last time I was in this room,
you wouldn't see many things blacker than me hair was.

TIPPIN (*moving a little down* R.). So you were borryin'
money before you met me at all!

JUDY (*turning sharply to* TIPPIN). I was not! Me
mother and me used to take fresh eggs and butter to the old
gentleman that lived here with his daughter. (*Turning
slowly to face up stage.*) A nice little thing she was too,
with goldish kind of hair and clever little hands with a
needle. (*Pointing.*) Why look, Tippin, there's the mark still
on the wall where the big candelabra was. Twenty-five
candles it had. (*She completes her turn, facing* TIPPIN.)

TIPPIN. Money to burn, surely. And hundreds sittin' in
the dark.

JUDY (*pointing to the* R. *wall, below the cabinet*). And
there beyant ye was a picture the size of the day and the
morrow, of a man by the name of *Addison,* dyin' in it. I
can see his eyes still . . .

TIPPIN (*turning to look at the wall*). Well—he must
be buried so. (*He wanders across to* L.) It's *"Travel in com-
fort by the Cunard Line"* that's in it now. (*Turning to* JUDY.)
How did that Farrelly fella get his nose in here anyway?

JUDY (*moving a little down* R. *and turning*). Sure, the

debts were heavier on it than a load o' coal. They be sayin' Farrelly bought it for a song, and that it was *spite* because Miss Kathleen Moira refused him . . . coarse clod that he was.

TIPPIN (*half sitting on the arm of the chair* L.). Was that what her name was?

JUDY. It was, faith, and it suited her too. She used to wear a long dress to her toes with flounces and frillies on it, and when the candles would be burnin' and her hair all wee lights, you'd think she stepped down out of one of the big frames. (*Sighing.*) She went to England with the old man himself. They say it was a dark day and a cryin' sea, and them goin'.

TIPPIN. Maybe it's *that,* that's making Farrelly the crusty little spider that he is.

JUDY (*moving up to the fireplace, back* C.). Och, sure it was all years ago. . . . (*She stares down at the fire.*)

TIPPIN. Still, it bates hell the way some o' these fellas keep mind of a defeat.

JUDY (*turning to face* TIPPIN). Would you mind o' *me* like that, Tippin?

TIPPIN (*with scoundrel emphasis*). If anythin' was to happen to ye, Judy . . . which the merciful God forbid . . .

JUDY. Y'oul' divil ye!

(*They look at each other and laugh softly.*)
God help us, why do we be laughin'?

TIPPIN (*rising, and moving up* L.C.). Arrah, Judy, isn't it because it's *given to us* to be laughin'.

(*The light fades a little, slowly.*)

JUDY. Maybe . . . maybe . . . (*She moves down to the chair* C.) We'll sit down, Tippin, and take the weight off our feet. Open that window till we hear the noise of the fair.

(TIPPIN *crosses and opens the window. Cows bawl, a few sheep bleat, a horse whinnies.*)

1ST VOICE (*outside*). It's a fine baste—none better.

2ND VOICE. It's not as good as your lyin' tongue would have us believe. Put out your hand there, Paddy Joe, and I'll split the difference with you.

1ST VOICE. Begod and you'll not!

TIPPIN. Here's Farrelly himself comin' through the fair.

1ST VOICE (*outside*). A fine healthy evening, Mr. Farrelly. Glory be to God.

FARRELLY'S VOICE (*roughly*). Well, Buck-teeth, you have your share of it, haven't you?

2ND VOICE. Good evenin', sir. Long days to you, sir.

FARRELLY'S VOICE. Ditto to you with dots, Joe McGinty, and don't forget your account's due on Wednesday morning.

3RD VOICE. Spare a copper, Mr. Farrelly, sir.

FARRELLY'S VOICE. Out to hell o' me way!

(TIPPIN *closes the window.*)

TIPPIN. He won't give much for nothin', the same Farrelly.

(MALONEY *opens the door, and stands there agitated.*)

MALONEY. Hurry! Quick! This way! He's on the stairs. (*He disappears.*)

JUDY (*jumping up, excitedly*). Come on, Tippin. (*Hurrying to the door.*) Run! Run!

TIPPIN (*following, breathless*). W-w-wait for me, Judy. Wait for me.

(*The door clangs as they hurriedly go out. A pause. Then it opens and clangs again peremptorily as* FARRELLY *enters, a powerful bully, coarse and cruel.*)

FARRELLY (*calling*). Are you there, *you*, Maloney! (*He crosses up* R.C. *above his desk.*)

MALONEY (*opening the door*). Yes, sir. (*He enters.*) You called me, sir.

(FARRELLY *picks up some papers, and runs through them.*)

161

FARRELLY (*reading*).   Has the evening mail arrived?

MALONEY (*coming down* L.C.).   I'm just goin' through it.

FARRELLY (*without turning*).   Is my money comin' in as it should?

MALONEY.   Very satisfactory, sir, except in a few cases that . . .

FARRELLY (*turning*).   A contradiction in terms. (*Looking at* MALONEY.) My money, according to your evidence, is *not* coming in well.

MALONEY.   Yes, sir.

FARRELLY.   Eh?

MALONEY.   No, sir.

FARRELLY.   Stop slobberin', and send out the usual tickler to these people *now*.

MALONEY.   Very good, sir. There's one of them, sir . . .

FARRELLY.   Them *all*, I said, Maloney.

MALONEY (*turning up* L.C. *to the door*).   Certainly, sir.

FARRELLY.   Wait!

(MALONEY *checks at the door*.)

I have been considering your request for a rise of pay. (*He moves round to his desk chair*.)

MALONEY (*approaching him with a slight smile, warmly*).   Oh, yes . . . yes, sir . . .

FARRELLY (*sitting, and going through his papers*).   My nephew-in-law has just got a certificate in bookkeeping, so any time you feel like leaving here to better your wages, just let me know.

MALONEY (*swallowing*).   I—I see, sir . . . It's not that I'm greedy, sir. It's just that . . . that I'll have to put off my marriage again.

FARRELLY.   If you weren't born a fool that would be a big consolation to you, Maloney. A—a lost lookin' craythur like that one, with straw-coloured hair!

MALONEY (*turning meekly*). Pardon *me,* Mr. Farrelly. It's not straw-coloured. It's coppery.

FARRELLY. Don't contradict me! Get to your work. You're impertinent.

MALONEY. By the way, sir, there's a woman here that . . .

FARRELLY (*rustling his papers*). Wait! I see here one and a quarter per cent deducted off Pat Murtagh's account. Why?

MALONEY. Well, I felt, sir, seein' that he paid it up so quick . . .

FARRELLY. You felt! . . . And what you felt swindled me out of three and sevenpence. Stop it out of your wages on Saturday.

MALONEY. But, Mr. Farrelly, I can't this week. My uncle that lives with me is ill and . . .

FARRELLY. I don't care if your uncle who lives with you was below playin' dominoes on the hobs of hell. And now to business. A woman, you say? What name?

MALONEY. Mrs. Judy Tippin, sir.

FARRELLY (*pensively*). Tippin . . . (*Puzzled.*) I don't know . . . Oh, yes, yes, Judy Brennan she was before she married that hound, Tippin.

MALONEY. He's with her, sir.

FARRELLY. I'll bet he is, if there's a jingle in her purse at all.

MALONEY. And she says she knows you, sir.

FARRELLY. Not a bit, Maloney. A mere accident.

MALONEY. She might be thinkin' it's a feather in her cap.

FARRELLY (*grimly*). So she might. And expect the percentage off, eh?

MALONEY. I'm not sure, Mr. Farrelly.

FARRELLY. You're not half as sure as I am. How much is her account?

MALONEY. Seventeen pounds, seventeen and six. She promised to clear it off when she sold her cow.

FARRELLY. And so she will, so she will. I saw the cow to-day in the fair. Send her in. I'll salt her.

(*He opens an account book.*)

MALONEY (*going up to the door*). Very good, Mr. Farrelly.

(*He opens the door, beckons off, and ushers in* JUDY *and* TIPPIN.)

Mr. Farrelly will see you now, Mrs. Tippin.

JUDY (*whispering as she enters*). Now mind your manners, Tippin, when our hand's in the dog's mouth.

TIPPIN (*entering with her*). Anythin' you say Judy. (*Moving* L.) But if I could just hit him once . . .

JUDY. Sssh! . . . (*She moves to* C., *below the desk.*) Sure, good day to you, Mr. Farrelly, sir.

(MALONEY *closes the door.*)

I needn't ask you how you're keepin' . . . sure I can see that for meself.

FARRELLY (*brusquely*). Sit down, and behave yourself, Judy Brennan.

(JUDY *sits meekly in the chair* C.)

TIPPIN (*above the chair* L.). *Tippin* the name is, if you please.

JUDY (*turning, reproachfully*). Your manners, Tippin!

FARRELLY (*looking at her*). You had a cow in the market to-day. I *saw* it.

JUDY (*demurely*). Faith, a cow's no fortune nowadays, sir. You'd be miles better with a greyhound.

FARRELLY. Now, now! (*He sits back in his chair.*) I refuse to be drawn into arguments with my clients. You sold your cow, and I take it you are here like a decent mannerly woman to clear off your account. It is due to-day. No, I beg your pardon, it was due yesterday at noon.

JUDY. You have it all off be heart.

FARRELLY.   I have. And I'd need to with the state morality's in, in this country.

(*The door opens.*)

MALONEY (*entering*).   The Auctioneer's on the 'phone, sir.

FARRELLY (*to* JUDY, *rising*).   One minute. (*Crossing below the desk to up* L.) Just a client I'm auctionin' out, that thought she was too able for me . . . and wasn't . . . (*To* TIPPIN *as he reaches him.*) What's *that* in your hand, Tippin?

TIPPIN (*sulkily*).   That's the pipe that was clutched in Michael Casey's dead hand, after the shunter didn't see him on the line.

(FARRELLY *checks at the door and comes down a little.*)

JUDY (*turning to* TIPPIN).   Put the pipe in your pocket, Tippin, in Mr. Farrelly's grand office.

TIPPIN.   So help me God, Judy, I'll do it for *you.*

FARRELLY (*looking* TIPPIN *up and down*).   A lazy, worthless loafer, that's what *you* are! (*As he turns up to the door.*) And you were once a decent woman, Judy Brennan.

TIPPIN.   I said her name was *Tippin* and be the seven saints . . .

JUDY.   Not another word now, Tippin!

(FARRELLY *exits, slamming the door.*)

TIPPIN.   God, isn't he the divil's own crab! I'll wait for you outside, Judy. I'm afraid o' meself now. If the . . . the thickness got up in me before him, and I'd hit him once, it wouldn't have to be twice.

JUDY.   'Tis maybe as well. Let you sit on the stone steps till I come out.

TIPPIN (*reluctantly*).   Aye . . . God be with poor Andy Noonan. It was that that gave him the pleurisy . . . sittin' on the stone steps.

JUDY.   Y'oul' divil ye, Tippin, you'd rather wait in Mc-Goran's Bar with your feet in the sawdust.

TIPPIN (*hurt*).   Now, Judy, you're wrongin' me before

God! (*He moves in, to* L.C.) Did I even breath a solitary word about a bar?

JUDY (*jingling coins*). There's a shillin' for you. (*She holds out the money.*) Let it never be said I was hard on you, Tippin.

TIPPIN (*taking the shilling*). May God send you twice as much. And He will. Wait till you see, now.

(JUDY *titters in spite of herself.*)

(*He jerks his head towards the door.*) You're wastin' your time with that crab, Judy. (*He goes to the door.*)

JUDY. Maybe I am. But if there's a way to get roun' him, I must find it. It's all that's between us and the road. Farrelly's not all bad. I mind of one day when I was just a girl he tossed me hair and gimme a penny.

TIPPIN (*turning up to the door*). That was when he had only tuppence, Judy. (*Turning.*) If a man has two pennies, he'll give ye one. But if he has two poun' he'll give ye nothin'.

JUDY. Go on, go on, he's comin' back.

TIPPIN (*going away: singing*). "Sure she looked so sweet from her two bare feet,
To the shade of her nut-brown hair,
Such a coaxing elf, I'd to shake meself,
For to see was she really there. . . ."

(*He slouches off with a laugh. A moment or two later,* FAR-RELLY *re-enters.*)

FARRELLY. A born loafer that fellow!

(*He crosses up stage to his desk.*)

JUDY. Sure, is it poor Tippin, sir?

FARRELLY. Poor Tippin! . . . (*Sitting.*) Come on! To business!

JUDY. Well, it's like this, Mr. Farrelly, sir. We sold the cow the day for eighteen pounds, and says we to ourselves, since cows is no good with the people that be makin' the laws in Dublin, we'll buy a whole flock of young hens and turkeys and rear poultry instead. That is, says we, if Mr. Farrelly agrees.

FARRELLY. Mr. Farrelly *doesn't* agree.

JUDY. But we could clear off everythin' at Christmas, sir.

FARRELLY. I might be dead by Christmas.

JUDY. You're a hard man, Mr. Farrelly.

FARRELLY. I am. As hard as flint. (*Calling.*) Are you there, Maloney? (*To* JUDY.) No woman ever got the better o' me, so save your breath, Judy Brennan.

MALONEY (*entering*). You called, sir?

FARRELLY. Make out Brennan's—I mean Tippin's—account, and mark it *paid.*

MALONEY. Right this minute, sir.
(*The light flickers.*)

FARRELLY. Wait! (*A pause.*) Did them lights flicker just now?

MALONEY. They did, sir!

FARRELLY. What the hell are they goin' in and out like that for? Who's monkeyin' with them switches?

MALONEY (*coming down a little* L.C.). They've been doing that all evening, sir. It must be some defect in the fuse box.

FARRELLY. It's that rotten wirin' of Logan's! If that rat, Logan, thinks he can do me . . . Get out and see to them!

MALONEY (*turning up to the door*). Yes, sir.
(*He exits.*)

FARRELLY. Come on, you, Judy Brennan, hand over that bag of yours. I can count quicker than you.
(JUDY *hands over her bag.*)

JUDY (*wistfully*). The catch is broke, sir. You'll have to open the knot on the ribbon.

FARRELLY (*shaking the bag*). Slovenly woman! (*Slapping the table repeatedly.*) What sort of a black knot is that?

Now if you were a good-doin', upstandin', careful little woman you'd have had the catch on that bag mended instead of a string round it like a tramp's bundle. Hand me over that knife, on the cabinet.

JUDY (*distressed*).   Oh, please don't cut it, Mr. Farrelly, sir.

FARRELLY.   And why not, will ye tell me, and me time flyin'?

JUDY.   It's a . . . a ribbon I used to hold up me hair with, a long time ago, when the long hair was in it. The times, sir, when they wore the rustlin' dresses and let the hair fall down over the flounces. Sure, you'll mind of them yourself, sir.

FARRELLY (*deliberately*).   I mind of . . . nothing.

JUDY (*innocently*).   But sure, in this very room, Mr. Farrelly . . .

FARRELLY.   I'll have none o' that now! Not a word!
(*The lights continue to flicker during the following.*)
There's them damn lights flickerin' again. If I had that rat, Logan, by the throat! . . . They're goin' . . . They're goin' out! . . .
(*The lights go out. The room is almost dark.*)
God's truth! They've gone out altogether. Now look at the mess we're in fumblin' in the dark! Damn that fellow's fuse wires! Damn the fellow's soul! (*Shouting.*) Hi, you, Maloney!

MALONEY (*entering*).   It's the main fuse that's gone, sir.

FARRELLY.   Get some candles quick! And tell that fellow Logan next door if the lights are not on in five minutes I'll break his back.

MALONEY.   Yes, sir! Right away, sir.
(*He hurries out.*)

FARRELLY (*fuming in the dark*).   Oh, that Logan fella. That rat! That crawlin' reptile! And one o' me own kind too.

Mass every mornin' and do ye up to the eyes. In the Guild of St. Patrick, and gut ye for a penny. Gives a pound to the priest to be a big fella and makes it up on rotten flex wire. Where are you, Judy Tippin?

JUDY (*who has not moved from her chair*). Sure, I'm just here, sir. Sure, it's just you not bein' used to the dark, sir. Sure, often Tippin and meself now be sittin' in the dark, havin' a crack, and think it grand.

FARRELLY. Grand! *Cattle!* Be quiet, woman! (*Jumping up.*) What's keepin' that fool with the candles?

JUDY. Faith, it's not in every shop you'll get candles nowadays, sir. Another of them small things that you'd be havin' little mind of in these times, like the long hair that used to be in it, and the flouncy dresses.

FARRELLY (*strongly*). Quiet, *quiet,* woman, with your lookin' back like that. You should *never* look back.

JUDY. Och, 'tis little choice we have. Back we look to the graves of poor things we loved, and on we look to our own graves.

FARRELLY (*sitting, slowly*). The clatterin' tong' of ye! Can ye not even let the dead rest?
(MALONEY *enters with two lighted candles.*)

MALONEY (*crossing to above the desk*). I just managed to get two candles, sir. I'll put them on your desk. (*He places the candles.*) Logan is busy at the fuse box in the hall.

FARRELLY. Tell the rat to hurry, and I'll fuse box him when he's done.

MALONEY (*hurrying to the door*). I will, sir.
(*He exits.*)

JUDY (*hushed*). The blessed candlelight, the way it was long ago. Let the good God bless all that has stayed on here, and let him give all their spirits great peace and long rest.

FARRELLY (*a little annoyed, but his voice hushed*).

Now, is that necessary? And it just the shadows of the candles flickerin'. 'Tis folks like you that coax the dead from their graves.

JUDY. Sure, a wee prayer won't do no harm, and them maybe wanderin'.

FARRELLY. There's a *time* for prayers, and a *place*. Isn't it the dickens when you're not used to the candlelight? It would make you to be thinkin' stupid things. . . . How strange everythin' looks. . . . You'd think we were . . . flung a long way back . . . a long way back.

JUDY (*as in a dream*). This room was just like this, grand and dim-lit . . . when I used to take the eggs to the old gentleman and his daughter. *She* had the flouncy dresses too, down to her toes they were, and long goldish kind of hair.

FARRELLY (*hushed*). Coppery hair it was.

JUDY. Was it? I forget.

FARRELLY. It was. (*Staring past* JUDY.) I remember . . .

JUDY (*pointing*). And look, sir, there's where the big candelabra was, and beyant there where the big ship is now was the big dyin' eyes of the man by the name of Addison. A man, they said, that was showin' men how to die . . . God help us, and there beside ye was the wicker chair with the work-basket and the little embroidered slips . . . and Kathleen Moira's little hands moving with the needle. . . .

FARRELLY (*tolerantly*). Hush, woman. Let these things be. . . .

JUDY. The whisperin' way you talk, sir! As if anyone could hear . . . Sure, aren't the dead . . . dead . . . ?

FARRELLY. There, there! For God's sake be quiet. I have crushed things out of this room with hammer and chisel, and I will not have them back. (*With a hint of hysteria.*) I will not have them even mentioned!

JUDY (*eerily*). 'Tis maybe so. But the candlelight was

theirs, not ours. 'Tis maybe that it has drawn them all back . . .

FARRELLY (*in hushed nervousness*). Such damn talk! Are you . . . crazy, woman?

JUDY. Why wouldn't they be for stealin' in again, and the chance given to them? . . . Think of the things that happened to them here . . . the dreams they had, the poor eyes that cried and their world tumblin' . . . the hearts that broke in them. . . .

FARRELLY (*touched*). I know . . . I was the breaker. . . . They owed me money and I took their home. . . . Isn't that the law of things?

JUDY. Aye . . . the law of Man made God. "Pay what thou owest." If you could have been just a little merciful . . .

FARRELLY (*magnanimously*). I *was* merciful. I offered to marry the daughter.

JUDY. And she . . . wouldn't? Kathleen Moira wouldn't.

FARRELLY (*not looking at* JUDY). No . . . She turned her back as if. . . .

JUDY. I can see the scorn in her beaten eyes, and the sweep of her petticoats past you. . . .

FARRELLY. Aye, it was like that . . . and her white arms were bare. . . . They maddened me . . . I swore by the God of us all . . . When a man like me loves . . .

JUDY. Or hates, terrible man.

FARRELLY. Aye, or hates. What is the difference? . . . I brought in the carpenters. I wanted to hear the sound of things crashin'. . . . But in the streams of dust I saw her face . . . with the coppery hair about it . . . and in the shavings on the floor I heard her small feet walkin'. . . .

JUDY (*rising slowly*). If she could see now the light fallin' on your face like that! . . .

FARRELLY (*nervous, disconcerted*). Like . . . Like what, woman? What . . . are you sayin' to me?

JUDY (*moving round to above his chair*). As if you were noble and kingly and brave, and the old spilt blood still unspilt in ye, like a miracle of the Lord, instead of mean and cruel like a man not out of the pain and the past at all . . .

FARRELLY (*hands to face*). Stop! Stop! Let . . . let me be now! . . . You are only imaginin' things. There is nothin' there at all. . . . (*Dropping his hands, and looking up at her.*) Didn't you say the dead are . . . dead? . . .

JUDY. Who knows, faith, what does and what doesn't die?

FARRELLY. Keep hold of me arm, Judy. (*Her hand touches his arm.*) I want to feel firm things . . . I want to be with a friend. . . . Judy, you owe me nothin', nothin' at all. Not a penny. Take all away, and we'll forget. (*A pause.*) Yes, there are things here I haven't smashed away. . . .

JUDY. Things beyond your hate.

FARRELLY (*head bowed*). Oh, I confess . . . I loved her, I adored her . . . I mind of her softness beside my coarseness . . . her sweetness beside my bitterness . . . (*He buries his face in his hands.*) I can still hear her small feet walkin' roun' and roun' me desk in circles forever. (*In anguish.*) I am tortured . . . I cannot bear it. . . . Take away this terrible mindin' o' things from me. . . . Out with them cursed candles! Out with them!

(*He hurls the two candles to the ground and the room is again in darkness.*)

Now I can see nothin'. . . . It is all hidden away. . . . Where are you, Judy? This dark is very heavy!

JUDY. Sure, just here beside ye now, sir, sayin' a little prayer. . . .

FARRELLY. Stay close to me, Judy. I need a friend. I

am . . . afraid . . . You owe me nothin' . . . nothin' . . .
We'll tear up your account.

JUDY. God love ye, and bless ye for that, sir.

FARRELLY. I owe it to you, Judy. "Pay what thou owest . . ."

JUDY. Not to me, sir, but to . . .

FARRELLY. Stop! Don't say *that* name . . . any name
that's . . . here. . . .

JUDY. Sure, we'll just stay quiet like me and Tippin in
the dark. . . .

FARRELLY. Aye . . . we'll be quiet . . . we'll say no
word at all. . . .

(*The lights suddenly go on.*)

JUDY. Look! Look! (*Moving to* L. *of the chair* C.) The
light's on again . . . the whole string o' them. Let ye lift up
your head, sir. Sure, it's all over now. (*She moves down to* L.
of the desk.)

MALONEY (*opening the door*). That's everything all
right now, sir.

FARRELLY. Get out! And tell that cutthroat, Logan, to
keep out o' *my* way!

(*The door slams. A pause.*)

Woman!

JUDY. Yes, sir.

FARRELLY. We were discussin' a business proposition.

JUDY. We—we were, sir.

FARRELLY. And you were impertinently asking for an
extension, which I very justly refused.

JUDY. That's right, sir.

FARRELLY (*fumbling with the bag*). And I was lec-
turing you on the stupidity, woman, of this string.

JUDY (*meekly*). And the bad-doin' woman I was, sir.

FARRELLY. Exactly. I hope you will benefit by these
remarks, and be more upstandin', honest and thrifty.

JUDY. I'll try, sir.

FARRELLY (*viciously shaking* JUDY'S *bag, and emptying it on the desk*). Seventeen pounds, seventeen and sixpence. (*He hands back the bag to* JUDY.) There's your bag back. Now that's you and I clear, woman, and if you were a more upright and conscientious woman, it would be a *big* satisfaction to you.

MALONEY (*entering with a paper*). Here's the account, sir.

FARRELLY. Hand it to Mrs. Tippin and go.

(MALONEY *gives her the account, and exits.*)

JUDY. You forgot, sir, to give me back me red ribbon, if you please.

FARRELLY. There's your rag for you! See if it will cure your hunger to-night.

JUDY. It will cure one sort of hunger, sir, away deep down. Have you anythin' that will cure *yours?*

(*The door opens and* TIPPIN *enters, smoking.*)

FARRELLY (*peremptorily*). Less of that! (*Rising.*) You will go now, Judy Tippin. Take her away, Tippin. I have work to do.

(*He turns* R., *and marches out vigorously to the inner office.*)

TIPPIN. Well, Judy, any luck?

JUDY. No luck at all, Tippin. I tried . . . ah, but sure it was no good.

TIPPIN. There now, Judy, there now! Sure, no matter at all.

JUDY. What'll we do, Tippin? There's nothing now . . .

TIPPIN. Arrah, sure, isn't there always somethin'! Amn't I always tellin' ye! With your worryin' and snufftherin'.

JUDY (*with some affection*). Y'oul' divil ye, Tippin.

TIPPIN. Sure, haven't we one another! Isn't that the secret that madmen like Farrelly will never learn. Come on now and I'll take your arm.

(*They go out slowly.* FARRELLY *re-enters* R., *and stands look-*

ing after them. He jingles JUDY's *money and laughs harshly.*)

FARRELLY.   Do you hear it, Kathleen Moira . . . Judy's cash. (*Moving slowly across* L.) She will sit with Tippin tonight in the dark on a stone floor and have cold potatoes and a mug of sour milk for supper. *I* own her. (*Staring out of the window.*) I own all that out there too.

(*Outside, in the market-place, cows bawl, horses neigh and sheep bleat.*)

Listen. There you are, Kathleen Moira! I own them all. And I own the wretches that drive them. I own their crops and their houses. I own their lives and their bodies and their souls! I am the Man of Property, the Man of Power and Money. (*He turns slowly and looks across the room.*) How much now, Kathleen Moira, for the sweep of your silk petticoats past me? How much now for that maddening little mouth you wouldn't let me taste? (*His voice grows weary and pathetic, as he moves to the chair* C.) Ah, Kathleen Moira, I can hear you answering me, and your voice is a little silver bell that I can never escape from. Ah, why do I try to lie to you when you know? Why do I go on living a lie? Why, Kathleen? Why? Why? Why? (*He sits down wearily, his head in his hands.*)

CURTAIN.

Three Act Play

The Devil Came from Dublin

A Satirical Extravaganza in Three Acts

CHARACTERS

UDOLPHUS McCLUSKEY (a District Justice about 50).

STANISLAUS BRANNIGAN (a Publican, middle-aged).

JUDY (his young Daughter).

MIKE MACNAMARA (a Smuggler, about 30).

SERGEANT WHISTLER (Sergeant of the Guards, middle-aged).

CRAMPSEY (a Civic Guard, about 35).

FATHER PHELIM (a Catholic Priest, elderly).

BARNEY KILLANE (a Smuggler, elderly).

IGNATIUS FARRELL (a Customs Officer, about 35).

RITA RONAN (a red-haired local beauty about 28).

MARIA (her housekeeper, elderly).

MRS. KATIE BANNON (a housewife, elderly).

MEN AND WOMEN SMUGGLERS

Note: This play is fully protected in the USA and Canada. Applications to perform it publicly should be addressed to The Richard J. Madden Play Co. Inc., 522 Fifth Ave. New York 18, N.Y.

The Devil Came from Dublin

A Satirical Extravaganza in Three Acts

SYNOPSIS OF SCENES

Act I: *A Lounge Bar*

Act II:
Scene I—*A Sitting Room*
Scene II—*Same as Act I*

Act III: *Same as Act II—Scene I*

The action passes in the Irish village of Chuckeyhead, near the Northern Border. The events take place during the Second World War, when the British food situation was very serious.

Note: *All of the characters in this extravaganza are entirely fictitious and bear no reference to any living person.*

ACT I

Scene: *The Lounge Bar of Stanislaus Brannigan's hotel in Chuckeyhead, a small village on the Ulster Border.*
The Tables and chairs are placed around the room.

181

The shelves are well lined with bottles, and there are the usual pictorial advertisements on the walls. There are swinging doors to the street, a door leading to the tap room in the right wall, and back right a few steps are visible of the stairs leading up to the bedrooms. In the left wall is a picture-panel, bearing the motto:

'AN HONEST MAN IS THE NOBLEST WORK OF GOD'

THE CURTAIN RISES *on a crowded stage, showing the Lounge Bar, with the smugglers in action. Amongst the smugglers on-stage are* BARNEY *and* PETER, KATIE BANNON, MAGGIE, SARAH, *and the three other men smugglers.* JUDY *is busy moving amongst them collecting their slips and fees which she places in a box that she carries around with her.*

THE SMUGGLERS, *for stage business, can be writing their slips, and also tying their parcels with string. Some are sitting and some standing.*

JUDY, *a winning and vivacious young girl, the daughter of Brannigan, keeps up a running commentary as she moves around.*

JUDY.   Come on now, with your chits and smugglin' fees. And no dodgin' mind, for Mike MacNamara is the divil himself when he's riz.

PETER.   Judy, are you sure that Mike's goin' over the Border tonight with the lorry?

JUDY.   He's goin' if his friend, Customs Officer Farrell, is on at the post. We'll know for sure when me dad comes in. He's out lookin' for more whiskey in Ballycrabbit town.

KATIE.   Fifty nylons, Judy, and there's me fee. (*She places slips in the box.*)

SARAH.   Two cooked hams, Judy. I could ate them meself this minute, only for the grand price I'll get for them across the Border. (*Places slip in box.*)

KATIE. The fast will do you good, Sarah, if you take it for your sins.

(*Laughter.*)

1ST MAN. A case of Scotch, Judy. Take it before I faint with temptation.

2ND MAN. Twelve pounds of fillet steak, Judy. The first Englishman that sees it will bless himself and turn into a Catholic.

3RD MAN. Two cases of American red salmon, Judy. Thanks be to God for Marshall Aid!

(*All give their slips and money to* JUDY *who puts it in her box.*)

BARNEY (*wheedlingly*). Judy, you could strike a match on me throat. Give us a drop of Irish.

JUDY (*sharply*). Now! Not till me Da comes back.

PETER (*coaxingly*). I'll bet you now, Judy, you have a drop hid under the counter.

JUDY (*tartly*). You must be able to see round corners, Peter. I'm under me Da's orders.

BARNEY. He has plenty to send across the Border anyway. And us oul' customers of his, with throats like lime-kilns.

JUDY. And do you think, Barney, he'd sell it to you at one-and-sixpence a shot when he can get double that in the town of Newry beyond the hill out there?

PETER. Ah, the same Border is the curse of the country. A bloody English crime.

BARNEY. Well, will yous listen to what's talkin'! A man that put a hundred platinum watches in his grandmother's coffin and it crossing the Border.

PETER. Will yous listen to Satan gettin' religious! A man that had to pretend to the Customs Officer that he was dumb, because his mouth was full of gold weddin' rings!

(*A loud knock sounds on the left wall. All look in that direction.* JUDY *hurries to the counter, pours out a generous measure of whiskey into a glass, crosses to the picture with the motto:* AN HONEST MAN IS THE NOBLEST WORK OF GOD, *draws a string that makes the picture ascend, to expose a little wooden panel in the wall.* JUDY *slides open the panel, passes the glass through it, closes it with a snap, and draws the picture back into its original position.* BARNEY *and* PETER *nudge each other knowingly, and the rest smile and wink.*)

BARNEY. The Sergeant can get his drink when he orders it anyway.

JUDY. God bless your brains, Barney. Do you want the Sergeant in there in the Barracks to sober up and put down his foot? And if he did, where's our whole smugglin' trade?

KATIE. Hear, hear, Judy! Yous men always want it both ways.

SARAH. Did yous ever see the man that didn't want to sell his cake and ate it at the one time?

JUDY. Come on, Barney, with your fees.

BARNEY. Five gross of lipsticks and perfumes for the Ulster lassies and them destroyed, God help them, with British austerity. (*He puts slip and money in box.*)

JUDY. And you, Peter?

PETER. Ten dozens of nylons for the darlin's, Judy, and a stuffed goose for me oul' grandmother in Ulster. The poor thing . . . her belly thinks her throat's cut. (*Puts fees in box.*) That's a fine adventurous blouse you have on, Judy.

JUDY. The only thing that's wrong with my blouse, Peter, is in your eye. And let your eye behave itself.

(STANISLAUS BRANNIGAN *enters carrying a jug.*)

Any luck, Da?

STANISLAUS. The divil's luck, Judy. A lousy two gallons of the native brew and Chuckeyhead with a thirst like an elephant that swallowed a cannister of rock salt.

BARNEY (*eagerly*). Is it for the customers or the Border, Stanislaus?

STANISLAUS (*mockingly*).   Are ye dry, Barney?

BARNEY (*mournfully*).   I'm as dry, Stanislaus, as the petrified shinbone of a prehistoric monster.

STANISLAUS.   God help us, that's dry enough surely! Judy, give Barney a drink.

PETER.   And don't let poor Peter petrify in his shoes with the thirst.

STANISLAUS.   And Peter, too, Judy.

(JUDY *gives them drinks.*)

Now, listen all! I met Customs Officer Farrell in the shakers for a drink, and I told him to slip in for the usual. He wants his usual fifty pounds to let Mike MacNamara through to the North with the lorry. Now, let yous keep your mouths shut tight about him being here in case some infidel's ear might hear more than it should.

BARNEY.   Depend on us, Stanislaus. We'll be as mum as a tombstone.

(*Murmurs of assent and expressions such as "ah, indeed we will!"*)

STANISLAUS.   He's lettin' Mike through with the lorry tonight. Where would Mike and our smugglin' trade be only for him?

PETER.   Oh, a dacent man, Customs Officer Farrell. I often wonder what he's like when he's sober.

STANISLAUS.   I saw him sober once, but he was sound asleep!

(*Laughter.*)

Into the taproom now, everyone, with the parcels for Mike's lorry. Yous never can tell what snoopin' divil from Dublin would blow in on an evil wind.

(*With words of approval, the* SMUGGLERS *gather their merchandise and pass into the taproom,* BARNEY *and* PETER *going last.*)

PETER.   Did I tell you the one, Barney, about the little chap whose friend said to him, "Who was that beautifully dressed lady I saw you with last night?" "Oh," says the little chap, "that was no lady. That was me big sister what was ruined."

JUDY. Stop tellin' them bad stories here, Peter Kenny. Father Phelim says I'm not to listen to them.

BARNEY. Ah, now, what's bad in that one, Judy?

JUDY. I'm too innocent to tell you that, thanks be to God.

(*All exit except* JUDY *and* STANISLAUS. *The peremptory knock comes again from the picture.* JUDY *and* STANISLAUS *pay immediate attention.*)

STANISLAUS. Hurry, Judy, girl. Give the Sergeant a bumper before he goes religious and has us all transported for life. I always dread a dacent man goin' religious.

(JUDY *runs with a drink to the panel and repeats the previous procedure. She then returns to the counter.*)

JUDY (*entering the drink in ledger*). Da, that's nearly two thousand bumpers again the Sergeant.

STANISLAUS. Judy, lass, isn't it a fair and dacent price for a blind eye?

(*Enter the* SERGEANT, *wearing glasses on the end of his nose. He is comfortably drunk, but holds it like a gentleman and a seasoned drinker, and has very definite inherent dignity which he never loses. He talks with the fruity tones of a well-oiled drinker.*)

SERGEANT (*at the door, sniffing pronouncedly, with mock severity*). Stanislaus Brannigan! I smell smugglers!

STANISLAUS (*affectionately*). Ah now, Sergeant, that's just your bad conscience havin' unneighbourly words with your liver. Pour the Sergeant a bumper, Judy.

(JUDY *busies herself with the drink.*)

SERGEANT (*taking off glasses and putting them in pocket*). I'd better take off me glasses, in case I see a . . . magnification of anythin' subversive and felonious. What the eye doesn't see, the nose daren't smell. As the poet said:

"We choose *this* cause or *that,* but still
The Everlasting works its will . . ."

Did any of yous see that able assistant of mine, Guard Crampsey?

STANISLAUS. I saw him, Sergeant, in Ballycrabbit town
this mornin'.

SERGEANT. That fellow bates hell. He's as mad as a hat-
ter on whiskey and widows.

(*At a table downstage, the* SERGEANT *leisurely takes two whiskey glasses from one pocket, two more from another,
then one from each of his two trouser pockets, places
them one inside the other and hands them to* STANIS-
LAUS.)

Your property, Stanislaus.

STANISLAUS (*taking glasses*). Did I ever refuse you,
Sergeant?

SERGEANT. You never did, Stanislaus.

STANISLAUS. Hell roast me if I ever do.

SERGEANT. Amen.

(*They shake hands affectionately.* JUDY *comes to him with
the drink.*)

JUDY. Will I put it down to you in me Da's book, Sergeant?

SERGEANT. Do, Judy, and it'll maybe shorten your time
in purgatory.

(*As* JUDY *moves away, he beckons* STANISLAUS, *and puts his
hand on his shoulder.*)

Stanislaus, when you and I were fightin' the Black and Tans,
do you remember Gogarty and his giant's laugh?

STANISLAUS. Ah, sure, wasn't it I, Sergeant, that whispered the Act of Contrition in his dyin' ear?

SERGEANT. I wrote a spasm about him today, when the
fiery mood was on me. Attention, Stanislaus!

(STANISLAUS *squares up, as the* SERGEANT *takes out a slip and reads:*)

> "Ah, now the years have lost their shapeliness,
>> For Gogarty is dead,
> And Larry too, and Shawn and Ned,
>> And left me here in tawdry dress
> In paltry times with love unwed
>> To the dancing curls that would sweeten
>>>> my bed. . . ."

STANISLAUS (*admiringly*). Begosh, Sergeant, that's masterly.

SERGEANT (*melancholily*). Just the rhymes of an old drunkard . . . Ah, we were all men of high stature then when the swords were crossed and the dream was alight. Now we're only drunkards and smugglers. (*He sits down heavily.*) Another drink, Judy, till the drunken turbine of me mind generates another spasm . . .

(JUDY *takes bottle and goes to him.*)

JUDY. Sergeant, maybe some day, if you were drunk enough, you'd put *me* in a poem, and then I'd be famous.

SERGEANT. Ah, Judy, aren't you your Da's daughter . . . the daughter of the man that whispered the Act of Contrition in Gogarty's dyin' ear!

> "Fill me a drink in Gogarty's mug,
>> That I may hear his giant's laugh
> Reverberatin' through the snug,
>> As Shawn and Ned and Larry quaff
> The brew they made for fightin' men . . ."

(*Touching* JUDY's *elbow and pouring a stiff bumper.*)

SERGEANT. God bless your elbow, Judy. It was born generous.

(BARNEY *and* PETER *come boisterously in from the taproom.*)

BARNEY (*gleefully*). And says she to Ignatius, "Bad

luck to you," says she, "but wasn't it the hard day for me the day I first humbled me body to you. Better for me if I was sellin' meself on the square of Mullingar, or maybe, God save us, to be havin' a bastard to a son of the gintry . . ."

(*They clap each other on the back and laugh heartily.*)

SERGEANT (*putting on his glasses and peering at them, comically*). Come round here, you pair of scoundrels, till I see if there's any bad in your mind.

PETER. Try our throats instead, Sergeant, and mind you don't get burned.

(*Laughter.*)

(*Customs Officer* IGNATIUS FARRELL *enters. He is a seedy, shrunken man, in a bad way for a drink, for his hands shake noticeably. Drink has made him loquacious and even at times obsequious. He is in uniform. He stands inside the swing doors and regards them quizzically.*)

FARRELL. Are you all dacent men here?

BARNEY. Every mother's son of us, Mr. Farrell.

FARRELL. Thanks be to God for his small mercies.

STANISLAUS. There's a bumper here for you, Mr. Farrell. Come on in.

FARRELL (*coming forward*). I will so. There's villainy afoot.

STANISLAUS (*questioningly*). Villainy?

FARRELL. An indeed there is. And maybe destruction forby. (*Clutching his drink.*) Wait now till I pour this into the maw of the Arch Demon of Necessity, and get the compis mentis back to me fingers.

(*As he drinks, his hand shakes violently. Having gulped down the whiskey, he holds up his hand and the fingers stop shivering. He smiles benignly.*)

There now! Isn't that as big a wonder as is in the world? The pendulum of dissipation rests.

SERGEANT (*crustily*). Officer Farrell, how many times have I advised you not to come in here in Customs uniform?

FARRELL.   And how else could I come when Murphy the Pawnbroker has every stitch I own.

SERGEANT.   You could come in civvies.

STANISLAUS (*he refills* FARRELL'S *glass*).   Some of these days you'll be fired for bein' drunk, and then where are we all? Where's our whole smugglin' trade? Where's Chuckeyhead?

(*The others shake their heads ruefully.*)

FARRELL.   How the hell could I be fired for bein' drunk? Sure when I'm drunk I'm efficient. But when I'm sober, I'm as stupid as an ox. Some day I'll be fired for bein' sober, and I'm warnin' yous.

PETER.   Did you say somethin' when you came in about villainy bein' afoot?

STANISLAUS.   Ah, he's just blatherin' out of him.

FARRELL.   Maybe I am, maybe I'm not. Let yous judge for yourselves. (*He takes a newspaper from his pocket.*) This is the Dublin mornin' paper. I got it early this mornin' off a dacent man in a motor car that was passin' through to the North. Them that have ears, let them hear!

(*He reads from the paper. They gather round—all attention.*) "In the Dail yesterday, the Minister for Justice, replying to numerous indignant complaints from Members of Parliament that every man, woman and child in Chuckeyhead was a smuggler . . ."

PETER.   Well, of all the damned lies!

FARRELL.   ". . . announced amid cheers that he had appointed a new District Justice in the person of Udolphus McCluskey, the eminent Barrister, with very special powers, to reside in Chuckeyhead and relentlessly suppress all smuggling with all the rigours of the law."

(*A sensation follows.*)

BARNEY.   Isn't McCluskey the cut-throat that sent to jail for six months the dacent man that fell off his bicycle between a policeman and a burglar?

PETER. Ay, indeed he is. The same villain that sent a poor man to bread and water in jail for just batin' his own wife. If it had been anyone else's wife . . .

JUDY. Da, this will be our ruination.

BARNEY. It'll be the ruination of all of us. What else is there to do in this place only smuggle?

PETER. We may all pack up and go on the dole. It's that or the jail.

STANISLAUS (*who has been shocked by the news, recovering*). That's a fine bloody grin you're wearin', Ignatius Farrell! If it's pullin' our legs you are . . .

FARRELL (*thrusting the paper at him*). Here, read it for yourself.

STANISLAUS (*reading*). Well, of all the misfortunes! (*Going to* SERGEANT.) Hey, Sergeant, it says here right enough that the antichrist McCluskey is appointed to Chuckeyhead sure enough. He must be one of them law-abidin' British immigrants that's invaded the country since the Socialists took over the government in England.

SERGEANT (*turning paper upside down*). Stanislaus, always read newspapers and government notices upside down. It's the secret of elementary intelligence. (*Lifting his glass.*)

"Me darlin' told me to drink no more,
    Or me life would be o'er in a little
            short while . . ."

BARNEY. You and your poetry! Sittin' there like an oul' hen trying to lay and Chuckeyhead ready to be wiped off the map. Are ye listenin' to us at all?

SERGEANT. Wouldn't it be the rainy day I'd start listenin' to a crowd of quackin' ducks every time it threatens to thunder!

PETER. Maybe then you'll tell us what to do.

SERGEANT. Do? Keep life rollin' along, Peter, and to

hell with the doctrinaires. When yous are as used to the official mind as meself, yous'll learn that between the announcement and the accomplishment, there's always in every government office a gentlemanly lapse of about three years.

JUDY.　Three years! Sergeant!

BARNEY.　Do you mean this new cut-throat of a District Justice won't be here for three years yet?

SERGEANT.　I'd say four, if I was cynical.

STANISLAUS (*jubilantly*).　Begosh, that's grand heartenin' news. The blessin' o' God on you, Sergeant. The drinks is on the house.

FARRELL.　The degenerate that first invented governments had a bad liver, a worse conscience and was plainly at variance with the Cosmos. (*Lifting a bottle of whiskey.*) Can I go upstairs for a sleep, Stanislaus, before I report at the Customs Post?

STANISLAUS.　Go right ahead, Ignatius, and when Mike MacNamara call, I'll send him up to you.

FARRELL.　Lift up your gates! I'll let Mike through with the lorry tonight in return for what the Scots call a small consideration.

(*He turns out the lining of his trousers pocket, grins, and carries his bottle upstairs.*)

Them and their bloody D.J.'s, with special powers! And to think they are our own lousy flesh and blood! God be with the poor British . . . it always took *them* at least ten years to make up their minds about anythin'. But sure of course, *they* were gentlemen.

(FARRELL *slouches upstairs.* JUDY *is touched and sorry for him.*)

JUDY.　Ah, Da, poor Mr. Farrell. (*She runs after him to the stairs.*) Oh Mr. Farrell, can I come up and put a blanket over you?

FARRELL (*maudlinly*).　No, Judy. Thirty years ago, I

loved someone very like you. But she expected me to be a hero instead of a man, and I lost her. Since then Ignatius Farrell ploughs a lone furrow and is responsible only to the Cosmos.

(FARRELL *slouches upwards.* JUDY *returns sadly to the counter. The swing doors open suddenly, and* GUARD CRAMPSEY *rushes in.*)

CRAMPSEY. Sergeant, Sergeant! I'm after pedallin' all the way from Ballycrabbit. There's atrocious news. Are ye sober?

SERGEANT (*rising unsteadily*). Am I what, Crampsey? Did you ever see me under the weather in your puff? Even when *you* were under the table? Deliver your message, Crampsey, and show some modicum of respect for your superior.

CRAMPSEY. The new District Justice is arrived . . . with the power of ten Archbishops in his pocket!

(*General consternation.*)

SERGEANT. Is it . . . the whiskey in you that's talkin', Crampsey? Out with it now!

CRAMPSEY. I'm tellin' ye, Sergeant, he's landed. He was on the train that's just in from Dublin. I have it out of the horse's mouth.

SERGEANT (*sags pathetically*). It's unheard of! A plain soda water, Crampsey. And you might be the better for one yourself. This new Government won't last a month if it's goin' to be as efficient as all that! It's an outrage on the people!

JUDY. Plain soda water! The reformin' is beginnin' already.

(CRAMPSEY *pours the* SERGEANT *a soda water which he does not relish.*)

CRAMPSEY. Even if it's tough, Sergeant, drink it all. It's best.

(*The* SERGEANT *holds his nose and drinks with a wry face.*)

I'm told he was at the railway station askin' everyone where he could find the Chuckeyhead bus!

STANISLAUS.   I hope there was nobody low enough to tell him.

CRAMPSEY.   Damn the one! I'm proud of Ballycrabbit, this great day. Wee Jamesey Burke that sells the papers at the station gate sent him to the other end of the town.

JUDY.   What make of a man is he at all, Crampsey?

CRAMPSEY.   A wee burley-barley man, I hear, carrying an umbrella like a gentleman, and as full of pomp as a petrol pump.

STANISLAUS.   This is the worst news yet. And the very night too that Mike's slippin' across the Border with the lorry!

SERGEANT.   This, Stanislaus, is an unparalleled phenomenon in the history of Ireland. It's what comes of introducin' American efficiency into a Christian country. Am I parade proof, Crampsey?

CRAMPSEY.   You're a wee bit dilated in the eyeballs, Sergeant. But with the help o' God it'll pass for flatulence.

SERGEANT.   Proceed before me, Crampsey, to the barracks—and bury the dead men.

CRAMPSEY.   You took the words out of me mouth, Sergeant. They'll not all pass for paraffin oil bottles.

(CRAMPSEY *goes out through the swing doors hurriedly*.)

SERGEANT (*to* JUDY).   A plain soda water, Judy.

JUDY.   Are you on a black fast or what? There's a drop of Irish for you.

STANISLAUS.   We all may as well throw in our cards. We're beat.

JUDY.   I'm ashamed of you, Da. Haven't we still Mike MacNamara?

BARNEY.   We have—if he's not safe across the Border by this.

JUDY.   Another word out of you, Barney, and you've

had your last drink in me da's pub. Take your drink, Sergeant, and be a man.

SERGEANT.   Slainthe, boys, here's what killed me father. (*Drinks.*) I'm goin' to be in the divil's own stew for a drink now. If only I was a camel I could carry a couple of quarts of malt in a convenient anteroom off me stomach.

STANISLAUS.   Sergeant—as long as there's a licensing law to be broken, I'll break it for you.

JUDY.   Good man, Da.

SERGEANT.   Let yous all remember—that if ever I have to arrest any of yous—which the All-merciful God forbid . . .

JUDY.   Ah, you poor Sergeant.

SERGEANT.   Gather round Mike, boys, and I'll be with you too—in spirit—even if that spirit lack liquefaction. (SERGEANT *exits by swing doors.*)

STANISLAUS.   The sun was shinin' this mornin', and life was good.

PETER.   Ah, now, you're sayin' it!

STANISLAUS.   But look at us now. Disaster and ruin starin' us in the face. Chuckeyhead in the dustbin.

BARNEY.   We might as well have no Border at all for all the good it is to us now.

STANISLAUS.   Who put the bad thought in me head about Mike? Was it you, Barney?

BARNEY.   All I'm askin' is—where is he? (*Enter* MIKE.)

MIKE.   He's here.

ALL.   Mike!

JUDY.   Ah, sure. Didn't I know it!

MIKE.   There was always a bit of the old woman about you, Barney. As for you, Peter, some of these days I'll buy you a petticoat.

JUDY.   Now, did he desert us, Barney Killane?

BARNEY.   I take it all back.

MIKE. You'd better, Barney. I have a bad habit of hoppin' traducers and backbiters off the chimney-pots. What's the matter with you, Stanislaus? Have you got toothache or is it your bad conscience?

STANISLAUS. I'm down, Mike. I'm far down. Did you hear the divil from Dublin is landed?

MIKE. Divil or no divil, a little bit of sanity is needed around here. If anybody wants any of it it's right here at the end of my fist. If this newcomer is to be beaten, he'll be beaten with his own weapons and within the law.

STANISLAUS. Within the law, Mike?

MIKE. That's what I said.

BARNEY. But how the hell do you expect dacent men like ourselves to work within the law?

STANISLAUS. Do you want our poor fathers and grandfathers to turn in their graves?

PETER. Answer that one, Mike, if you're able.

MIKE. This man, believe it or not, has a terrible respect for law. And of course he's too learned a man—and therefore too big an ejot to know any better. There's his weakness. That's where we must re-educate him in the dacent human and Christian weaknesses. We must de-Puritanise him for his own good, and for the greater glory of the race.

STANISLAUS. There's sense in that. Begod, Mike, you didn't think that one out in your sleep.

MIKE. I always sleep with one of me eyes open, Stan, it's a good Christian habit. Suppose for a minute we went outside the law and chucked the fellow in a boghole.

STANISLAUS. It's unfortunately not to be thought of.

MIKE. We'd have seven devils worse than himself down here from Dublin. Instead of violence, we've got to win this fellow over to be one of ourselves. We've got to make him see that the Border—

ALL (*raising their hats*). God bless it!

MIKE. Amen!—is an English crime.

ALL.   Hear, hear! We're agin it to the death!

JUDY.   It's the only way out . . . make him one of ourselves. And if whiskey is needed, Mike, count me and me Da.

BARNEY.   Are you goin' across the Border with the lorry tonight, Mike?

MIKE.   It all depends on Farrell. If he plays ball we'll make a dash for it.

STANISLAUS.   He's upstairs sleepin' it off. But if this divil from Dublin arrives, Mike?

MIKE.   Divil, or no divil, we've got to go over. This village has got to live, law or no law.

JUDY.   Ah, good old Mike! I have all the money and the slips ready for you, Mike.

MIKE.   Judy, you're a divil and a darlin'. If only you had been born with a pair of pants on, instead of a plungin' neckline!

(MIKE *pats her on the cheek and is about to go, when* BAR- NEY, *who is looking from the window, announces* RITA'S *entrance.*)

BARNEY.   Hi! Hi! Attention, Mike! Here's Rita Ronan, your mad redhead, comin'.

MIKE.   Not so much of the *mad*, Barney Killane.

STANISLAUS.   Arrah, go aisy with that pest, Mike. Since her father died and left her all that money and that darlin' oul' house, she's put dozens of men through her hands, and the hussy'll marry none o' them. "I'll marry no one short of a hero," says she.

PETER.   Do you think for a minute that she'll marry *you*, Mike?

MIKE.   That's enough! The others *asked* her to marry them, I just *tell* her. Does everyone here understand that, or does he want it *explained* to him?

BARNEY.   She's out of breath runnin'. She must have heard about the D.J.

(*Both swing doors are thrown open, simultaneously, and*

RITA *stands framed in them.*)

RITA. Is it true?

MIKE. Is what true, Rita?

RITA. The splendid news!

MIKE (*going to her*). What the blazes is splendid about it, you madhead?

RITA. Ah, but think of the terrific thrills we'll have dodging his high Dublin lordship! Mike, me darling, you'll be in terrible danger—you'll be inches away from the handcuffs every minute that passes—think of it! Nero descending on the Arena! Cromwell descending on Drogheda! Napoleon at the Gates of Moscow. (*Sensing the silence, lamely.*) Well, won't it be wonderful?

MIKE. Now will you get off this high horse of yours, and come down to earth.

RITA. But we'll be living breathlessly. And it's going to give you the chance to be a hero—a *real* hero! I'm warnin' you, Mike. I've sworn never to marry anyone short of a hero. And that includes *you!*

MIKE. Ah, you've got heroes on the brain!

PETER. Put the puck back into us, Rita.

RITA. I'll put it back into you. I'm coming with you across the Border tonight, Mike.

MIKE. God, what am I going to do with *you?*

(IGNATIUS FARRELL *comes down the stairs, and slouches on, in trousers and shirt. He shows no trace of his uniform.*)

FARRELL (*woefully*). It's no good. I can't sleep. I'm not drunk enough to sleep; and I'm too drunk to keep awake. So I lie in bewitched suspension between the Sphinx and Morpheus!

RITA (*caressing him*). Ah, me poor, poor Ignatius, who sleeps so beautifully under my window whenever his legs refuse to own each other.

MIKE. Here, what the hell is all . . .

RITA. Mike, will you spare us these crude Anglo-Saxon interjections. Speak to me, my poor Ignatius.

FARRELL (*looking at her wistfully*). You strange, beautiful, lovely, velvety creature, why do you torture me? You are the murmur that haunts the pillows of bald men who dream fiercely of rustling petticoats and an impossible positivism.

RITA (*entranced*). Oh, what a heavenly speech! Say it again, Ignatius.

FARRELL. I never say things twice. I always forget them. What was I sayin' just now?

MIKE. Now look, Farrell, this drinking of yours will ruin us all. We've got to be ten times more careful now with this new D.J.

STANISLAUS. Can you not take the pledge and save plenty of money with all the bribes we're giving you?

FARRELL. Certainly, but mark my dilemma! Every morning I say to my image in the glass, no drink today. I start to shave—I find shaving an impossible operation. I say, one drink so that I may shave. Mark the subtlety of the demon in me! I drink deep, shave unerringly, and present myself. Ignatius Farrell presents himself!

MIKE. Very well then—one a day.

FARRELL. But the hour moves on, and my seven demons who dance attendance to the Arch Demon of Necessity, request a drink, suggest a drink, require a drink, DEMAND a drink. I feed them with fire, and they suck their tails contentedly and muse comically over the inscrutable, the inexorable and the unanswerable.

RITA (*fondling him*). Ah, me poor darlin' tortured Ignatius.

MIKE. Pest! Don't make him worse than he is. (*He pushes* RITA *away.*) Here's your fifty pounds for the right of way at midnight, and don't let me down.

(FARRELL *takes the notes, kisses them and puts them in his pocket.*)

FARRELL. The gates will lift, Mike, and the road is yours.

MIKE. And go teetotal for a while, or you'll ruin us all.

(THREE MEN SMUGGLERS *rush in excitedly.*)

THREE MEN. The bus! The bus! It's comin' in at the Square, and the new D.J. is gettin' out of it with Father Phelim.

STANISLAUS. They'll be comin' in here. Up the stairs to hell out of the way, Farrell.

FARRELL (*throwing a pound on the counter, lifting a bottle*). I'll take this for company. I wonder how tee-totallers pass their time. (*He goes upstairs.*)

MIKE. I'd better get out of here before this Dublin chiseller smells the villainy off me. Come on, Rita.

RITA. No, I want to stay, Mike. I want to be an example to me wild darlings. I want to show you how heroes should behave! I want to throw defiance in the face of this . . .

MIKE. You crazy madhead! Do you want us all in jail this night? You're coming whether you like it or not.

(MIKE *carries* RITA *off, back behind the bar.*)

STANISLAUS. Look respectable now, you chaps, if you're able at all—and hide everything that's to be hidden, and let law and order prevail. Judy, look at you girl. Heighten the plumbline of that dress this minute . . . and take them sexy ear-rings off you.

JUDY. Aw, Da! Me poor ear-rings and me grand plunging neckline.

BARNEY. Pull in your paunch a bit, Peter. You're looking terrible prosperous.

(*All go to the window and look out.*)

JUDY. He looks very foreign, God between us.

PETER. Isn't it a quare sight to see a man with an umbrella. And the sun splitting the trees.

STANISLAUS. There's no red on his nose—that's a bad sign.

BARNEY. Ah, I'd say he was a teetotaller by the gob of him.

JUDY. I wonder if he's married, God help her.

(ALL *move back to the counter*. FATHER PHELIM *and* UDOL-PHUS McCLUSKEY *enter*. FATHER PHELIM *is elderly and benign but shrewd.* McCLUSKEY *is about 32, with horn-rimmed glasses, meticulous, exacting, a bit of a snob and very much on his dignity.*)

STANISLAUS. Look out!

ALL. Good morning to you, Father.

PHELIM. Good morning. Now, my good people, this as you'll all have guessed, is Mr. Udolphus McCluskey, the eminent barrister-at-law who is to be our new District Justice. He has been sent to us for our sins and I'm afraid his penances will be stiffer than mine. I have given you all a fine, upstanding character, so don't let your poor old priest down.

STANISLAUS. His honour can depend on us to make him one of ourselves.

UDOLPHUS. People of Chuckeyhead, I cannot lay claim to be a Chuckeyheadonian, but in spite of this grave initial drawback I have, as you know, been advanced to a position of eminence in the Irish Bar. Need I tell you that the name of your picturesque village stinks in the nostrils of the Irish administration? As a consequence, I solemnly warn you all that I am here to *see* all, to *believe* nothing and to regard each and every *one* of you as a two-faced . . .

PHELIM (*stung*). One moment, District Justice Mc-Cluskey. As a born and bred Chuckeyheadonian and proud of it, I'm afraid I must register a protest against such a sweeping indictment.

UDOLPHUS (*severely*).   My powers are plenary, Father Phelim.

PHELIM.   Your powers may well be plenary, Mr. McCluskey, but I'd proceed cautiously with my Chuckeyheadonians if you insist on including their priest amongst the pigeons, so to speak!
(*Murmurs of ugly tempers.*)

UDOLPHUS (*realizing*).   Perhaps in my honest, forthright and single-minded way, I have given a wrong impression (*bowing to Father Phelim*). My apologies, Father Phelim, for some obscure insult which was not intended.
(*They nod in appeasement and smile in a scoundrelish way.*
The PRIEST *smilingly bows.*)

PHELIM (*authoritatively*).   My good people, you will under my orders continue to listen politely and dutifully, to the further fulminations of his honour (*to* UDOLPHUS, *sweetly*). You may *safely* proceed, Mr. McCluskey.

UDOLPHUS.   Good people! As your very excellent priest, Father Phelim, has implied, I am here to uplift the *Civil* law, readorn the *moral* law, and restore Chuckeyhead to its jewelled place in the Irish firmament.

ALL (*clapping heartily*).   Hear, hear! Your honour!

UDOLPHUS.   People of Chuckeyhead, save your applause to cool your porridge. I am not easily impressed by popular exhibitions of mass emotion. (*Pointing to one of the three smugglers.*) Here you, my good man, stir yourself and bring my luggage in from the sidewalk. It will keep you from scratching yourself in eminent company.

SMUGGLER.   It's a pleasure, your honour. (*He goes out.*)

UDOLPHUS.   Who is the proprietor here, Father Phelim?

PHELIM.   Stanislaus Brannigan, present yourself.

STANISLAUS.   At your service, your honour.

UDOLPHUS.   In the task before me, Mr. Brannigan, I must require and demand your unswerving co-operation.

STANISLAUS. Your honour can count on me to keep a watchful eye on you every hour of the day and night.

UDOLPHUS. With your long experience of people, Mr. Brannigan, I take it you would know a smuggler at sight?

STANISLAUS. I could pick out one in five thousand, your honour. I could even smell one in my sleep . . . the damn crowd of villainous and lawless . . .

PHELIM. Control your language before his honour and meself, Stanislaus Brannigan.

STANISLAUS. I beg both your pardons. At times me feelin's . . .

UDOLPHUS. Your feelings if genuine do you great credit, Mr. Brannigan. I can venture to assume that these law-breakers do not frequent your premises?

STANISLAUS. Is it here, your honour? If one of them gentry showed his hawk's nose in here, I wouldn't wait for the Sergeant. He'd go through that window there head first. You'll testify to that, boys?

BARNEY. Indeed we will, indeed we will.

PETER. We're dacent men, your honour.

STANISLAUS. Ah, sure, in no time at all, sir, you'll be able to tell the difference between the smugglers and dacent men, like me own customers here.

(STANISLAUS *indicates the others, and* UDOLPHUS *moves around and scrutinises them closely.*)

UDOLPHUS. Unfortunately, my instructions are that there are no *dacent* men, as you term it, in Chuckeyhead . . . that every man, woman and child is a chronic smuggler. The fair name of your picturesque little village here on the Ulster Border has been befouled. Every year thirty thousand pounds' worth of contraband is smuggled in this area alone across the Border out there. A blot, a grave and shameful blot. But the remedy is *here* . . . (*touches his breast*).

(*The* SMUGGLER *re-enters with two travelling cases and a*

large telescope on a tripod. He slips over the steps and falls with the tripod.)

Careful, you foolish fellow, careful with that valuable telescope.

(UDOLPHUS *goes to swing doors and rescues the telescope which he handles very lovingly and carefully.*)

I borrowed this telescope, in my official capacity, from De Valera who has a passion for star-gazing. Father Phelim, may I graciously invite you to have a look?

(UDOLPHUS *points the telescope through the window.* FATHER PHELIM *puts his eye to the barrel.*)

PHELIM. It's incredible. I can see the sheep on the mountain right here beside me.

UDOLPHUS. Ah, Father Phelim, you'll see more than sheep on those hills by the time I have swept this place clean of smuggling and chronic lawlessness. Father Phelim, may I again have audience with the proprietor?

PHELIM. Stanislaus Brannigan, again present yourself.

STANISLAUS. Call on me day or night, your honour.

UDOLPHUS. Mr. Brannigan, assuming you are an honest man, you will, I am sure, be pleased to learn that I have decided to make your premises here not only my living quarters, but the vital centre of my activities.

STANISLAUS (*stunned*). Your honour, this is terrible over-powerin'. Me rooms, sir, are not used to the—the gentry.

UDOLPHUS. All that your rooms require, Mr. Brannigan, is a liberal libation of elbow grease—a product in very short supply in rural Ireland. I have observed on entering, that your two front rooms command an excellent view of the Border. As I have full commandeering powers, I now decree that you move your family to the back of your premises and leave me free not only to live at the front, but to erect this powerful telescope that will sweep the vantage points of the Border with an all-seeing eye.

STANISLAUS. But, your honour, sure it wouldn't work at

all, at all. Them two front rooms, your honour, sure they—they haven't been lived in for—for three years.

UDOLPHUS.   And may I ask, Mr. Brannigan, why this illogical boycott of a beautiful view?

STANISLAUS.   Sure they're—they're *haunted,* sir. There's a . . . a *ghost* in them. I can't say more because it's a . . . a family secret.

UDOLPHUS.   In law, Mr. Brannigan, there is no such thing as a ghost. So let the rooms be prepared immediately for my reception. Nothing extraneous must stand in the way of the regeneration of Chuckeyhead. My mission is a first priority. I am, as you know, a power that has no truck whatever with lawlessness. My cure for chronic lawlessness is jail and plenty of it.

(*He sits down beside the* PRIEST.)

STANISLAUS (*coming to them*).   The usual ginger wine for yourself, I suppose, Father?

PHELIM.   That's correct.

STANISLAUS.   Half or fully fortified, Father?

PHELIM.   Isn't the chill in the air the answer to that, Stanislaus Brannigan?

STANISLAUS.   I'm an ejot, Father. And what will his honour be takin'?

UDOLPHUS.   A tomato cocktail, Mr. Brannigan.

STANISLAUS (*returning to bar; gasping*).   With . . . with pleasure, sir.

(*The* MEN *at the bar are nudging, whispering and smiling at each other. The conversation of* UDOLPHUS *and the* PRIEST *is reduced to dumb show.* UDOLPHUS *shows the* PRIEST *certain legal documents out of his brief case.*)
Judy, a large Irish with ginger wine for the Priest. And what do you put in a tomato cocktail for his nibs?

JUDY.   A . . . a . . . what did you say, Da?

STANISLAUS.   What do you put in a tomato cocktail, boys?

PETER. It's a phenomenon I saw drunk in certain Puritan quarters in Dublin. Squeeze the juice of a fresh tomato into a glass.

(JUDY *rapidly presents the juice.*)

JUDY. There y'are. Go on, Peter and don't go too quick.

PETER. That's it all.

JUDY. All?

STANISLAUS. But what . . . what . . . fortification, Peter?

PETER. I'm telling you, that's it all.

STANISLAUS. But, my God, that's a Protestant minister's drink. Bad and all as he is, I can't give him that!

PETER. It's what he asked for.

BARNEY. Ah, isn't it good enough for the weasel?

STANISLAUS. God stiffen him, I hate teetotallers! I'll just put in a small fortification of brandy, and the blessing of God. There now . . . that'll either civilise him, or paralyse him.

(*He crosses to table.*)

Ginger wine for you, Father, and tomato cocktail for his honour.

(FATHER PHELIM *offers* STANISLAUS *money.*)

Indeed I will not, Father. Sure, me house is honoured.

(FATHER PHELIM *nods to him and he goes back to the bar.*)

UDOLPHUS. Drunken Dublin motorists laughed at me, until I gave them jail without the option. But I showed them, as I'll show them here!

PHELIM. The trouble about our jail, Mr. McCluskey, is that they turned it into a dance hall when the British left. They're divils for dancin' in my parish.

UDOLPHUS. Ridiculous! That goes to show the very lax state of the law in the whole area. I'll be pestering you, Father, for your help and co-operation.

PHELIM. My job, Mr. McCluskey, is the divine law, and I'm old enough now to have the wisdom to stick to it.

UDOLPHUS.   But incontrovertibly smuggling across the Border is sinful.

PHELIM.   If a man smuggles and *thinks* it's a sin, it *is* a sin.

UDOLPHUS.   Is that good theology, Father?

PHELIM.   The best of theology.

UDOLPHUS.   I wouldn't call it good law.

PHELIM.   Mr. McCluskey, law at *its best* is no more than a bastard child of theology at its worst. Your good health, sir.

(*They drink.* UDOLPHUS *splutters.* FATHER PHELIM *claps him on the back.*)

UDOLPHUS.   Phew. That's the strongest tomato I ever tasted.

PHELIM.   That's just Stanislaus Brannigan's good nature. A dacent man.

UDOLPHUS.   Now that it's down, it feels fine and comforting, but I think, Father, as a pure matter of principle, Mr. Brannigan should be suitably reprimanded, even for erring on the right side.

PHELIM.   Well, if you insist. Stanislaus Brannigan!

STANISLAUS.   Yes, Father?

PHELIM.   Present yourself!

STANISLAUS.   Your honour?

UDOLPHUS.   Brannigan, I like my tomatoes as God made them. In law, to err, even on the right side, is wrong.

STANISLAUS.   Your honour, when there's an honoured guest in me poor house, it's not law I think about. But sure, maybe I was wrong.

UDOLPHUS.   Spurious sentiment, Mr. Brannigan. You stand reprimanded and admonished.

STANISLAUS.   It won't happen again, sir.

UDOLPHUS.   It better not! Be good enough to direct me to your local Sergeant of the Guards.

STANISLAUS. Sure the police barracks are just next door, your honour . . . more's the pity.

UDOLPHUS. One moment, Mr. Brannigan. Explain your rather cryptic comment.

STANISLAUS. Ah, sure, on two highly lamentable occasions, your honour, I was a split second of the clock late in closing, and the Sergeant popped on me like a ton of bricks and gave me such a dressing down that even the dogs wouldn't drink me blood.

UDOLPHUS. Nevertheless, I commend the Sergeant. In law, Mr. Brannigan, a split second is a definite lapse of time, and therefore a breach of the licensing laws.

STANISLAUS. Ah, sure, your honour, we live and learn, God help us.

PHELIM. Come, Mr. McCluskey, and I'll introduce you myself to the Sergeant.

UDOLPHUS. Thank you, Father. Have my luggage sent upstairs, Mr. Brannigan. I will soon wipe this smuggling racket out of existence. Before I left Dublin, I assured my close friend, the Minister of Justice . . .

(*All groan.*)

What on earth is the meaning of this rebellious outburst against the lawful government?

PHELIM. If the twelve Apostles, Mr. McCluskey, came down and formed the Government of this country, my parishioners would be against them. They are, you will admit, perfectly entitled to be against them!

UDOLPHUS. Regrettable, but democratically permissible.

(UDOLPHUS *exits.* FATHER PHELIM *goes to the door. There is general chatter from those at the bar.* FATHER PHELIM *turns to them.*)

PHELIM. During . . .

(*Chatter ceases.*)

During my sermon on Sunday, I will dwell for a few mo-

ments on this exhibition of bad manners. Stanislaus Brannigan!

STANISLAUS. Yes, Father?

PHELIM (*handing him a parcel*). You will see that
Michael MacNamara delivers this ham to my half starved sister in Belfast, Border or no Border!

(FATHER PHELIM *exits.* STANISLAUS *grins at the others and
puts the ham away.*)

(*Enter* MIKE *from back of counter.*)

STANISLAUS. Begosh, Mike, you missed the furore. I'm
a ruined and destroyed man.

MIKE. I missed nothing. I had me ear to the door. "In
law, Mr. Brannigan, a split second is a definite lapse of
time . . ."

ALL. "And therefore a breach of the licensing laws."

STANISLAUS. Are we goin' over with the lorry tonight or
are we not? Let you tell us now.

MIKE. Have we any choice? We go *over*, or we go
under.

PETER. Will you look at the D.J.'s telescope, Mike?

MIKE. Does the learned ejot imagine we smuggle during the day? He forgot the searchlights.

(*All laugh.*)

STANISLAUS. It's easy for yous to laugh. But here am I,
saddled with him upstairs, and his eye like a burnin' coal on
every move I make.

MIKE. We'll think of somethin', Stanislaus. For every
poison there's an antidote. Come on, boys, let's get on with
the job. Chuckeyhead has got to live. I've got a full list of
the stuff here (*consults paper*). Who the hell's sendin' anyone a stuffed goose?

PETER. It's mine, Mike. Just a small present for me poor
grandmother across the Border.

MIKE. Indeed! And valued at a pound. That's only one
and six to me, Peter.

PETER.   Ah, sure, I'll make it half a crown, Mike.

MIKE.   You're damn generous, Peter. Judy, go and bring that goose here till I have a look at her.

PETER.   Ah, now, wait a minute, Mike. You wouldn't belittle a dacent man on his word.

(JUDY *brings the goose and* MIKE *shakes it.*)

MIKE.   Would I not? Come on, Peter, cough it up. What's in this goose's backside?

PETER.   Ah, just a few cheap watches, and a handful of petrol lighters.

MIKE.   The value, Peter? Come on, you old snake! You may dodge the Customs, but you won't dodge me.

PETER.   Twenty pounds, Mike.

MIKE.   That means thirty pounds at least, you robber! Hand over forty five shillings for service to be rendered to that goose with the golden eggs.

JUDY.   I'd never have believed that you'd try to defraud Mike, Peter.

STANISLAUS.   It's terrible dishonest. I'll maybe be forced to expel you from the Smugglers' Association.

MIKE (*reading*).   In the name of God, what's this? "A gross job lot of ladies' foundations." What the blazes is a lady's foundation?

PETER.   Can we not keep the trade respectable?

STANISLAUS.   Are you there, Judy?

(JUDY *comes from the back.*)

Tell your poor Da . . . what is a lady's . . .

MIKE.   Foundation.

STANISLAUS.   Foundation.

(JUDY *whispers details in* STANISLAUS' *ear. He nods eloquently a few times.*)

STANISLAUS (*trying to explain to* MIKE).   It's a class of elastic bridle, Mike, that bundles the stomach, the bile, the kidneys, the liver and the ribs all in the one symmetrical line.

It seems you can't buy them in the North for love or money, and the lassies' husbands are leaving them in droves.

MIKE. I'll let them go this time for the sake of the Northern lassies, bless them! Tonight, then with the help of God. If the District Justice has anything to be smuggled, get his money in advance.

STANISLAUS. He might have a stuffed goose, like Peter's there, and its stomach full of bad thoughts.

(MIKE *goes out back. The* SERGEANT *enters, looking very worried and woebegone.*)

(*Vehemently*) Sergeant! If it's the last thing you do, you've got to get this antichrist to hell out of me house.

SERGEANT. Sure, is it me you're blaming? And I under what is called a . . . a peremptory mandate from himself within. Sure, that's not a spit short of martial law. Sure, at least I had to pretend I was all with him.

STANISLAUS. Pretend, is it? To saddle me, and me orphan Judy there too, God help us, with a puritan-minded D.J. stuck there, with a nose like a vacuum cleaner. What, I ask you in all fairness, is going to happen to me after hours trade at the bar? And don't you know as well as meself that all me dacentest customers are in the . . . smuggling profession. Sure, I might as well close down and have done with it. Mightn't I, boys?

ALL. Ah, indeed you might, indeed you might!

(*The* SERGEANT *sits down miserably.* STANISLAUS *takes up a large moth-eaten ledger and throws it open at a folio before the Sergeant.*)

STANISLAUS. Look at that, Sergeant. It's totted up at the end there. One thousand, seven hundred and fifty-five pints of the best double X, and an untotted and unspecified number of half ones of the best Irish whiskey . . . none of which was ever begrudged you as a dacent man . . . you'll bear me out, boys?

ALL. Ah, indeed we will, indeed we will!

STANISLAUS. And, Sergeant, did I ever ask you to clear it off me books?

SERGEANT. You did not.

STANISLAUS. Or, in fairness to me, did I ever ask your father before you . . . the Lord be good to him . . .

(ALL *lift their hats.*)

ALL. Amen!

STANISLAUS. . . . to do the same?

SERGEANT (*also raising his hat*). You never did.

STANISLAUS. Then in all Christian fairness, Sergeant, act if you ever acted. I told him me rooms had a ghost in them, but it was no good. He said the law didn't recognise them. Can you think of a bigger lie?

SERGEANT. I'll exercise all the reserves and resources of me nature to manufacture a whopper that will put the peter on him.

(STANISLAUS *signs to* JUDY *who hands him a large whiskey. He planks it in front of the* SERGEANT.)

STANISLAUS. Well now, put that in your gob before you go, and it'll put a bit of honest puck into you.

SERGEANT. I will, I will indeed. (*He takes it neatly.*) Ah, man, that was good, after that sermon on Genesis and jurisprudence.

(*Enter* UDOLPHUS *and* CRAMPSEY.)

A word in your ear, your honour.

UDOLPHUS. Presumably, Sergeant, you mean in confidence. Sit down.

(MEN *at the bar chatter as the three sit at a table.*)

And now, Sergeant?

SERGEANT. I have a report to make, your honour . . . under the lip, so to speak.

UDOLPHUS. Wait! Seeing as we are using this man's premises for our conference, we'll have a little refreshment first.

SERGEANT. Never on duty, sir . . . thank you, sir, all

the same. And of course, Guard Crampsey here has been a strict teetotaller since his birth, thanks be to God.

CRAMPSEY. I promised me mother, your honour.

UDOLPHUS. Yes, yes . . . I too had a mother who was a truly providential influence in my life. Nevertheless, I feel we should justify the rules of ordinary courtesy (*calling*) Mr. Branningan.

STANISLAUS (*coming forward*). At your service . . . always, your honour.

UDOLPHUS. Three—tomato cocktails, Mr. Brannigan.

STANISLAUS (*gasping*). Instantly, sir.

UDOLPHUS. And Mr. Brannigan . . . as God made them.

STANISLAUS. Ex—exactly, sir.

(STANISLAUS *returns unsteadily to the counter, and begins the business of making the tomato cocktails, while the customers grin.*)

UDOLPHUS. And now, Sergeant, that word in me ear, as you so realistically term it.

SERGEANT. It's an extremely delicate matter, your honour. For a moment, sir, I'll have to—er—uncover the indelicate.

UDOLPHUS. The law has no pruderies. Uncover it, Sergeant.

SERGEANT. Felix Brannigan, sir, the brother of the proprietor here, went wrong in London, sir, if you understand me, and married a Protestant woman.

UDOLPHUS. Proceed!

SERGEANT. Seein' the error of his ways he arrived home and married a Catholic woman, with the result that he was unaccountably charged with bigamy.

UDOLPHUS. Ah, yes, yes, an unfortunate and incongruous clash with the Civil law. Proceed!

SERGEANT. He—he—Crampsey, tell it to his honour. You have a stronger constitution than meself.

CRAMPSEY. He cut his throat above in the bathroom, sir, and he's not—not at rest, if you know what I mean, sir. (ALL *at the counter are nudging each other and laughing secretively.*)

CRAMPSEY. Your honour, Stanislaus Brannigan closed up the room and it was all hushed up.

SERGEANT. But they say, sir, that he walks the upstairs corridor, God between us.

(STANISLAUS *comes and serves the three tomato juice.*)

STANISLAUS. The tomato cocktails, your honour, as— as God made them.

UDOLPHUS. But this is ridiculous! The law which is composed of an infinite succession of mathematical exactitudes does not admit of ghosts and wraiths and such like. Mr. Brannigan, do you believe in ghosts?

STANISLAUS. Oh, indeed I didn't, your honour, until the dreadful night I met me poor wayward brother, Felix, with his poor darlin' head under his arm. Sure it was poor Judy, God help the child, who kept pouring brandy down me neck, until I came round. Father Phelim said Mass in the room but it didn't shift him. Ah, sure, poor Felix was never aisy to shift. But we never mention it now, sir. Two and sixpence, sir. Thank you, sir.

SERGEANT. Ah, indeed, sir. This is a tragic house and family! But they keep it all very quiet, sir. There's more than meets the eye.

UDOLPHUS. This report of yours is very distressing, Sergeant. I don't think this is a desirable place for me after all . . .

SERGEANT. Now, there's a load off me mind that you agree with me, your honour.

CRAMPSEY. No place at all for a man in your position, no place at all.

RITA (*off-stage*). Sergeant . . .

(RITA *enters excitedly, carrying a huge cardboard box, tied*

214

with twine and conspicuously labelled 'Mushrooms.'
She holds up the box to the SERGEANT. *All are secretly*
in the jitters in case she gives the game away.)

RITA. Sergeant! Look! Contraband!

(*The* SERGEANT *goes to her fearfully.*)

SERGEANT. Rita, what on earth is all this about? What
have you here? Calm yourself now . . . it says mushrooms.

RITA. Mushrooms, me eye. It's a contraband parcel.
I've just seen a smuggler.

SERGEANT. A smuggler! Attention, Crampsey!

(*Both make for the door.*)

RITA. Wait! He's far away by now. He recognised me
as one of our Anti-Smugglers Committee and he dropped
this box and took to his heels.

(ALL *hide their faces in terror, fearful of what is coming*
out next.

STANISLAUS (*aside*). That's the biggest lie yet!

SERGEANT. This fine action of yours, Rita, deserves to
be brought to the immediate notice of our new District Justice.

RITA (*pretending to be surprised*). Oh, heavens, is this
his honour? I've heard the most wonderful things about him.
They call him in Dublin the lawbreakers' Waterloo.

SERGEANT. Your honour, allow me to present our most
charming resident, Miss Rita Ronan. A lady, your honour,
of the most unusual talents.

UDOLPHUS. Charmed, Miss Ronan. A lady, I can see
instantly, with a high and commendable sense of public duty.
Allow me to shake your hand.

(RITA *drops the box and they shake hands.*)

RITA. Your honour, I thought I was going to be terrified
of you, and here I am quite at ease with you already.

(*Secret groans from the counter.*)

UDOLPHUS. Believe me, Miss Ronan, I have my moments.

RITA. Oh! If you just knew the dodges these smugglers stoop to. Look, your honour, inside is one innocent layer of harmless mushrooms, and six layers of expensive nylons. Could you beat that for villainy?

UDOLPHUS. Incredible! The rot here is even worse than I thought. Did you say, Miss Ronan, that you were a member of the Anti-Smugglers Committee here?

RITA. Sure, I'm the president of it, your honour. Mr. Brannigan and I formed it to help the poor overworked Sergeant here.

UDOLPHUS. This pleases me considerably. Chuckey-head has indeed its occasional bright spots.

SERGEANT. I'll take charge of this parcel, Rita, and have it examined for fingerprints. Crampsey, make a careful and accurate examination of its contents.

CRAMPSEY. I will, Sergeant.

UDOLPHUS. Can you recollect having seen this smuggler before, Miss Ronan?

RITA. I'm not sure, but . . . Sergeant, it's just dawned on me . . . it could well be Midnight Mickie!

SERGEANT. Who . . . who . . . did you say?

RITA (*kicking him on the shin*). Midnight Mickie . . . the sinister chief of them all!

SERGEANT. Yes . . . er . . . yes . . . it could be Midnight Mickie. Check on his whereabouts, Crampsey.

CRAMPSEY. I will indeed, Sergeant.

UDOLPHUS. Miss Ronan, you have such a resourceful nature that perhaps you could help me. I am at a loss as to where I can stay. I cannot stay here for a reason possibly well known to you.

SERGEANT (*winking*). I was telling him in confidence about poor Felix Brannigan haunting the front rooms above.

RITA. Oh, God between us, the night I went upstairs to see Judy, he was rolling his head in front of him as if he was playing bowls. This is no place for his honour at all. I

have a rambling old house that my father left me, with a top floor to let and the use of my sitting room downstairs.

(*Consternation at the counter.*)

UDOLPHUS. This is most charming of you. Sergeant Whistler, why wasn't this suggestion made to me before?

SERGEANT. Because, your honour, I did not consider it a right and proper suggestion to make. Miss Ronan is a single lady and is, socially speaking, alone in the house.

RITA. What nonsense! I'm not alone. My old house-keeper, Maria, is always with me.

UDOLPHUS. Miss Ronan, I most gratefully accept your generous offer . . . Sergeant, see to my things.

SERGEANT. Crampsey, proceed before his honour with his luggage.

CRAMPSEY. I will this minute.

(CRAMPSEY *goes off with the luggage and telescope.*)

(*There is a violent noise, as if someone falling downstairs, and* IGNATIUS FARRELL *appears dishevelled, in trousers and shirt.* UDOLPHUS *swings round and stares at him. The others hold their breath and are at a loss what to say or do.*)

FARRELL. I know *him*. He's the new bejaysus from Dublin. I'll tell you who I am. I'm a smuggler.

(*Consternation.*)

UDOLPHUS. Sergeant, attention! Arrest this man and have him brought before me for summary conviction.

(*The* SERGEANT *moves towards him.* RITA *signs frantically to* UDOLPHUS *and pushes the* SERGEANT *away.*)

RITA. There, there now, poor Jerome, of course you're a smuggler. (*She soothes him and signs to* UDOLPHUS). Your honour, this is poor Jerome O'Brien, Stanislaus Brannigan's unfortunate brother-in-law.

(STANISLAUS *gasps.*)

His poor wife dropped dead milkin' a cow and he's never got over it.

UDOLPHUS. But he should be properly looked after. Why isn't he certified?

RITA. Ah, now, who would certify poor Jerome and him always capturin' London at the head of ten thousand Irish Fusiliers.

UDOLPHUS. You seem to have a very tragic family history, Mr. Brannigan.

STANISLAUS. I try to cloak it, your honour, but sure the —the skeletons will rattle.

FARRELL. I want to tell that old blunderbuss why I smuggle. I smuggle on principle.

UDOLPHUS. Principle?

FARRELL. That's it. That Border out there is in direct variance with the Cosmos.

STANISLAUS. For God's sake, your honour, pay him no heed. The poor mind is gone. Come on now, J-J-Jerome, back to your bed, like a dacent brother-in-law.

FARRELL. My name's not Jerome. It's Ignatius.

(ALL *look startled.*)

RITA (*saving the situation*). Ah now, sure it'll be Cornelius or Jeremiah in another minute. A wee kiss first, and he'll go quietly, won't you, Cornelius? Or is it Ignatius?

FARRELL. Call me what you like so long as you give me one poor scruple of your beauty.

(RITA *kisses him and* BARNEY *and* PETER *drag him away.*)

UDOLPHUS. What a splendid person you are! Tactful, understanding, discreet, diplomatic—your handling of that unfortunate was exemplary.

RITA (*archly*). Now, mind my poor head, your honour. It's easily turned.

(RITA *takes* UDOLPHUS *off, and secretively waves back at them.*)

STANISLAUS. There's a ton weight off me mind now that that Colossus is out of here, even if our troubles are only beginnin'.

SERGEANT (*pouring out wads of paper from* RITA's *box.*)
Look! Isn't it amazin' what a woman's mind will think up!

STANISLAUS.   The darlin'! And me mad brother-in-law,
Jerome, was a masterpiece. Only for her, we were sunk!

SERGEANT.   We'll be sunk with a vengeance if Farrell
doesn't take the pledge.

STANISLAUS.   You're right! Barney, bring on that mis-
begotten brother-in-law of mine, till I make him a teetotaller.
(BARNEY *and* PETER *are dragging* FARRELL *on as*)

The CURTAIN *falls.*

ACT II

Scene I

SCENE: *A Sitting Room in Rita Ronan's house in Chuckey-*
head.

TIME: *A few weeks later.*

It is cosily furnished and commands a fine view of
the adjacent mountains from the window c. *back. The*
door to the hallway is to the left, and the fireplace in
the right wall. UDOLPHUS's *telescope and stand are vis-*
ible on top of the sideboard. RITA's *photograph stands*
on the mantelpiece. Heavy curtains screen a small ante-
room back R. *On the wall back is a striking framed*
water-colour of RITA's *head. It is afternoon of a sunny*
day. RITA *is discovered fussing around and firing ques-*
tions at MARIA *who has just come in from shopping and*
is carrying a shopping bag.

RITA (*excited*). Did you manage to get the green
olives in Ballycrabbit for his honour, Maria?

MARIA.   I got them after a struggle. What the hell does he want with olives anyway?

RITA.   Gentlemen like to eat olives.

MARIA.   Well, I tasted one o' them and thank God I'm no gentleman.

(*She makes a wry face.*)

RITA (*admonishes her*).   Less of that, Maria.

(MIKE MACNAMARA *comes to the window.* RITA *fussily waves him away but we realise she is doing it to tease him.*)

RITA.   Go away, Mike. Can't you see I'm busy arranging his honour's dinner? (*She looks at* MARIA.) And the paté de fois gras for his honour. I hope you didn't forget it.

(MIKE *sits sullenly on the edge of a couch.*)

MARIA.   The grocer said it was out of fashion now and he gave me a tin of spinach. "That's nearest to it," says he.

RITA.   Spinach.

(MIKE *laughs dryly.*)

MARIA.   The grocer said if it's good enough for Pop-Eye it's good enough for the honourable Delphie-Doodle.

(MARIA *laughs and* MIKE *splutters sarcastically.* RITA *eyes them both contemptuously.*)

RITA.   Get out of here, Maria, and start preparing his honour's dinner. Oh dear, I have to sew a button on his jacket. Ah! Here it is!

(As RITA *lifts a jacket from a chair,* MARIA *with a snort goes off, closing the door.* MIKE *watches* RITA *sullenly.* RITA, *as she sews, covertly regards* MIKE *from under her eyelashes. She is obviously teasing him. A tense, silence follows. Finally* MIKE *rises, snatches the jacket from her, throws it on the ground and walks on it. She is inwardly delighted to get him so disturbed.*)

(*outraged*) Mike MacNamara, you—clodhopper!

(*She rescues the jacket and presses it to her breast provokingly.*)

Poor Udolphus's jacket!

MIKE (*angrily*).   The name's McCluskey, isn't it?

RITA (*archly*).   But it's so formal and such a mouthful.

MIKE.   I don't care if it's ten mouthfuls, you'll mouth every one of them! I knew this would happen. I'll break his calf's neck!

RITA.   How crude! You should learn instead to say some of the beautiful things that Udolphus says to me.

MIKE.   I have neither the education nor the villainy that's needed to flatter a maddenin' hussy like you.

RITA.   Nonsense! I remember once, after you finished a bottle, you said I had the same legs as the Venus de Medici. Where did you get *that* one, Mike?

MIKE (*curtly*).   I was drunk. I heard Peter Kenny sayin' it to a Dublin barmaid, and I pinched it.

RITA.   And had she, Mike? I mean the barmaid?

MIKE.   How the hell do I know? Forget it, can't you?

RITA.   I see . . . I suppose you had a mean, common, sordid affair with her behind my back!

MIKE.   Rita! You'll take that back! This minute!

RITA.   I have no such intention. These insults are not so easily put out of sight!

MIKE.   Well, of all the wicked . . .

(MARIA *puts her head in at the door.*)

MARIA.   Will yous two stop that sparrin'! That antichrist will be in any minute from the Coort. What's between yous now?

RITA.   Maria, Mike's been having a low affair with a barmaid.

MARIA.   He what!

MIKE.   Well, of all the filthiest lies! Very well, then, I'll go straight out and give myself up and admit everything.

(MIKE *goes towards door.* RITA *springs from* MARIA'S *arms to his.*)

RITA.   Mike, how dare you offer to go to jail in a com-

222

mon cowardly way like that! When you go I want you dramatically arrested like Robert Emmet, found guilty before a petrified audience and dragged in chains to a prison cell!

MIKE. I've warned you before I'm not interested in hero stuff. Now, cut it right out!

RITA (*contempt*). You little man! You haven't the puff of heroes in you! (*Going to the striking water-colour on the wall.*) Oh, God be with my poor darlin' Englishman who threw himself off the bridge for me!

MARIA. That's her, Mike, on the high-romantic again. I'd take her aisy till it passes. And don't cross the Border with the lorry tonight, after all them jail sentences. It's too dangerous.

RITA (*swinging round*). He must! He must always *dare!* Let nothing ever stop you daring or I'll hate you!

MARIA. Oh, the twisted villainy that's in that head of yours!

(MARIA *sweeps out in disgust.*)

MIKE (*evenly*). I *must* cross tonight. This village must go on living in spite of puritans and cutthroats. (*Crosses to* RITA.) If I had six more runs with the lorry, I'd have saved enough for that wedding you want in Dublin.

RITA (*angrily*). Poor man! It's not money you want to marry *me*. I have too much of it already. It's *heroism.* And remember this, Mike MacNamara, no hero, no wedding!

MIKE (*exasperated*). But you said you wanted to be married in Dublin!

RITA. I've changed my mind. It's a redhead's privilege! (*She points to a mountain on the Border.*) See that mountain out there where great queens and heroic lovers lie buried. I want to be married to a *hero* on *top* of that.

(MIKE *regards her in an exasperated mood.*)

MIKE. Redhead, you've asked for it! You're goin' to get kissed.

RITA. How dare you, Mike! Control your—sexual impetuosities!

(*MIKE venomously chases her round the room. She keeps crying out for MARIA. He catches her and swinging her over a couch, rains wild passionate kisses on her. She fights hard for a moment and then submissively puts her arms round him and makes contented noises with her lips.*)

(*Looking up at him, the master.*) Ah, Mike, I was dreaming about us last night.

MIKE. That's better, redhead! Were we very happy?

RITA. Unspeakably happy, Mike.

MIKE. I can see you all in white like a lily and I looking splendid and helping you into a motor boat in Dublin Bay.

RITA (*releasing herself*). No! It was nothing common or bourgeois like that at all. It was too soulful and exquisite. I was all in black, sobbing heartbreakingly by a fire of grey ashes, and you were in a prison cell, thirsting madly for freedom and for *me!* Ah, why did I waken to *this*. (*Rising and regarding him.*) You look very ordinary to me today, Mike MacNamara!

MIKE (*surlily*). I'm the same as I was yesterday. *And* the day before!

RITA. Maybe I just love a dream hero and you are merely his shadow.

MIKE. If ever a redhead wanted a wallopin', that one is *you!*

RITA. It will be my husband's privilege to wallop me. You will go now, Mike MacNamara, and remember, no hero, no petticoats!

(*MARIA comes rushing in. The wailing of CHILDREN, off, becomes audible.*)

MARIA. Rita! Bertie Bannon's wife is here and her five

children all weepin' and wailin'. That Dublin devil is after sendin' poor Bertie to jail.

MIKE (*perturbed*).   This is terrible news. Bertie's one of my best men. That makes eight men in jail in less than two weeks. Isn't it amazin' the respect that Tiberius has for law. The brute must have English blood in him somewhere.

RITA.   He's not a brute, Mike. He's a well-meaning Puritan with a conscience like a mouse-trap.

MIKE (*angrily*).   Well, we don't *grow* Puritans in *this* country. And *you'd* stand up for him anyway.

(MRS. BERTIE BANNON *appears in the door crying. Her* FIVE CHILDREN *are wailing off.* MARIA *puts a solicitous arm about her.*)

CHILDREN (*off*).   Me poor Da! Me poor Da! Me poor Da!

MRS. BANNON.   He's after sendin' me poor Bertie to jail, without bail or mercy—me poor Bertie that hardly ever battered me in his life.

RITA (*going to her*).   There, there, Mrs. Bannon. We're all your friends and we'll see you through everything. (*Looking sideways at Mike.*) You should be proud that your brave Bertie is in jail suffering for freedom.

CHILDREN (*off*).   Me poor Da! Me poor Da! Me poor Da!

MIKE.   I'll see you don't want, Katie, while Bertie's away.

(*He claps her on the shoulder and hands her a few banknotes. She grabs them greedily.*)

MRS. BANNON.   The blessin' o' God on ye, Mike. Sure it's not *you* I want to skin but that foreign Viking from Dublin!

CHILDREN (*off*).   Me poor Da! Me poor Da! Me poor Da!

MARIA (*at window excited*).   Here he comes, slouching

along like the Devil himself in human shape, God between us! Out by the window, Mike! Fly! Rush! And don't dare cross the Border tonight after this!

RITA (*rebellious*). Do Mike! Dare, like a hero! Dare and dare and dare!

MIKE. Hussy! Wouldn't you just give your eye for the glory of visitin' me in prison and feelin' good about it!

MARIA. Go on, go on! And I'll be prayin' for you, Mike.

MIKE. I wouldn't put it past you!

(MIKE *goes rapidly. The front door can be heard closing.*
RITA *runs to* MRS. BANNON *and gives her some bank-notes.*)

RITA. Now, Katie dear, count on me not to let you want while Bertie's sufferin' for the cause. And we'll get up a concert for you and a raffle and we'll stage "The Girl that Took the Wrong Turning" and you'll have plenty of money.

MRS. BANNON (*eagerly pocketing the money*). Begod, I'm doin' grand. If I'm goin' to be as well off as this, I'll just let Bertie cool his heels and welcome. He's a tight-fisted wee pishogue anyway. All the same, I'd like to get a crack at oul' Skin-the-Goat from Dublin. If only I had an egg bad enough to waste on him! (*Calling towards the door.*) Yous are very quiet out there, children. Don't yous know your poor Da's in jail, sittin' on a cold stone with black ace-of-spades bread in one hand, and in the other nothin' but a mug of the cold water he was never used to!

CHILDREN (*off*). Me poor Da! Me poor Da! Me poor Da!

(*To this tune* UDOLPHUS *enters. He is erect and self-assured.*
He takes in the scene with a gesture of disgust.)

MARIA. There now, Mrs. Bannon! Keep your mind off it. Bertie will soon be back to you again.

UDOLPHUS. What on earth is the matter here?

MRS. BANNON (*rising viciously*). So well you might ask, you villain unhung! Look at me and me poor orphaned children after you sending our poor Da to his death o'cold in jail!

UDOLPHUS. Mrs. Bannon, as I tried to tell you in Court, the law, which *I* did *not* make, must take its course. Now you must get out of here. This is sheer impertinence.

MRS. BANNON. I'll go when the mistress of this house says it!

UDOLPHUS (*evenly*). Rita. Please.

MARIA (*quickly*). Is it your poor dead father you'd have to turn in the grave, and the widows and orphans stoned from his ever-open door? It would be the poor day that outrage would happen.

(RITA *looks uncertainly from one to the other.*)

UDOLPHUS. Rita, my apologies. I have the deepest respect for you and for the memory of your father, who was, I am certain, a splendid gentleman. But I will not be blackmailed by any lawbreaker's wife, and I will not weaken or compromise in the task before me. Either this woman leaves or *I* do!

RITA. Your honour, I thoroughly understand. Come, Mrs. Bannon, don't worry—all will be taken care of.

MRS. BANNON (*angrily*). You oul' Dublin chiseller, you! (*She goes with* RITA; *at door.*) Away before me, children, till we sit around our lonely fireplace and say the rosary for your poor persecuted Da. (*Turns to* UDOLPHUS.) Did you fall down a well or what? If you did, the jackass that pulled you out had little to do!

CHILDREN (*off*). Me poor Da! Me poor Da! Me poor Da!

(RITA *takes* MRS. BANNON *off.* UDOLPHUS *hands* MARIA *his hat. She refuses it, sniffs and sweeps out.* UDOLPHUS *looks after her severely.* RITA *re-enters in a moment, closes the door and gives him a flashing smile and an admiring look.*)

Rita. Udolphus, you were wonderful! You were larger than life! If you had weakened, I'd have despised you.

Udolphus (*very pleased and flattered*). I have schooled myself, Rita, never to weaken. (*He comes to her and touches her shoulder.*) But if there is one woman in the whole world that I'd have . . .

Rita (*protesting*). No! Don't say it!

Udolphus (*looking at her*). The loveliest things are always better left unsaid, Rita. Breath makes them common.

Rita. What a lovely thought, Udolphus! If only I could get beautiful thoughts like that from—(*She stops short.*)

Udolphus (*looking enquiringly at her*). From who, Rita?

Rita. No one that matters.

Udolphus. Are you in love, Rita?

Rita (*surprised*). Why, of course! Not to be in love with someone is the earth's edition of hell.

Udolphus. What an embarrassing notion! (*Looks at water-colour.*) Was *he* in love with you?

Rita (*looking wistfully at picture*). That was my poor darlin' Englishman that made that. He was so obedient in his love, so subservient, so pathetically eager to please me! Only for that I could have loved him.

Udolphus. I suppose he didn't understand that you worshipped the unbending and the inexorable.

Rita. It must have been that. One day he said to me, "Rita, you don't love me and so I must die."

Udolphus. Good heavens, do these fellows ever learn discipline? What did you say?

Rita. I said, "How beautiful!" And he went and threw himself off the bridge for me.

Udolphus (*shocked*). Do you mean the fellow—drowned himself?

Rita. Ah, indeed, it wasn't the poor darlin's fault that

he got a mudbath instead of love's watery grave. Please don't speak of it. It was a wretched fiasco.

(UDOLPHUS *looks at her and laughs indulgently.*)

UDOLPHUS.   You demand much, Rita.

RITA.   How can I help it? I cannot lower my standards. I worship the heroic and the exalted. I love the rock that the sea beats on in vain. Like a hero whom no price can buy! Like—you on the Bench, Udolphus.

(*Looking at him, as he smiles at this flattery.*) Were you *very* severe at today's Court, Udolphus?

UDOLPHUS.   Indubitably so, Rita. (*Sternly.*) A fire must be quenched. A mad dog must be curbed.

RITA (*admiringly*).   How splendidly you say that! (*Imitating him.*) "A fire must be quenched! A mad dog must be curbed!" (*Appealingly.*) Please, Udolphus, sentence me to jail till I get the thrill of it!

UDOLPHUS (*surprised*).   You!

RITA.   Please, Udolphus.

UDOLPHUS: Perish the hour! (*He puts his hands on her shoulders.*) Those eyes in the dock! And that red glory!

RITA.   What would you do?

UDOLPHUS.   Shut my eyes and pray for guidance.

RITA.   Would you sentence me with your eyes closed?

UDOLPHUS (*after a pause*).   Yes, ruthlessly, if you were guilty.

RITA (*shaking*).   You brute, Udolphus! But I admire you more than ever.

UDOLPHUS.   You'd despise me otherwise. Tell me, Rita, whose is that red house next to the Court house in Emmet Street?

RITA.   That's Ignatius Maloney's place.

UDOLPHUS.   Ah, that accounts for something that's been puzzling me. A flowerpot was dropped on me from the top storey today as I passed.

229

RITA. A what? But surely it was an accident—an act of God?

UDOLPHUS. I'm afraid God had nothing to do with it. I sent Ignatius Maloney to jail for two months today for chronic smuggling.

RITA (*pretending*). Ignatius a smuggler! You're crazy! He's been known to spit in the face of a smuggler. And he's Father Phelim's collector in the chapel.

UDOLPHUS. I am aware of that. Father Phelim made an eloquent plea for him in Court. But I had to inform his reverence that Ignatius's holy activities didn't prevent him from smuggling cases of nylons and labelling them "Holy Pictures —handle with reverence."

RITA (*hiding her merriment*). Udolphus! You could knock me down with a feather! (*Keeping her expression serious.*) And to think Maggie, his wife, tried to murder you with an—aspidistra!

UDOLPHUS. Attempts on my life, Rita, merely strengthen my integrity. No human factor can deter me from making an example of this grossly unprincipled neighbourhood.

RITA. I'm afraid, Udolphus, I'm going to shock you.
(*He stares at her.*)
The fault I find in you is that you jail the *lambs* and let the *lion* roam free.

UDOLPHUS (*starting*). Ah!

RITA (*insinuatingly*). There *must* be a lion, you know.

UDOLPHUS. Rita, you very, very wise little person! Of course there's a lion, a chief thug, a hidden evil genius!

RITA (*egging him on*). Why not seize him dramatically, sentence him handcuffed in a crowded Court and smash the conspiracy with one master blow?

UDOLPHUS (*excited*). That is the solution! But who is he? There's the rub!

RITA. His nickname is Midnight Mickie. I mentioned him to you before.

UDOLPHUS. Yes, yes. I remember. But who is he?

RITA. That's the puzzle. It's whispered that he's tall and good looking—they generally are, you know.

UDOLPHUS. Yes, yes, spurious romanticism. Wait! (*Suddenly recalls something.*) I got a whisper today about a questionable character that owns the garage here. His name is—(*Consults a paper.*)—Mike MacNamara.

RITA. Heavens! The initials are the same—M.M.

UDOLPHUS. So they are. But we have no evidence, of course. I'll get the Sergeant to trail him.

RITA. Better trail him yourself to make sure. That reminds me. You can see right into his garage from your bedroom window above.

UDOLPHUS. Terrific! My telescope! I'll keep it focussed on him day and night.

(UDOLPHUS *takes up the telescope that is folded on the sideboard and excitedly makes to go upstairs.*)

RITA. Udolphus, please make a terrific speech when you're sentencing him. I want to digest every syllable of it.

UDOLPHUS. Rest assured, Rita, the iron will enter his soul when he faces *me* for sentence.

RITA. It will be wonderful! You, there on the Bench—the embodiment of Justice, the dispenser of life and death! Feared and hated! Alone! Aloof!

UDOLPHUS. Yes, Rita, the man that is married to Justice must tread a lone and loveless path.

RITA. Poor Udolphus! If only you could keep a little secret bit of the romantic up your legal sleeve!

UDOLPHUS (*wryly*). I once did—as a student, when I fell in love with—er—an impossible creature.

RITA (*involuntarily*). Don't tell me she was—a barmaid!

UDOLPHUS.   In fact she was.

RITA.   Good Heavens! Every presentable man I meet falls in love with a barmaid. I must take a good look at the next one I meet to see what she has that I haven't.

UDOLPHUS.   My dear, you mustn't compare yourself. It's like German measles. Luckily, my excellent mother rescued me.

RITA.   Your mother?

UDOLPHUS.   Ah, yes, a splendid lady, upright, just, impeccable and morally ruthless. I owe all my strength to her.

RITA.   She showed you the way up?

UDOLPHUS.   Yes, from my very infancy. She put me in long trousers when I was ten. She said they were more dignified. She made me pray with her every night for integrity, purity, loyalty and moral stamina.

RITA.   Poor Udolphus. Did she never even mention love?

UDOLPHUS.   She said that love was for the weak-willed, the dim wits and the lecherous and that the future population of the world could safely be left to them.

RITA (*in a secret horror*).   What a woman!

UDOLPHUS (*admiringly*).   Ah, yes, a tower! A beacon!

RITA.   But, Udolphus, the cry of the soul and the call of the blood! What of that?

UDOLPHUS (*smiling*).   What a madhead you are, Rita! Supposing the romantic, as you term it, didn't work out?

RITA (*reprovingly*).   Afraid, Udolphus?

UDOLPHUS.   Of tragedy, yes, sensibly afraid.

RITA.   Tragedy? The song you will never sing, the book you will never write, the mountain you will never climb, the woman you will love but never win . . . These are not tragedies! They are the poems of living.

UDOLPHUS (*pensively*).   "The woman you will love and never win." That must be *hell*.

RITA.   That, Udolphus, is the royalty of living. Pursuit!

And the hounds of love after you! The pain and the glory!—
who will separate these two?

UDOLPHUS.   There's maybe something in it, Rita. May I
venture to say something to you?

RITA.   If it's exciting, yes!

UDOLPHUS.   Please don't think I presume, or take un-
warranted liberties. Your curls are all very lovely, but there's
one small one behind your left ear that is always just too
lovely for any uninspired word of mine.

RITA (*breathless*).   Udolphus!

UDOLPHUS.   Please, Rita, can—can I—can I have it?

RITA.   Udolphus, I said *just* exciting, not electrifying!
Do you want your sainted mother to turn in her grave?

UDOLPHUS.   Rita, I think mother would understand.

(RITA *swings round to her work basket, grabs a small pair of
scissors, and hands them tremblingly to* UDOLPHUS.)

RITA.   Hurry, Udolphus, before I waken. Er—help
yourself!

(UDOLPHUS *takes the scissors nervously and stares unnerved
at the lovely head which* RITA *pushes against his shoulder.*)

UDOLPHUS (*uncertainly*).   It's the one exquisite little
thing that I—I—oh, never mind. Every Achilles has his vulnerable heel. (*He begins nervously the operation.*) I'm afraid
I'm trembling.

RITA.   That's what's worrying me. Mind me ear—it's
not for hire. (*She puts her arms maddeningly on his shoulders.*) There! Is that steadier?

(UDOLPHUS *clips off his curl, and* RITA *watches him as he
tenderly examines it. He takes out a small diary and
places it between two pages. Then he lifts* RITA's *hand
and reverently kisses it.* RITA *stares entranced at her
kissed fingers.*)

RITA (*entranced*).   Udolphus! I didn't know that girls
still get kissed on the hands. It's wonderful.

UDOLPHUS (*embarrassed*). You'll think me a bit of a fool, Rita.

RITA (*looking seductively at him*). Ah, Udolphus, a great man once said, "He who is afraid of making a fool of himself needn't worry—because he is already a fool!"

UDOLPHUS. Thank you for that, Rita. It gives me courage and confidence.

(*He draws her to him and their lips meet gently. Then he kisses her neck and shoulders.*)

Rita, dear, I wish, after all, that my mother had had a little crumb of the romantic in her.

(*He crosses and lifts the telescope and stand.*)

I'll go up and focus this for awhile on this—this suspect's garage.

RITA. Do please, Udolphus. I have a strong suspicion that there's more in that scoundrel's smile than meets the eye.

UDOLPHUS. If there is, let *me* unmask him! The Minister of Justice once referred to me as a ferret!

RITA. Good for the Minister. But at the same time, Udolphus, there's a blonde virago lives over that garage. I do hope nobody thinks you're focussing on her. She has been known to go to bed in the altogether.

UDOLPHUS. I'll keep the altitude of the telescope within bounds. I think the folks here know me better than that!

(UDOLPHUS *moves awkwardly towards the door carrying the telescope! He turns and looks shyly back at her. She smiles roguishly at him and gives him a little wave of her hand. He waves boyishly back, smiles and goes out. Immediately* RITA *goes to the mirror, looks at her hair, and makes a wry face.* MARIA *enters and regards her.*)

MARIA (*truculently*). Rita! Do you know that poor Ignatius Maloney is away to jail too?

RITA (*calmly*). I know, Maria. (*Taking money from*

her handbag.) I want you to take round this money to his wife. Tell her we'll see her through.

MARIA. How many more of them are you goin' to support? (*She takes the money.*)

RITA. What does money matter when me ould darlin's are sufferin' for the cause?

MARIA. Of all the crazy crackpots! (*Looking closely at her.*) What's the matter with your hair?

RITA (*archly*). I gave his honour a curl.

MARIA. You what! I'll stand no more of this. I'll tell Mike and he'll batter the daylights out of you!

RITA. If only he'd be a hero for me, Maria, I'd let him hop me off the picture rail! But at the moment it looks as if his honour is me fate!

(MARIA *looks at her, sighs, looks at the banknotes in her hand and goes. The* SERGEANT *appears forlornly at the window. He is tired and disturbed.*)

SERGEANT (*appealingly*). Rita!

RITA (*looking round eagerly*). Sergeant!

SERGEANT. If I was to come in, would I be botherin' you?

RITA (*welcoming him*). Botherin' me! And you one o' me darlin's!

(*The* SERGEANT *comes in wearily.*)

SERGEANT. Ah, sure, I'm botherin' everyone nowadays, Rita, and it's gettin' me down. I'm here to have a word with the menace!

(RITA *pours him out a stiff whiskey.*)

RITA. He's changing upstairs. See if that will rise you a storey or two.

SERGEANT (*shakes his head*). He'd smell if off me, he has a nose like a bloodhound. Put it away before the temptation knocks me out o' me standin's.

RITA. Aren't you my guest? And hasn't he the manners to know you can't refuse a drink from your hostess?

SERGEANT (*beaming*).   Begosh, that's a cast iron alibi. (*He drains the drink, and she puts the glass away.*)

RITA.   You're not very happy, Sergeant?

SERGEANT.   Ah now, between ourselves, Rita, indeed I'm not. It's the looks I get from all them poor chaps in jail. "Traitor," says one woman to me today. "Cut-throat," says another; "Black and Tan," says a third. And I slink past my own people with the policeman's scowl. I wish I was ten thousand miles away!

RITA.   It wouldn't matter, Sergeant. The humbugs and the doctrinaires are everywhere now, and we all slavishly toe the party line. 'Shun, you swine! Look up the rules! Tot up the totals! Examine the precedents! Go by the signboards! But, we here, Sergeant, are the children of disobedience before the God of law! We're the last of the rebel breed! (*A door clangs off.*) Sober yourself, Sergeant. And be respectable! The high God of efficiency approaches.

SERGEANT.   Ah, the poor man! Sure his mother put the peter on him before his eye began to rove. Thanks be to God my poor little mother was a mannerly woman that knew her place! Ssssh! (*UDOLPHUS enters impressively and sizes up the SERGEANT.*)

UDOLPHUS (*energetically*).   Well, Sergeant Whistler, you haven't come I hope to arrest Miss Rita.

SERGEANT.   I'm afraid, your honour, I'd need to call out the military for *that!*

RITA.   Sergeant, I'd go quietly with *you.* (*They smile at each other.*) Dinner in five minutes, Udolphus. And it's time that overworked Sergeant had another stripe!

UDOLPHUS.   I'll consider it, Rita. I'll either hang him or promote him. (*RITA goes laughingly. The SERGEANT and UDOLPHUS size each other up.*)

SERGEANT. Am I intruding on your privacy, your honour?

UDOLPHUS. Not in the slightest, Sergeant. I'm all for the closest co-operation with the Guards. (*Scrutinising him.*) Did you brush your uniform this morning, Sergeant?

SERGEANT (*abjectly*). I—I didn't get time, your honour.

UDOLPHUS. I used to say that too, until my excellent mother taught me that all things I had no time to do could be done easily by rising half an hour earlier. (*Pointing to uniform.*) These include, Sergeant, the button missing on your uniform the day I landed here—and *still* missing.

SERGEANT. Me eyes is too far gone for threadin' a needle, your honour, and the women are none too friendly with me now, with so many of their men in jail.

UDOLPHUS. My mother, Sergeant, taught me from birth to be self-reliant in all these matters. She also taught me to adopt a correct posture in the presence of superiors. Attention!

(*The* SERGEANT *abjectly comes to attention, pulls in his stomach, and throws out his chest.* UDOLPHUS *surveys him critically.*)

Mm . . . quite an improvement. The Guards progress! . . . yourself and your assistant Guard Crampsey will in future report to me each morning at seven for a little physical exercise. Another of my mother's excellent rules.

SERGEANT (*appalled*). The—the oul' back's none too good, your honour, since I missed Midnight Mickie by inches and fell over the railway bridge.

UDOLPHUS. Lack of exercise, Sergeant, and a chronic ignorance of the motions of the blood stream. And now, your business with me?

SERGEANT (*erect*). There's terrible bad blood about, sir, over the imprisonments today and the—the severity of the fines.

UDOLPHUS. That's only to be expected. Disobedient children never like their medicine. Are you afraid, Sergeant?

SERGEANT. Ah, it's the people passin' me by without speakin', your honour. It's a thing that I thought we had buried. You'd imagine I was a Black and Tan back from the grave, God between us!

UDOLPHUS. Come, come, Sergeant! This is just mere sentiment. The Irish people must grow up. They must learn to chase responsibilities instead of butterflies. Then they'll start obeying the laws—their own laws, mark you! Tell me, Sergeant, do you know a man called Mike MacNamara?

SERGEANT (*wilting*). Er—vaguely, sir. He runs a garage at the end of the main street.

UDOLPHUS. Indeed.

SERGEANT. Och, a dacent man, sir.

UDOLPHUS. Everyone in this place seems to be termed "a dacent man." Are there no indacent men?

SERGEANT. What I meant, your honour, was that he has never been up.

UDOLPHUS. Up?

SERGEANT. In Coort, sir. Nothin' again him at all, at all.

UDOLPHUS. Mmm . . . I've heard whispers, Sergeant . . . very distinct whispers.

SERGEANT. Your honour, if you put all the whispers in this place together, they'd make a thunder clap that would submerge the country.

UDOLPHUS. I have strong suspicions that this Mike MacNamara is a leader of the smugglers. I can't tell you more than that, but I want you to trail him everywhere.

SERGEANT (*gasping*). That's incredible, sir! It's unheard of!

UDOLPHUS. Nothing is incredible here, Sergeant! Once we get the ringleader in jail, this smuggling racket will collapse. Then the people will turn to honest work.

SERGEANT. That will be the trouble, sir—gettin' the work to be honest at.

UDOLPHUS. We'll recommend to the Government that they start a small factory hereabouts. That will solve the matter.

SERGEANT. Is it that crowd of *chancers* that's in power now? Sure, they couldn't start a hen-house!

UDOLPHUS. Come, come Sergeant! The Guards must have no politics.

(*Suddenly from the hallway without comes the noise of brawling and of voices raised. The voices are those of* MARIA *and* IGNATIUS FARRELL. UDOLPHUS *and the* SERGEANT *listen in—the latter very nervous.*)

MARIA (*off*). I said you can't go in there! His honour is with the Sergeant.

FARRELL (*off*). The Cosmic word is *"must"!* Ignatius Farrell advances on the road of rectitude.

MARIA (*off*). You can't. You mustn't. You're drunk!

FARRELL (*off*). It's all part of the inexorable law of the Cosmos.

(*The door opens and* IGNATIUS FARRELL *is seen standing drunkenly, holding a bottle of whiskey and saluting* UDOLPHUS. *He is in Customs uniform.* MARIA *is behind him, wringing her hands. He shuts* MARIA *out by closing the door. The* SERGEANT *is squirming with fear.*)

UDOLPHUS (*angrily*). What on earth is the meaning of this drunken intrusion?

SERGEANT (*trying to save the situation, officiously*). Just let me handle this, your honour. (*Secretively.*) A dangerous character, sir, if he's crossed, and not too strong in the mind.

(*The* SERGEANT *goes to* FARRELL *and tries to push him out.*) Now! Now! Out of his honour's presence this minute! On your way now, or I'll run you in!

(*The* SERGEANT *gives* FARRELL *a secretive wink but* FARRELL
obstinately resists.)

FARRELL (*drunkenly*). Sergeant, no man—can stop
the march of the inevitable! The clock of the Cosmos has
chimed! Ignatius Farrell must take the plunge—I mean
pledge. He's battling his way against seven demons to Father
Phelim to confess all! "Tell nothin'," says me seven demons.
"Tell all," says me conscience. Straighten the crooked! Open
up the secretive! Uncover the covered!

UDOLPHUS. Sergeant! Is this man not known to me? Is
he not Stanislaus Brannigan's unfortunate brother-in-law?

SERGEANT (*secretively*). Ah, indeed he is, your honour.
A bitter pill in the mouth of a dacent man.

UDOLPHUS. Then what is he doing with a Customs uniform on him?

SERGEANT. A—a pardonable vanity, sir. The poor man
thinks, at times, he's anyone from Napoleon to Saint Patrick
himself. On your way now, Ignatius! On your way!
(FARRELL *still resists the* SERGEANT.)

FARRELL. The truth must out, Sergeant, and the see-
saw of the Cosmos be adjusted. The way to Father Phelim
lies through the demon-infested jungles of the mind of
Ignatius Farrell.

UDOLPHUS. Wait, Sergeant! Under this man's lunacy,
there may be stray wisps of vital information. (*To* FARRELL.)
My good man, how can you go to Father Phelim to make
your confession and take the pledge in this drunken condition?

FARRELL. Your honour, how the hell could I discuss
with Father Phelim my vital relationship with the Cosmos in
me sober senses? "Pipe down," says me seven demons. "Pipe
up," says me conscience. And there's Father Phelim waitin'
for me a million miles away, armed with the stole, the holy-
water pot and the Absolve te votre peccavi!

UDOLPHUS.   Then off with you to the priest and make a clean breast of everything!

FARRELL.   How can I face Father Phelim in his capacity of Celestial Chuckerout, with *that* on my soul?

(FARRELL *takes out an envelope and throws it dramatically on the table.* UDOLPHUS *stares at it. The* SERGEANT *is stiff with fear.*)

UDOLPHUS.   Examine this document, Sergeant, and decide as to its relevance.

(*The* SERGEANT, *with a show of official thoroughness, pockets the package.*)

SERGEANT.   Your honour, I'll explore the document thoroughly the moment I get back to the barracks.

UDOLPHUS (*impatiently*).   You'll explore it *now*, Sergeant. Procrastination is an Irish national cancer!

(*The* SERGEANT *lamely produces the envelope and extracts a letter and ten five pound notes. He looks fearfully at* UDOLPHUS.)

SERGEANT.   Me eyes is bad, your honour and I haven't me glasses.

UDOLPHUS (*peremptorily*).   Give it here. (*He reads.*) "To Customs Officer Ignatius Farrell." Are you one of our Customs Officers, my man?

FARRELL.   I am, for me sins, your honour.

UDOLPHUS.   Then, Sergeant, I have been maliciously misled as to this man's status and identity!

SERGEANT.   We tried to cover him up, your honour.

UDOLPHUS.   Cover him up?

SERGEANT.   Er—wink the—the blind eye at his faults, sir, because, apart from his terrible thirst, he's a dacent man.

UDOLPHUS (*exasperated*).   *Another* dacent man. For this, Sergeant Whistler, I must recommend that you be reduced to the ranks!

(*The* SERGEANT *abjectly bows his head.*)

FARRELL (*drunkenly*). His honour's right. When we're all shriven and unadorned and adjusted to the Cosmos, we'll swing ecstatically between the might-have-been and the impossible!

UDOLPHUS (*sternly*). Sober yourself, sir. (*Examining letter.*) This is obviously a bribe of fifty pounds to allow a lorry load of contraband through to the North at midnight tonight. Do *you* know, Sergeant, whose the signature is?

SERGEANT (*abjectly*). I'm far from well as it is, your honour. Don't surprise me too much.

UDOLPHUS (*dramatically*). Mike MacNamara!

SERGEANT (*brokenly*). This is a terrible shock to me, your honour. Mike MacNamara of all people. I'd as soon suspect Father Phelim himself.

UDOLPHUS. You must suspect *everyone—even* Father Phelim. I have fairly conclusive evidence that Father Phelim is smuggling wax candles and paraffin oil into this village. I'm considering his arrest.

SERGEANT (*aghast*). Arrest! Your honour, do you want the third world war fought out on Irish soil!

UDOLPHUS. There you see! Privilege! You can't arrest *this* one because he's a priest!

FARRELL (*maudlinly*). You can *not*.

UDOLPHUS. You can't arrest *that* one because his uncle's in the Dail.

FARRELL. True!

UDOLPHUS. You can't arrest the next one because his mother's grandfather was a Fenian!

FARRELL. True!

UDOLPHUS (*angrily*). Who then is not immune from arrest in this country of legal exceptions?

FARRELL (*maudlinly*). His honour's right! In this island menagerie of ours, the exception is the law and the law is an ass. We're a disgrace to the Cosmos!

UDOLPHUS (*sizing* FARRELL *up severely*). Customs Officer Farrell, consider yourself suspended from all official duties.

FARRELL. Suspended! There you see! That's what comes to Ignatius Farrell for making an epic stand against the seven demons that infest him! "Scram!" says his fiends. "Scram not," says his conscience. And look at him now abjectly suspended between the Court house and the confession box!

UDOLPHUS. Silence before me, sir! And take yourself and that disgraceful bottle out of here!

FARRELL. Go, and he goeth! Ignatius Farrell now that he has handed in his bribe and adjusted himself to the Cosmos, must now advance towards Father Phelim and his ghostly advisers. But *this* must *not* go! (*He holds up the bottle.*) A shocking act of renunciation is called for, and the demand must be met heroically and as befits us!

(FARRELL *dramatically crosses to a vase of flowers beside the door, uncorks the bottle, and empties it into the vase.*)

"Pipe down," says me fiends. "Pipe up!" says me conscience.

(*The* SERGEANT's *face is a study in pain and torture before such criminal waste.* FARRELL *turns and with a heroic gesture throws the empty bottle in the waste paper basket.*)

FARRELL. Gentlemen! The battle is won! Ignatius Farrell sounds the Cosmic note of jubilation and the defence rests!

(FARRELL *dramatically staggers out and closes the door. The* SERGEANT *looks fearfully at* UDOLPHUS *who sternly regards him.*)

UDOLPHUS. Sergeant Whistler, out of such evil as this comes the good, the vital evidence we require. The decisive battle of Chuckeyhead is about to be won! Go out, on my orders and bring Mike MacNamara in!

SERGEANT (*almost speechless with fear*). Do you mean . . . arrest him, your honour?

UDOLPHUS. Decidedly. And also arrange a surprise police raid on his place of business.

SERGEANT. He's . . . a terrible strong man, your
honour. Six foot in his socks, the chest of a bull, and a fist
like the top of a shillelagh!

UDOLPHUS. What? Are you implying, Sergeant, that he
would have the nerve to resist arrest?

SERGEANT. It's unfortunately not outside the—the
probabilities, sir?

UDOLPHUS. Then in addition to the charges of smuggling and bribery, charge him further with . . . causing
grievous bodily harm to an officer of the law.

SERGEANT (*weakly*). I will, your honour . . . if I'm
able . . .

(*The* SERGEANT *dons his cap and crosses to the door, where
he turns.*)

There's one small matter, sir . . . (*Nods towards kitchen.*)
Herself within is liable to throw things about when she's
upset.

UDOLPHUS. And who, pray, is *herself?*

SERGEANT. Miss Rita, your honour.

UDOLPHUS. And why should Miss Rita be upset over
this scoundrel's arrest?

SERGEANT. Did you not know, your honour? Sure she's
mad in the head about Mike?

UDOLPHUS. She's what?

SERGEANT. Ah, indeed she is, sir. Sure she jilted a
Member of the Dail and a farmer with three hundred acres
and a grand Englishman that made that picture of her head
(*Points to water-colour.*)—all for the same boyo.

(UDOLPHUS *is thunderstruck. He looks miserable. The* SER-
GEANT *watches him covertly, hoping he'll retract.*)

(*Insinuatingly.*) Of course, your honour, if it would avoid
embarrassin' you in awkward circumstances like these here,

I could always give him the . . . quick nod to clear at once across the Border out of the . . . jurisdiction.

UDOLPHUS (*angrily*). What? Another scoundrel who is immune from arrest because a redhead loves him! Can any administrative idiocy surpass that? Could legal dodging be worse, even in America?

SERGEANT (*apologetically*). Sure I was only tryin' to be helpful, sir, in a sad pickle o' bother.

UDOLPHUS. You stand severely reprimanded, Sergeant. Go out, with your eyes seeing straight for once, and bring this lawbreaker in!

(*The* SERGEANT *bows abjectly and nervously fumbles with the door.* UDOLPHUS *turns away towards the mantelpiece and contemplates* RITA's *head in water-colour. The* SERGEANT *turns, eyes him secretively, deftly lifts vase of flowers, and tiptoes out.*)

ACT II

Scene II

SCENE: *The Lounge Bar as in Act I.*
TIME: *About an hour later.*

MIKE MACNAMARA *is seated at the table down L.,
adding up a battered account book.* JUDY BRANNIGAN
comes across with a drink for him.

JUDY.   Did you pack the red salmon, Mike, that Matt
Coleman left in the taproom?

MIKE.   It's in the lorry in the yard, Judy. I see here just
a two pound roll of butter in Jamsie McCoombe's name. It
looks suspiciously small. Did you check it?

JUDY.   Catch me trustin' Jamsie! I stuck two fingers in
it and they came out with the finest cigarette lighter I ever
laid an eye on.

MIKE.   Good man, Judy! You're your Da's daughter!
Isn't this a helluva country! You can trust no one! Give it
back to him, Judy. I'll have fair dealin' or no dealin'. That's
all the stuff checked. I'm all set now for a quick run across in
the name o' God. I hope Farrell's on the job all right. I sent

246

him the fifty quid for the road in advance. I'm always afraid
of him collapsin' sudden with heart disease or the D.T.'s.

JUDY.   Don't worry, Mike. He told me this morning he
was on his way to Father Phelim to take the pledge for life.

(*The* SERGEANT *enters. He looks nervous and worried. When
he sees* MIKE *out of the corner of his eye he starts and
gives a deep sigh.*)

JUDY.   Sergeant, me Da left a bumper for you for gettin'
us rid of the D.J.

(*She planks a glass of Irish on the counter, and the* SERGEANT
takes it eagerly.)

SERGEANT.   The blessin' o' God on him! And the choice
of ten good men and true for yourself, Judy. (*Nodding towards* MIKE.) I want a word with Mike.

JUDY.   He's countin' up the stuff that's on the lorry in
the yard . . .

(*The* SERGEANT *eyes* MIKE *nervously as he checks his accounts.*)

SERGEANT.   Believe it or not, Judy, I'm here to arrest
him.

JUDY.   Arrest *him,* is it? You're havin' your joke, Sergeant.

SERGEANT.   Ah, I wish I was. But it's true.

JUDY.   Ah, you poor thing! You'd better have another
bumper.

SERGEANT.   I'd better. I won't feel the murderin' so
much if I'm well fortified.

(JUDY *hands him a stiff drink.*)

JUDY (*bursting into tears*).   'Tis maybe I'm givin' you
the last drink you'll ever have.

(*The* SERGEANT *consoles her by clapping her on the shoulder.*)

SERGEANT.   There now, Judy, there now! If the worst
comes, let yous ever remember I was always a dacent man
to your Da and the boys.

JUDY (*sobbing*). Ah, indeed you were, indeed you were, you poor thing. As long as I'm alive, no one will say the hard word agin ye, after your funeral.

(*The* SERGEANT *drains his glass, and summons up his courage.*)

SERGEANT. Here goes, in the name o' God.

(*He crosses towards* MIKE, *who goes on checking as he talks to him. The* SERGEANT *takes the chair beside him and begins ingratiatingly.*)

The . . . the little woman is well, I trust, Mike?

MIKE. The best, Sergeant. That red mop of hers gives me the grandest nightmares. Four or five more loads like this one, and with the help o' God I'll take her by the scruff o' the neck to the altar. Judy! Bring the Sergeant a bumper and put it down to me.

JUDY (*sadly, bringing drink*). Take it quick, Sergeant, and say a wee prayer after it.

(*She suddenly is overcome with tears and emotion, and runs hysterically into the bar room.* MIKE *regards her, puzzled.*)

MIKE. A wee prayer for what? What's the matter with the lassie?

SERGEANT (*evasively*). It's—the oul' grannie above in the attic that's near her end. Ninety if she's a day.

MIKE (*sarcastically*). That one, is it? She'd guzzle a bottle a day if she got it. If she ever dies, it'll be of thirst. (*Looks at the* SERGEANT.) Go on, Sergeant, knock it back. By the look of you, you could be doin' with it.

SERGEANT (*nervously*). God between us and all harm! (*He drinks nervously.*)

MIKE. You're very peely-wally lookin'! What's on your mind?

SERGEANT (*sorrowfully*). Ah, a ton weight of trouble, Mike.

MIKE. Arrah, amn't *I* here beside you always? (*Dramatically displaying a huge fist.*) I once put a man to sleep for thirty-six hours with *that!*

SERGEANT (*quaking*). God help us!

MIKE. And when he woke, he as much as looked sideways at me, and I put him back to sleep for forty-eight hours.

SERGEANT. Just for lookin' sideways at you?

MIKE. Just for that! He'd be asleep yet only he wakened up for a cup o' tay. He was always a divil for tay.

SERGEANT. You'd do the same again, I suppose?

MIKE. I would if I was riz! I'm a divil when I'm riz— friends or enemies, it's all the one to me. I once in a temper threw a great friend o' mine through a window. As close a friend as yourself! Of course, I paid for him in the hospital and got him a new set of teeth. But there it is! I wallop first and get sorry afterwards.

(*This conversation entirely unnerves the* SERGEANT, *who eyes* MIKE *apprehensively as he adds figures.*)

SERGEANT. The little woman is well, I hope, Mike.

MIKE. Sure, you asked me that before! What the hell's the matter with you?

SERGEANT. I'm maybe a bit low in the bones. You'll maybe understand, Mike, that since I had that operation last year I'm not the man I was at all, at all.

MIKE. Ah now, I'm well aware of that, Sergeant. Sure there wasn't a dry eye in the village that day the rumour got around that you died sudden in the hospital. (*He continues checking.*)

SERGEANT. Ah, now, you wouldn't think to look at me that the pains be on me in the night and I gaspin' for the smallest breath.

MIKE. That's a terrible state of affairs. I'll take you to the doctor tonight, that's what I'll do.

SERGEANT (*fearfully*). Ah, indeed I wouldn't be a bit

surprised . . . Mike, I have a . . . a class of a message for you. Would you have a drink with me first, in the interests of Christianity and human decency?

MIKE. Do you want to have me too drunk to drive the lorry? What's the matter with you?

SERGEANT. Well, it's like this, Mike. I'm here, Mike . . . I'm here to arrest you by order of the D.J.

MIKE (*adding*). . . . seventy-five and eight are eighty-three and seven are ninety . . . What was that you were sayin', Sergeant?

SERGEANT (*breathlessly*). Ah, just, Mike, that . . . that I'm here to arrest you on the D.J.'s orders.

(MIKE *stares at him and then, lying back, laughs heartily as* STANISLAUS *enters carrying a case of stout, and* JUDY *reappears at the bar.*)

MIKE (*laughing*). Stan! Bring us two bumpers! The Sergeant is here to arrest me!

(STANISLAUS, *who has moved up to the bar to get the drinks, stares owlishly at the* SERGEANT *as he brings them. Then he suddenly bursts into hyena-like laughter, so that he and* MIKE *become like two monstrous roosters on a barn floor. The* SERGEANT *sits miserably between them, staring at his empty glass.*)

STANISLAUS. Sure, that was a grand one of the Sergeant's!

SERGEANT (*venturing*). If you'd come quietly, Mike, I could get you off with a fine. A great help it would be and I under peremptory orders to use all the reserves of the law.

STANISLAUS (*with decision*). Mike, will I pitch the Sergeant through the window or down the cellar steps? It's all the one to me!

JUDY (*running over*). Ah, Da! The poor Sergeant!

MIKE. Ah, leave the dacent man alone. Isn't he entitled to his fun, as much as the rest of us?

SERGEANT. I'll recommend strong that it be only a fine, Mike, if you'd only come quiet and get it over.

STANISLAUS (*sternly*). Quiet, did ye say? This is gone far enough! Get Mike in jail before that oul' divil on the Bench, and where's the town? In the dustbin! Where's the workers? Starvin' on the kerbstones! Where's me own business? Bankrupt and shuttered up! Why don't ye drop a bomb on us dacently and wipe us out in a Christian way that we'd understand?

(*The* SERGEANT *suddenly rises, full of resolution, and moves towards the door.* MIKE *notices his sudden resolve and intentness.*)

SERGEANT. I know what I'll do. I'll put an end to this!

MIKE. Wait, Sergeant. What the hell are you up to now?

SERGEANT (*turning dramatically*). I have one fine staunch friend in this town. And that friend is Rita Ronan. I'm goin' straight round to her now to tell her the disgraceful way you're treatin' me!

(*He is making for the door in a temper when* MIKE *springs from his chair and bars his way.*)

MIKE. Ah, begod, Sergeant, that's below the belt! Friends is friends! Do you want to see me wandering the streets a broken and destroyed man robbed of the one thing in life that I thirst for?

SERGEANT. It's up to yourself! Rita's the medicine for you! And when you get a dose of her temper, it won't go down as aisy as a bumper of the best!

STANISLAUS. Judy! For God's sake bring a drink to the Sergeant before he destroys the world! Now, Sergeant, I never knew the man that interfered between future man and wife that ever had any luck. What God will join together, let no law or Sergeant put apart . . . Isn't that straight from the Gospel?

(JUDY *arrives with the drink.*)

Here now, down with that bumper. And let you lose your policeman's senses and talk like a dacent man. Isn't clarity the word, and isn't clarity called for?

(STANISLAUS *and* MIKE *persuade the* SERGEANT *to accept the drink.*)

MIKE. Take it aisy, Sergeant. Sure, the D.J. can prove nothin' again me anyway.

SERGEANT. You may as well know now, Mike, that Customs Officer Farrell got drunk on his way to Father Phelim's to take the pledge, and because he wanted to make a clean breast of everything, he handed over your letter and fifty quid to the D.J.

(*Consternation follows.* MIKE *and* STANISLAUS *react strongly.*)

STANISLAUS. This is the worst news since the Titanic disaster!

JUDY. There now! Yous *would* make a teetotaller of him!

MIKE. Judy's right! We blundered! I never met the teetotaller yet that I'd trust an inch!

STANISLAUS (*briskly*). Judy! Get the men in the yard to unload the lorry at once.

SERGEANT. And be sure to put the cargo under your grannie's bed in the attic where I won't think of lookin' when I'm searchin'!

STANISLAUS. The very thing! Run, Judy, run!

JUDY. But there's cases of whiskey in the load! You can't put *that* under me grannie's bed.

STANISLAUS. You can *not*, begod, Judy! She has a nose like a wireless aerial! Come on, lassie—think of something! (*He and* JUDY *hurry out through the bar.*)

SERGEANT. We're oul' friends, Mike. So if you decide to skip across the Border out of the jurisdiction, you'll unfortunately have to knock me out first, or I'll lose me stripes. I know you'll be dacent enough to make it aisy and merciful.

MIKE. Thanks, Sergeant, but that's no good. I'm not leavin' Rita. That barrel of tomato juice is soft on her, and you never know what Rita would do in one of her tantrums. Could you get me off with a fine?

SERGEANT. I can! You can take that from me! I'll put up a plea for you that'll be cast iron. It's a great help that you have no previous convictions. A clean sheet's a big thing before the Bench.

MIKE. Then I'll come quiet, Sergeant. But if anything goes wrong with the works it'll be you and me for it and no quarter asked or given.

(*The* SERGEANT *shakes hands with him.* STANISLAUS *comes back in.*)

STANISLAUS. Judy and the men are as busy as nailers on the lorry.

MIKE. I'm goin' quiet with the Sergeant, Stan. He's guaranteein' it'll be a fine only. Can I get bail, Sergeant?

SERGEANT. And why not? It's a civilised country, in spite of the villains that's runnin' it!

MIKE. Come on with me, Stan, and take a few pounds with you to bail me out.

STANISLAUS. I will to be sure. The money for the cargo is in the back.

(*He goes to collect it.*)

SERGEANT. Sure, it won't take me a minute to charge you with bribery and corruption, and then, please God, we can make out the bail bonds in a jiffy and have a dram afterwards before I report progress to that . . . that son of a . . . *good* mother.

(STANISLAUS *returns and mixes drinks.*)

STANISLAUS. A last dram before the unholy ritual!

MIKE. Seconded!

SERGEANT (*laughing*). An important capture! They'll maybe give me an extra stripe for this!

MIKE. Or maybe a headstone with an angel sittin' on it.

STANISLAUS (*handing round glasses*).   To temperance!
SERGEANT.   Christianity!
MIKE.   Fair dealin'!
STANISLAUS.   Common dacency!
SERGEANT.   And the wind that shakes the barley!
(*They drink. The* SERGEANT *starts up a song. The others join in as the* SERGEANT *grips* MIKE *by the wrist and the scruff of his neck in mock arrest.* STANISLAUS *leads the way towards the door, waving the wad of pound notes. As the others follow, singing—"Nellie Dean."*)

The CURTAIN falls.

ACT III

SCENE: RITA's *sitting room as before.*

TIME: *It is about two weeks later.*

MARIA *is discovered dusting.* RITA *comes in dressed all in black, and with a black scarf round her red curls. She goes to the mirror to view her appearance.* MARIA *stares at her in wonderment.*

MARIA. What in the name of Heaven are you all in black for, madhead?

RITA (*turning*). Why shouldn't I be in black? Don't you know my poor Mike is above in the Court on trial?

MARIA. Will you take that funeral stuff off you, and behave yourself!

RITA. How dare you, Maria! The women of Ireland have always mourned for their heroes in deep black.

MARIA. Didn't Mike make it plain enough to you that he doesn't want to be a hero?

RITA. It's not what Mike wants—it's what I want. I'm off now to the Court to see my poor darling suffering.

(RITA *is making for the window, much to* MARIA's *amuse-*

255

ment, when IGNATIUS FARRELL *comes to it and stands
looking in. He looks bewildered and rather lost and uncertain.* RITA *stops short.*)

Ignatius! You look bewitched! What's the matter?

MARIA (*angrily*).   Don't let that dirty informer in here,
or I'll walk out!

RITA (*pertly*).   Walk out then, woman! Poor Ignatius
is the fateful instrument by which Mike reaches heroism.

(MARIA, *with a gesture of disgust, throws her feather duster
at him, and sweeps out of the room.* RITA *takes* IGNATIUS
forward.)

FARRELL (*with half dazed expression*).   That woman
is ignorant of the Cosmic immensities.

RITA.   Let her be. She can never understand the debt
of gratitude I owe you, Ignatius, in having Mike arrested. I
can marry him at last. Where were you going now, Ignatius?

FARRELL.   I was on my way to Father Phelim to take
the pledge.

RITA.   But you've been weeks going to Father Phelim!

FARRELL.   Bear with me. The way to Father Phelim is
immeasurable. Every time I get drunk I chase him to give
me the pledge and he runs. Every time I'm sober, *he* chases
me to give me the pledge and *I* run. And there we are, dodging each other around the boulders of the impossible.

RITA (*sympathetically*).   Ah me poor Ignatius! It's just
that in the heart you're a poet and no one understands poetry
only *me*.

FARRELL (*half dazed*).   I'm in a strange state of suspension. I'm in me sober senses as late in the morning as this, and
it's never happened to me before. It's queer! It's like clay
bein' poured on a coffin. It's only now I'm beginnin' to understand the hell that teetotallers live in.

RITA.   A stiff drink might raise you up, Ignatius.

FARRELL (*hand up*).   No! For God's sake, don't start

up me seven demons. The battle between them and Father Phelim must be won.

RITA. But you're in a bad way. Surely you could take one drink if I put it in a *medicine bottle* for you.

FARRELL. "Stay," says me fiends. "Go," says me conscience. (*Pause.*) Rita is there a—a medicine bottle reasonably handy?

RITA. There's one here with stuff that I use for curling my hair. I'll pour it out.

(RITA *pours out the lotion and fills the bottle with whiskey. IGNATIUS takes it and eyes it glassily.*)

FARRELL. Oh, for the subtle mind of a woman! I'd never have thought of the medicine bottle. Here goes! Round seventy-nine! Ignatius Farrell is again hammered through the ropes, but Father Phelim refuses to throw in the towel.

(IGNATIUS *drinks long and with great relish. He puts down the empty bottle with a great smile of relief and lovingly regards* RITA.)

RITA. Is the poetry comin' back, Ignatius?

FARRELL. The Cosmos is again rolling beautifully on to its destiny.

(MARIA *comes rushing in.*)

MARIA. Rita, I hear boohin' and yellin' round at the Court! It's maybe that Mike's escaped!

RITA. Terrific! Mike to be a hunted felon! Oh glory!

(STANISLAUS BRANNIGAN *comes rushing in, by the window, in great excitement.*)

STANISLAUS. Rita! There's terrific news! Mike got cocky in the dock and the D.J. insisted on his left arm being handcuffed to Crampsey's right. The sweat that poured off poor little Crampsey would have wrung out a pair of blankets.

MARIA. Come on, Stanislaus! What happened to Mike?

STANISLAUS. The Sergeant couldn't find the stuff in the lorry, and the smuggling charge broke down. But he was found guilty of bribery, and the D.J. gave him three months without the option.

RITA. Three months! A hero at last!

MARIA. Behave yourelf, Rita! Go on, Stanislaus. Did Mike go mad?

STANISLAUS. Mad, did you say! The Sergeant took one look at the murder in Mike's eyes, and made for the door like a mad dog with a squib at his tail!

MARIA. And the D.J.?

STANISLAUS. A paraffin lamp whizzed past his head and he made for his room and locked himself in. And there was poor Crampsey tied to a madman being dragged all over the place!

RITA. It's wonderful! It's heavenly! Oh, I'm so happy . . . I must see me Mike in chains . . . in the dread talons of the law . . . Will he be coming this way, Stanislaus?

STANISLAUS. He will, if he doesn't murder Crampsey and him locked to him with the handcuffs.

RITA. This is the most wonderful moment of my life! Always I have regretted that Mike was too young for the revolution. Ah, but now, thank God, he wears the chains at last. They're coming!

(*She moves to open window.*)

STANISLAUS (*at window*). Here he comes, still hand-cuffed, with poor Crampsey on his feet one minute and on his head the next and the Sergeant has the key away with him! Will you look at the crowd that's after them!

RITA. It's fate, it's destiny! Mike must wear his chains! (*Shouting out of the window.*) Mike me hero, I'm suffering with you, darling.

STANISLAUS. Look out everyone! He's comin' in, and the temper's leppin' out of him. I'm all for dyin' in me bed.

(*Exit* STANISLAUS *by window.*)

RITA. High drama! The Venus de Medici be damned!

She's a hussy with barmaid's legs. I'm Helen of the Thousand Ships.

MIKE (*off-stage*). Where is he?

RITA (*kneeling on one knee, head bowed and arm outstretched in submission*). Make way for Mike!

FARRELL. And give Ignatius Farrell a drink.

(FARRELL *helps himself to a drink and sits musing in a chair.* MIKE *comes striding in, dragging the half dead* CRAMPSEY *with him.*)

RITA. Mike! Me hero! In chains at last!

MIKE. Where's that bloody Sergeant? He belied and belittled me! I'll not rest till I hop him off the chimney pots.

MARIA. He's over the Border by this, Mike.

MIKE. I don't care if he's over the equator—I must get him. (*He seizes* RITA *by the arm.*) You always had a soft spot for him. You have him hid in the cupboard. Out with him.

MARIA. Behave yourself this minute, Mike. The Sergeant is not here. And don't you touch Rita.

MIKE. I'll spring clean the carpet with her.

RITA (*with her arms about him*). Do, Mike! It would be wonderful!

(*He seizes her again and puts his arms passionately round her.* CRAMPSEY *is jerked into a fierce embrace.*)

MIKE. And what's more, if this is a plot to get rid of me between you and that walking barrel of tomato juice on the Bench, do you know what I'll do with you?

RITA. Tell me, Mike. Tell me!

MIKE. You lovely maddening redheaded she-devil. I'll make a red rope of your hair and strangle you with it!

RITA. Ah, what a death! Kiss me, Mike. I adore you.

(CRAMPSEY *is again jerked into the embrace as* MIKE *kisses* RITA *passionately.*)

FARRELL (*half-dazedly*). Begod, that's lovin' on a Cosmic scale!

CRAMPSEY. Mike, there's not much of me left. Will you listen to what may well be me last words before I pass out?

MIKE. Ah, you've been grinin' for hours. I'll listen to nothin'.

CRAMPSEY. Do you want to be harnessed to a corpse, and to be laid out along with me on the deathbed? Do you want the De Profoundis said over you and a wax candle at your head?

MIKE. I want me bloody left arm back, that's all.

CRAMPSEY. Come around then to the blacksmith and let him hammer us apart, for it wasn't God that put *us* together.

MIKE. Fair enough, come on! I'm sick of dragging you after me as if you were an oversized guardian angel.

RITA (*angrily*). Stop! How dare you accept such a suggestion, Mike, when you know I love you.

MIKE. And what the hell's that got to do with it?

RITA. Do you think for a moment that I could remain in love with you after you had reduced yourself to a little man?

MIKE. So you want me to go to jail!

RITA. I want you to wear your chains like a hero and be numbered with the famous! I want you to look through your cell window and dream fiercely of freedom. I want you to hate law like hell, and love life with passion. I want to sit here, tortured at the thought of you tasting the tasteless water and eating the stale heel of a loaf.

MIKE. Damn your contrariness. I'll go to jail for no one, love or no love!

MARIA. You ought to be ashamed of yourself, Rita!

RITA. Away, woman, and cook the cabbage!

(MARIA, *with a gesture of disgust, sweeps out.* RITA *turns to* FARRELL *who is sitting pensively, his eyes on a bottle.*) I appeal to you, Ignatius. Well, my poet of the Cosmos, what is love?

FARRELL (*rising, bemused*). Love, Rita, in terms of the Cosmos, is the breathless combination of the heroic and the romantic!

RITA (*to Mike*). Small man. You're answered! Take him away, Crampsey; I hate him.

(MIKE *looks venomously at* FARRELL, *and chucks* CRAMPSEY *after him.*)

MIKE. Come on, Crampsey! I've always wanted to beat the bejaysus out of a poet!

(MIKE, *dragging* CRAMPSEY, *rushes after* FARRELL *who runs unsteadily round and out through the window.* RITA, *with arms outspread, prevents* MIKE *from following him.*)

RITA. Back, small man! The poets have their privileges!

MIKE (*snorting*). Jail, me foot! Did we banish the British and their jails just to set up bloody jails of our own!

CRAMPSEY (*whining*). Come on, before you go for her again and destroy meself in the battle!

MIKE (*roughly to* CRAMPSEY). Come on! Take me away, Crampsey!

(MIKE *stalks through the doorway, violently dragging* CRAMPSEY *after him.* RITA *throws herself face downwards on the couch, sobs loudly and kicks her heels in temper. The* SERGEANT's *head appears furtively at the window.*)

SERGEANT. Rita, let the bad word not be said of you, that you let me expire in the open street.

RITA (*jumping up, surprised*). Ah, me poor darling Sergeant! Come in this minute to me. Are you murdered and destroyed?

(*She runs to him solicitously. He is worn out and dishevelled. His uniform is creased and irregular.*)

SERGEANT. Destroyed is the word, Rita.

RITA. Were you running, or what?

SERGEANT. Ah now, if I ran one mile, I ran ten miles,

and if I'd been able I'd have run ten more after seeing the murder in Mike's eyes. Let you look on a man that's not long for this world.

(RITA *pours him a large whiskey and takes it to him. He takes a large gulp.*)

RITA.   You were never meant to be a policeman, Sergeant.

SERGEANT.   It's true. But me father was one before me. That's the curse of this country. A nation of mad misfits, all wanting to be something else. At twenty, I wanted to die for Ireland; at thirty I wanted to live for her; at forty, I realised I should have been a poet. And now I sit and make drunken rhymes about great men and great days that are gone.

RITA (*softly, reclining on the floor by him*).   A poet! And never a poem at all for a poor redhead?

SERGEANT.   Ah, sure, I wrote one about you the day the mad Englishman jumped off the bridge for you.

RITA.   And you never told me! Me poor darlin' Augustus that broke his heart over me and married a cook! Out with it, Sergeant!

SERGEANT.   Ah, now, would you have us raking the dead ashes?

RITA.   Love never dies, or beauty or the heroic. They wander the Irish streets like old-fashioned ghosts in a drab tasteless world. Drink! And deliver up my poem!

(*He drains the glass, goes to the water-colour on the wall, contemplates it, and, turning to her, recites:*)

SERGEANT.

"At the edge of the lake at Lercan
    I have builded a silver tower
With all the words you have spoken.
    And under the layers of thinking,
Like a coin out of old days buried
    By mud wall and long rain drinking,

Reposes the thought how I loved you,
    With the beech leaves flaming your hair
And the birds in their flight around you."

RITA.   Sergeant, it's out of this world! From this min-
ute, I'm immortal. Imagine that bogman, Mike, making a
poem like that! Like every other woman the world over, I
have fallen in love with the wrong man . . . But no matter,
I have inspired a poem!
(*Enter* MARIA.)
MARIA.   Rita, will you come off that chariot of yours?
The dinner's destroyed.
RITA.   Damn the dinner, Maria! I'm terrifically happy.
The Sergeant has immortalised my hair.
MARIA.   Three more drinks and he'll immortalise your
grandmother.
(*Distant booing is heard through the window.*)
They say an old fool's the worst fool. Listen! (*Goes to the
window and looks out.*) Sacred Saints! The whole village
is booing the D.J. and pelting him with tomatoes and vege-
tables. It looks like another revolution!
SERGEANT.   Begod, I'm destroyed! He'll charge me with
neglect of duty and desertion.
RITA.   Ah, me poor downtrodden Sergeant, in with you
here behind the curtain and he'll be none the wiser.
(RITA *leads him to anteroom upstage and draws the curtains.*
    He looks through them at the bottle.)
SERGEANT.   Could I take a little bit of company with
me, Rita, to keep the—the petrification away?
(RITA *hands him the bottle.*)
RITA.   The poets in ancient Ireland, Sergeant, always
had their privileges.
SERGEANT.   The blessin' o' God on you!
(*The booing dies away.*)
MARIA.   He's making his way in, in a woebegone state.

RITA. Spare me from his mathematical mind! I'm off to me bedroom to have a headache.

(RITA *exits.* MARIA *remains to tidy the room. The front door is heard to slam. After a slight pause* UDOLPHUS *enters, looking the picture of misery. His clothes are stained and dishevelled.* MARIA *gives him a look and exits without a word.* UDOLPHUS *goes to the fire, then sees it is not lighted. This is the last straw.*)

UDOLPHUS. Oh, this . . . this villain of a country! This despair of all law and order! If only we could be like respectable Ulster . . . the gentleman's gentleman of the Empire! But no! We prefer to be the *enfant terrible* of the west. Oh, isn't it the pity of me . . . the man of law!

(*He sits down miserably in an armchair,* MARIA *enters with a tray to collect the dirty glasses.*)

MARIA. Excuse me.

(*She crosses, collects the glasses and moves to the door.*)

UDOLPHUS. Wait, Maria, my fire has not been lighted.

MARIA (*angrily*). Light it yourself! I'll be a blackleg and a scab for no man livin'. Poor orphan boy condemned to bread and water in a foreign jail!

UDOLPHUS (*exasperated*). It's not a foreign jail, woman; it's an *Irish* jail.

MARIA. Oh, we have jails of our own now, have we? We're gettin' as grand as the English.

UDOLPHUS. There is definitely no answer to that! Please go away. I'll light the fire myself.

MARIA. Light it, then.

(*As* UDOLPHUS *lights a match.*)

That match will be a great help. I never lit that fire yet without at least half a pint of paraffin.

UDOLPHUS. Paraffin! Isn't that just like the whole mad crowd of you! No system! No training! The easiest and laziest way out.

MARIA. Arrah, isn't God looking after us, and what the

hell do we want with systems and things? (*She sweeps towards the door.*)

UDOLPHUS. Wait! Ask Miss Rita to come in. I must talk to someone who is sane and sensible.

MARIA. You can't see her now. She's not out of it yet.

UDOLPHUS. Out of . . . what?

MARIA. The faint, of course. She's been in and out of forty faints at least, since the inhuman villainy was perpetrated at midday?

UDOLPHUS. Surely Miss Rita is not . . . not ill?

MARIA. Do you think, your honour, that she's a horse, that she could suffer your foul and murderous blow without the life in her dying down to such a low ebb that if you blew on it, it would go out like a smuggled candle?

(MARIA *bursts into tears and goes.* UDOLPHUS *goes to the mantel and takes down the photograph of* RITA *and looks at it lovingly.*)

UDOLPHUS. Oh, Rita. I wonder if my mother who made me so instinctively orderly and law-abiding was *always* right? Even the saints had their weaknesses.

(*During this speech the* SERGEANT'S *head appears through the curtains. At the end of the speech,* UDOLPHUS *reverently kisses the photograph and the* SERGEANT'S *eyes turn to anger.* UDOLPHUS *replaces the photograph and crosses to the sideboard, takes out a bottle of tomato juice and pours some into a glass. The* SERGEANT *tiptoes to the mantel, takes down the photograph, rubs* UDOLPHUS'S *kiss off with his sleeve and puts his own in its place. Then he goes back to the alcove. All this passes unnoticed by* UDOLPHUS, *who takes a sip of his tomato juice and makes a wry face.* STANISLAUS *appears at the window.*)

STANISLAUS. Is Miss Rita at home, your honour?

UDOLPHUS. She's lying down, Brannigan. Come in. I want to talk to you.

(STANISLAUS *comes in, by the window. He is well on his guard and defensive.* UDOLPHUS *stands cold, shivering and forlorn before him.*)

STANISLAUS (*surlily*). Me pub's bankrupt, me shutters are up. What more do you want of me now?

UDOLPHUS (*forlornly*). You all hate me, don't you?

STANISLAUS. Ah, indeed we do, sir.

UDOLPHUS. Brannigan, I have been insulted, belittled and pelted with all sorts of filth. Look at me!

STANISLAUS. That, your honour, is the human spirit assertin' itself. That spirit hated and overcame Nero. It hated and overcame Hannibal. It hated and overcame Cromwell and Castlereagh and it hates and will overcome *you!*

UDOLPHUS. My mother taught me otherwise, Brannigan. My mother was a good woman.

STANISLAUS. Your honour, there's a long queue of good women at the gates of hell!

UDOLPHUS. I'm very miserable and shivering with cold. Will you mix a tomato cocktail for me?

STANISLAUS. Do you mean with a—a Stanislavian fortification?

UDOLPHUS. I mean with—the human spirit in it.

STANISLAUS. It's a trade secret, but no matter. The greater the moment, the greater the deed. (*Starting to get drinks from different bottles.*) There now! First a basis of tomato to disguise it, if it's after hours! A finger of brandy to neutralise the tomato. And a whisper of rum to switch on the power. There now!

UDOLPHUS (*miserably*). It looks good.

STANISLAUS. It tastes better.

UDOLPHUS (*as he drinks he splutters*). It's very hard on the throat.

STANISLAUS. Ah, sure, the throat never yet had a good word to say about the stomach. Do you feel a sort of hilarity beginnin' in the bones?

UDOLPHUS (*pensively*).   I do.

STANISLAUS.   Thanks be to God.

UDOLPHUS.   I'm a little bit warmer now.

STANISLAUS (*starts mixing again*).   You'll be twice as warm after the second one. I once cured a man of double pneumonia with ten of these. But I might have saved myself the trouble. The silly ass turned round and died in me arms of delirium tremens.

UDOLPHUS.   Is this wise?

(*Watching him mixing.*)

STANISLAUS.   Is what wise?

UDOLPHUS.   The second.

STANILAUS.   Ah, indeed it's not. But sure if we lived by wisdom we'd all kill one another with holy intentions.

UDOLPHUS.   I'm a very miserable and lonely man, Mr. Brannigan. Do *you* hate me too?

STANISLAUS.   Ah, begod, sir, you could ate all that *I* like of you.

UDOLPHUS.   Here I am, a man of law, without a single friend, deserted by the police, ignored by the priest and pelted with vegetables by the very people that made the laws that I administer.

STANISLAUS.   It's just, your honour, that you don't understand.

UDOLPHUS.   Understand *what*, will you tell me?

STANISLAUS.   Sure, man, we love makin' laws, but we're far too intelligent ever to obey them. Take, for instance that grand timetable down there at the oul' bus depot. It's on fine glossy cardboard with a harp at the top and a St. Christopher medal at the bottom, and there you'll get to the very split second the times of buses that don't even exist.

UDOLPHUS.   But what is it there for?

STANISLAUS.   What's the clock in the little square there for? It never goes. What's the dozen's of oul' hens you meet at every door there for? They never lay. What's the spittoons below in my pub for? Nobody ever uses them so long as they have the carpet. What's all our pretty Chuckeyhead girls there for? Nobody ever marries them . . . except of course the tourists who fall in love with their accents instead of their ankles, God help them.

(*He hands* UDOLPHUS *a new drink.*)

Here now, knock that one back in the name o' God.

UDOLPHUS (*drinks and splutters again*). That was like a flock of wasps goin' down my throat.

STANISLAUS. That's just the rum and the brandy arguin'. I wouldn't give them a bit of heed. (*He starts mixing again.*)

UDOLPHUS. I feel very sore with Father Phelim. He's never once invited me to dinner. That, to me, is below the social belt.

STANISLAUS. And how could the poor man invite you to dinner when the paraffin in his lamps, his candles, his tay, his tapioca, his gorgonzola and the linen dinner clothes on his table are all smuggled from across the Border! Sure, begod, with that ferret's eye of yours, before you reached the plums and cream you'd have him under arrest!

(UDOLPHUS *is provoked into laughter.*)

Begosh, are ye laughin', your honour? They say that when a puritan laughs, there's laughter in Heaven!

(*He hands* UDOLPHUS *a new drink.*)

There now. The third one is always the grandest. They say it takes a gastronomical expert to tell the difference between the third one and the grace o' God.

UDOLPHUS. We'll drink to that! (*He drinks it neatly; benignly.*) That one went down like a lamb.

STANISLAUS. That's your throat acceptin' the facts of life.

(*They drink heartily—the cocktails are beginning to tell on them.*)

UDOLPHUS. I feel happy now, Brannigan, as if I was lifted up for the first time. Tremendous things are happening to me—yes, even love.

STANISLAUS (*heartfully*). Thanks be to God. The best pick-me up for a heart that never rejoices is a divilish head of red curls.

(UDOLPHUS *has crossed, having given a comic little stagger, to the water-colour portrait of* RITA, *and is gazing wistfully at it.*)

UDOLPHUS (*soulfully*). "The woman you will love and never win . . ." That's what she said to me one day and she called the pain of it the poetry of living. My mother used to say there's an affinity between red curls and the flames of hell. But I don't think now that she was right. In fact, she was wrong. There is also a *heavenly* red. Why should the devil have all the entrancing colours?

STANISLAUS. Ah, I wouldn't have heeded her. I never yet heard one woman sayin' a good word about another woman.

(JUDY *comes to the window, alarmed and excited.*)

JUDY. Come down this minute to the pub, Da. The smith is below with a chisel and a sledge hammer and the sweat pourin' off him, tryin' to hammer Mike and Crampsey apart, and the three of them's gettin' drunker and drunker.

STANISLAUS. Is it Paddy the smith, and him as blind as a bat?

JUDY. Every time he misses the lock of the handcuffs and hits Mike's wrist, Mike gets ravin' mad and pucks the two of them on the chin.

(STANISLAUS *laughs heartily.*)

Stop your laughin', Da. They'll be apart by the time we get back, and Mike will have the mallet you open the beer barrels with. He's mad to crack in the skulls of the D.J. and the Sergeant.

STANISLAUS. Run, Judy, run! Before there's another revolution.

(STANISLAUS *and* JUDY *run wildly out by the window.* UDOLPHUS *stands dazed looking after them. The* SERGEANT *pokes his head through the curtains and his features are contorted with fright. He tiptoes secretively and rather unsteadily towards the window, but trips and spins round to face* UDOLPHUS. *They stare at each other.* UDOLPHUS *tries to steady himself and stand on his dignity but his words give him away.* RITA *comes in by the door and regards them both.*)

UDOLPHUS (*braving it out*). Sergeant Whistler! Halt! Attention!

(*He gives another comic little stagger and sees* RITA *who smiles in secret amusement.*)

One moment, Rita dear! This calls for drastic treatment! Sergeant Whistler, if you dare desert your post in the face of the enemy I'll have you summarily dismissed!

SERGEANT (*grandly drunk*). No man will dismiss *me*, your honour, I'm a Sergeant of the Guards of the Republic . . . not the Black and Tan you want me to be! I resign! There's me hat!

(*Throws it on the ground.*)

And there's me tunic!

(*His tunic follows.*)

Take them, your honour, and put them on the same breed of men as yourself!

RITA (*breathless*). Sergeant! Me darlin' poet! All the pride of the heroic dead are alive in you, this great minute!

(UDOLPHUS *stares at him fiercely and then at* RITA. *Then he takes his stained briefcase from the sideboard.*)

UDOLPHUS (*dramatically*). And I'll be a dispenser of law for no man either! There!

(*Hurls briefcase on the floor.*)

I'd rather be a dispenser of cough cures. If they do no good, at least they do no harm, and that's more than can be said of the law.

RITA (*ecstatically*). Udolphus! You wonderful person! You have defied the mouldering shinbones of ten million dead lawyers.

(RITA *links the two by the arms and gives each a kiss.*)

UDOLPHUS. Rita, darling, my mother was wrong. He who misses love misses all. Today I sentenced my hated rival, Mike MacNamara, to jail because I adore you.

RITA (*ecstatically*). Udolphus! You wonderful scoundrel! Brother of King David! Cousin of Julius Caesar! Great grandson of Casanova!

(RITA *and* UDOLPHUS *embrace and they both fall on the couch, with their arms round each other. The* SERGEANT *scratches his head in wonder, and goes morosely and pours himself a drink.*)

UDOLPHUS (*fondling* RITA). Yes . . . my world is lost for you . . . my honour, my integrity, my mathematical mind . . . all utterly gone . . . My beautiful, my adorable Achilles' heel . . . for this, great men died or made fools of themselves or both. So be me! I am no longer a man of law. Law is a pretence, a veneer, a professional conspiracy, a presumptuous corollary of the Divine decree, an insidious concoction that shrivels the heart and the soul into two dried peas that are equally contemptuous, a scientific indoctrination of human nature, a mad mathematician's attempt to square the human circle, a . . .

(*There is a thunderous knocking at the door.*)

Holy St. Christopher, that's Mike with the mallet!

RITA (*sweetly*). What do I care that a barbarian comes for common vengeance! I can safely leave him to my two warriors! And let History speak of it!

(RITA *exits smilingly. The* SERGEANT *and* UDOLPHUS *grab each other in fear and trembling and make simultaneously for the window.*)

(MIKE *enters swiftly by the window, in a very dishevelled condition, angry and tempestuous. He has a broken handcuff attached to his wrist. As the* SERGEANT *and* UDOLPHUS *reach the window he grabs each of them by the scruff of their necks.*)

MIKE.   At last! You two villains unhung! I'll give yous poetry and law with the lid off.

SERGEANT.   Take it aisy, Mike, till we explain.

MIKE.   And what is there to explain short of lies, treachery, deceit and villainy?

(MIKE *holds them both in a vicious grip.*)

SERGEANT.   Ah, now, Mike, if you'd only listen. I'm not a policeman any longer. I resigned. And his honour here has resigned from the law. We're dacent men.

(MIKE *stares at them flabbergasted, relaxes his grip on them and contemplates them in wonderment.*)

MIKE.   And why the hell didn't yous say that before? Put it there, the two of yous.

(*He shakes them by the hand.*)

It's a fine class of man that sees the error of his way, and redeems himself before it's too late. You'll both have a drink with me. Are you certain sure now that the two of yous resigned?

(*He pours out drinks.*)

UDOLPHUS.   You have our word of honour, Mike.

MIKE.   And are yous now dacent men?

SERGEANT.   We're dacent men.

MIKE.   Thanks be to God. The lawyers and the polis are the curse of this country. (*To* UDOLPHUS, *suspiciously.*) How can I be certain, your honour, that when you sober up, you'll not fall back into legal villainy again?

UDOLPHUS.   That's what's worrying myself. My mother trained me night and day to keep strictly to timetables, speed limits and licensing laws, and to declare everything at the Customs.

MIKE (*to* SERGEANT). Begod, that's terrible serious! It'll destroy his character in the end.

SERGEANT. It's maybe a foreign drop he has in him somewhere. I once knew a poor chap in Dublin that had a Chinese mother and he couldn't keep his hands out of his sleeves.

MIKE. You've struck it, Sergeant. Have you vetted that Amazon mother of yours and your poor moreen of a father?

UDOLPHUS. They were both Irish.

MIKE. Go back further then. It's bound to be there. They say it takes seven generations to get a flaw out of the blood.

UDOLPHUS. My grandmother was a Rodney.

SERGEANT (*in horror*).

MIKE. A what?

UDOLPHUS. A Rodney. She came from Nottingham.

SERGEANT. Ah, that's what's done it.

MIKE. There's the germ. The English. The most law-abidin' poor devils on the face of the earth.

SERGEANT. When their Government put sixpence on their pint and a murderous shillin' on their tobacco, they grinned and bore it like gentlemen.

MIKE. They did so. But when our crowd of cut-throats above in the Dail put a penny on the porter and tuppence on the fags, what did *we* do?

SERGEANT. Chucked them in the Liffey.

MIKE. We did so. And one wheep out of this new crowd of bloody chancers, and what'll we do?

SERGEANT. Chuck them in the Liffey.

MIKE. With the help o' God.

UDOLPHUS. I'm afraid I'm a hopeless misfit here. I'm going to emigrate to London. I must work this out, this catastrophe that has swamped all my values. (*Picks up his briefcase.*) The law in the dust . . . the democratic Acts of their own Parliament in the gutter . . . Oh, this valley of inverted values! If only my mother hadn't made me her dignified little man in long trousers. If only she hadn't said, "Udolphus dear, a little gentleman is never in doubt as to truth and the right."

(UDOLPHUS *exits by the door.*)

MIKE. Isn't it a terrible thing—the difference between a good man and a dacent man.

(*Noises off-stage become audible, as if apples are being thrown. The* SERGEANT *and* MIKE *look at each other wonderingly.* MARIA *enters in an exasperated mood.*)

MARIA. Mike, for God's sake, will you *do* something with that pest in there?

MIKE. What's the hussy up to now?

MARIA. She's hoppin' cookin' apples off your photograph because you won't go to jail for her and be a hero.

MIKE (*ominously*). Oh, she is, is she? Wait till you see *me* hoppin' *her!*

(MIKE *goes off truculently.* MARIA *grins and winks at the* SERGEANT.)

MARIA. Wait now till you hear the music—and it's long overdue.

(MARIA *goes off. The* SERGEANT *sits woefully listening, as the hullabulloo starts off-stage, and* MIKE *begins walloping* RITA. *He puts his hand to his head to shut out the noise.*)

(FATHER PHELIM *comes in by the window and hears the row off-stage.*)

PHELIM. What on earth is going on in this place?

SERGEANT (*sadly*). It's Mike, Father, that's askin' Rita to marry him.

PHELIM. *Askin'* her, did you say?

SERGEANT. It'll be murder or a spit in the eye off it. Me poor darlin' that I wrote the poem for . . . Dammit, let it never be said that I didn't unsheathe the warrior's sword for her. It's a disgrace to the race! (*He seizes the poker.*) Forward!

(*The* SERGEANT, *with poker aloft, runs across to go to the rescue, but* FATHER PHELIM *interposes.*)

PHELIM. Ah, sit down, you oul' fool! That in there is the beginnin' of a sensible Christian marriage.

(RITA *enters, her hair wildly tossed, her face smudged and her dress torn. She looks half dazed at them.*)

RITA (*dazedly*). I'm going to marry Mike . . . it's wonderful . . .

(FATHER PHELIM *smiles. The* SERGEANT *looks wistfully at her.*)

SERGEANT. Ah, you poor thing.

(MIKE *enters, stern and commanding.*)

MIKE (*to* RITA). No further nonsense, redhead! (*To* FATHER PHELIM.) Father, I want our marriage banns put up right away.

PHELIM. I take it that Rita has said "Yes"?

RITA (*dazedly*). He held my head under the tap till I said it.

PHELIM. Well, that's *one* way.

(STANISLAUS *comes bursting in by the window, very excited.*)

STANISLAUS. There's *thunderin'* news. Poor Andy Flanagan's funeral was passin' me pub, and one o' the mournin' coaches is after givin' the D.J. a lift to Ballycrabbit railway station.

PHELIM (*sternly*). It's not for you, Stanislaus Brannigan, to say whether the departure of our late revered and respected D.J. is thunderin' or otherwise. Such matters involve abstruse theological considerations outside the orbit of the lay mind! (*To* MIKE.) Michael MacNamara, you and Rita will becomingly present yourselves at my house tomorrow.

(FATHER PHELIM *goes out primly by the window.* STANISLAUS *and* MIKE *laugh knowingly.*)

STANISLAUS. Did you see the twinkle in his eye? Sure he's delighted, only he daren't say it.

(*Cheers from outside.*)

Will you listen to the people cheerin' me to open up the pub again! Come on out and say a word to them.

MIKE. I will so. And it's solid hard work for all to get this starved village back to plenty. And I'll have no romantics! (*To the* SERGEANT, *sternly.*) One more line of poetry from you, Sergeant, and I'll brain you! And as for the redhead. I'll put the peter on her!

(STANISLAUS *and* MIKE *go out by the window.* RITA *looks forlornly at the* SERGEANT, *who's sitting morosely on a chair, with head down.*)

RITA (*sadly*). Me wild darlin's are all dead. I'm Helen of Troy no longer.

(*The* SERGEANT *rises slowly and moves morosely and funereally towards the window.*)

SERGEANT (*mumbling as he goes*). ". . . and they are no longer separate persons, but two in one flesh with one aim and purpose, in a union that only death can break . . ."

RITA (*in pain, her hands to her head*). No, no! Sergeant! Don't say it to me! It's too horrible! I'd just be a redheaded hag with—

(RITA *is interrupted by* JUDY *who comes excitedly to the window and runs to* RITA.)

JUDY. Rita! Do you know whose after comin' in to me Da's pub to stay for a month? The mad Englishman that painted your head and threw himself off the bridge for you! (RITA *gets wildly excited.*)

RITA (*ecstatically*). Oh, me poor darlin' Augustus! I'm crazy about him! (*Running and looking at his water-colour.*) Ah, look how he loved me! Imagine that clod, Mike, painting a beautiful head like that! Run, Judy! Dash! Tell him I'm rushing to his arms.

JUDY. But he says that this time he's goin' to *wallop* you!

RITA. Terrific! I'll adore him! Mike and he will have a mighty battle over me! It'll be wonderful! Run, Judy, run! (JUDY *rushes off. The* SERGEANT *standing in the window, lifts up his head and laughs happily.*)

SERGEANT. Ha! Ha! Ha! The romantic gods are laughin' still!

(*Chuckling, he disappears from the window.* RITA, *gesticulating, flings a scarf about her head and again looks at the water-colour.* MARIA *comes in calmly carrying a tray with tea-things on it. She looks askance at* RITA.)

RITA. Maria, me darlin' Augustus, the mad Englishman, has arrived to battle for me with Mike. It's going to be petrifyin'. (*As she rushes towards the window.*) I've always wanted to be Deirdre of the Sorrows!

(*As she dashes through the window, she runs into the arms of* MIKE *who is coming sternly in.* MARIA *bursts into hearty cackles and goes off with the tray and* RITA *finds herself gazing up at* MIKE *in wonder.*)

(*In wonder.*) Mike! Oh, you poor darlin', I was just dashing off to see Augustus. He's back in Stanislaus's pub and he wants to run away with me. (*Dragging him in by the hands.*) Thank God, Mike, you have saved me in the nick of time! You're a hero at last!

MIKE. What on God's earth am I goin' to do with you, you infernal madhead?

RITA. To begin with, Mike, smother me with kisses.

(*She holds up her face and he kisses her wildly.*)

MIKE. It looks as if I'll have to batter you again!

RITA. Oh, Mike, it'll be wonderful! And will you make me a nice quiet girl?

MIKE. No! You're my darlin' maddenin' redhead and I'd rather have you than all the quiet girls that ever lived. And I'll give you a son that will grow up like a lion, and he'll abolish the Border!

277

RITA. Oh, Mike, could anything be more wonderful! The mother of a hero!

(RITA *is wrapped ecstatically in* MIKE's *arms as*)

The CURTAIN *falls.*